No Matter What

STEPHEN SUFFRON

CLAY BRIDGES
PRESS

No Matter What

Published by Clay Bridges Press in Houston, TX
www.ClayBridgesPress.com

ISBN: 978-1-68488-155-0
eISBN: 978-1-68488-156-7

Special Sales: Most Clay Bridges titles are available in special quantity discounts. Custom imprinting or excerpting can also be done to fit special needs. Contact Clay Bridges at Info@ClayBridgesPress.com

To Liz, my real dream girl.
Thanks for loving me no matter what.

CONTENTS

Chapter 1

SUMMER DETOX

It used to be that when a guy liked a girl, he couldn't send a quick "Hey" to her phone or inbox and hope for the best. He couldn't hide behind text or a computer screen to maintain the façade of being cool or aloof. No. He had to walk to the front door of her house, knock on the door, and tell her father to his face that he was there to call on his daughter. Imagine how exposed he would have felt when she finally appeared in the doorway. All pretenses are gone. He is there for one purpose: to win her heart.

Thankfully for my kids, I didn't grow up during that time or they would never have existed. But we did have to use the phone and actually speak to someone. It took me a long time to get bold enough to pick up the phone, but once I did, it usually went something like this:

Well . . . first came the phone book—I used the white pages instead of asking for the number. One fewer terrifying interaction. Then I'd sit there, staring at the phone, heart pounding. Back then, there was a button on the phone that was the "hook," and if you pressed it, the phone was hung up, and when it was released, there was a dial tone. I would hold that button down and rehearse dialing the number again and again. Staring at the phone as my hands shook, sometimes I would gain the courage to release the button and dial for real.

Then the rings would come. You know the sound. It was the point of no return. Brrrrrrrrrrrrr . . . my heart rate has just doubled . . . Brrrrrrrrrrrrr . . . I think I'm going to throw up . . . Brrrrrrrrrrrrr . . . that's three rings—maybe I can hang up now without it being weird . . . Brrrrrrrrrrrrr . . . answering machine! Click!

Hanging up represented both relief and frustration. Relief because no matter who or what picked up the phone, it was bad—if the girl herself picked up, I would have to get enough moisture back into my mouth to identify myself (and after that, to make conversation), and if she didn't pick up, I had to squeak out "Is so-and-so there?" and if she wasn't, I had to awkwardly stutter out some sort of message. And the machine was even worse, because it *recorded* all of that for posterity.

But hanging up was also frustrating, because all that mustered courage came to nothing. There was rarely even caller ID then, so hanging up saved your anonymity but didn't give her the opportunity to call you back if she wanted.

But I am thankful for one thing: no pictures. There was no Facebook or Instagram where someone could go browse dozens of selfies of all the girls from school. If a guy liked a girl, he saw her when he *saw* her. For me, that meant summer was a break. Sure, I could obsess about girls anytime, but since I could go all summer without actually laying eyes on most of these girls, it allowed me to clear my mind a bit.

Every summer from middle school on, I needed that break more than the year before. At the end of my sophomore year, it was Nicole Ellis. Really, it was always Nicole Ellis ever since we moved to town at the beginning of sixth grade, but this was the year I finally had real interactions with her. She was in most of my classes, and every day, I would thrill at every chance to make her laugh, and I found I was good at it. I didn't feel invisible anymore, but I never felt like I had a legitimate shot with her, either. I didn't even go through the whole stare-at-the-phone routine when it came to her. But by the time school was out, I could hardly think of anything else.

June was a good "detox" month for me, though I wouldn't have thought of it that way at the time. By the beginning of July, I was back in my summer routines and pursuits, and basketball—shots I made, missed, or should have taken—increasingly became the thoughts that filled my mind as I lay in bed to sleep.

As I drifted off to sleep on the night of July 12, 1993—the day before my dad's birthday—one thought lingered in my mind: how I'd been brutally stuffed going up for a shot in the lane that afternoon. *I would have had him if I'd pump-faked*, I told myself, picturing myself scooping under him for an easy layup as he flew past, trying to block my shot.

I didn't know then that my carefree, late-night replays were coming to an end. My summer detox was about to be over. And the events that followed would set the stage for the story of my junior year.

Every teenage guy has to figure out what life is about—who he is, what it means to be a man, and what it means to love. Unfortunately, it usually happens through a series of humiliating catastrophes. We all want to be different. I was *determined* to be different.

One of the ways I wanted to be different was in how I saw Nicole. Even before I knew her at all, my feelings for her had always been strangely warm and protective. Thinking of her in terms of her body parts, as so many of my friends did, made me feel wrong. Even dirty.

I came to this realization that morning as I prepared to take my shower. Even in the summer, she had a way of creeping into my thoughts at that groggy, vulnerable hour. As the water poured over my head, I reflected on my emotional depth—on my maturity compared to the walking hormones that surrounded her. *I wonder if she knows I'm better than that*, I thought as I stepped out.

I wrapped my towel around my waist and wiped a hole in the condensation on the mirror. I opened the door to let the water vapor escape into the hallway while I put on my contact lenses. Even after a couple of months, prying my eyelids open to jam those foreign objects onto my cornea was still a struggle. But once they were in, I hardly noticed them.

With the contacts in place, I could see my face clearly. It was still sort of a new face to me, without the constantly crooked, heavy glasses that had hidden my face for so long. Without the oppressive coke bottles, what remained wasn't so bad. Some girls had even started to notice. I wasn't sure of what to make of it, but I started to get a few more friendly glances and second looks than usual as the school year ran down.

"I don't look so bad," I mumbled to myself as I fixed my hair. I turned my face to admire my strong jaw line, beginning to be defined by the hint of a facial-hair shadow. I smiled to look at the straight, white teeth that God (and milk with dinner every night) had blessed me with. Yup, I looked *good* . . . except my lips were too big. And my arms weren't big enough. And then there was that zit . . .

I leaned forward toward the mirror and brought both index fingers to the side of my right nostril. A sharp sting, a pop, a squirt—and a small white object stuck to the mirror.

"You had nice velocity on that one, Jay." Roger's voice cut through my concentration, making me jump. He loved to do that to me. "Are you going to stand there naked all day or are we going to go?"

"Just a minute." I grabbed a Kleenex and went to my room to get dressed.

Most summer afternoons, I'd be in a steamy gym with eight or nine other guys, playing basketball. Today, Roger and I had to go find a present for our dad's birthday.

Since we hated shopping and we loved eating, we decided the outing needed to include lunch—Mexican, of course. There weren't any decent Mexican restaurants in Missouri where Roger went to college.

"Hey," Roger garbled through a mouthful of burrito, "I hear that a bunch of girls go to your summer league games."

I hardly glanced up from my plate. "Not really. Just people's girlfriends."

"What about Amanda? She likes basketball."

"Yeah. I guess she's there sometimes."

Roger grinned. "Didn't you say that she was acting pretty friendly toward you toward the end of the year?"

"I guess so."

He handed his glass over his shoulder to the waitress. "And now she shows up at your summer league basketball games. She likes you. You ought to go for that, Jay."

"I don't know," I mumbled.

Roger dropped his fork and shook his head. "Now what's wrong with *her*?"

I shrugged. "She's a little tall."

Roger rolled his eyes. "OK. Amanda's too tall. Amy Wilson has 'kind of a weird nose.' And Donna DiPoto is a little 'hairy' for you. Oh—and Tammy! What was wrong with her?"

"She's kind of annoying."

"You're just making excuses." Roger glared at me, exasperated. "I know what it is. You're still stuck on that Nicole Ellis trip, aren't you? It's not going to happen."

"I know." I stared at my plate, pushing my rice around with my fork.

"Move on! All these girls like you. Granted, one's got a mustache, but you're just being picky about the others."

"I know . . . but if I still like Nicole, it's not fair to me or to any other girl I would date."

"Whatever." Roger scraped the last bit of queso off his plate, sipped his coke, and called for the check.

We didn't talk as much during the unpleasant chore of shopping. After not finding anything at the mall bookstore, we tried Montgomery Ward. Roger found an Old Spice display and started sorting through some gift packs. I wandered over to the clearance rack to look at shirts.

I picked up one of the shirts and held it up in front of my face, trying to picture my dad in this blue and orange plaid pattern with his only pair of casual slacks. When I lowered my hands, my eyes closed in on a blonde head across the store, about forty yards away. My pulse instantly doubled.

I could spot Nicole Ellis anywhere—across a crowded hallway or from forty yards away in a department store. I had studied her enough to know every detail: the athletic, toned legs that hinted at hours of cheer practice, the effortless way she carried herself, the golden waves of her hair. But beyond all that, it was her smile. Someone could nitpick her eyes, nose, or lips, but to me, when she smiled, everything aligned into something radiant, something that made the rest of the world fade away.

"Are you going to get that?" Roger's voice yanked me from my lovesick trance.

I glanced down at the shirt, now crumpled up in my hands. "Yeah, I guess."

"That's her over there, isn't it?" (I must have been obvious). He nudged me toward her.

I turned abruptly. "Let's go."

Roger paid for his bottle of Old Spice, and I paid for my orange and blue plaid. We left the store without looking back.

The detox was over.

Chapter 2

THE LETTER

Our standard birthday celebration for my dad was not enough to distract me from the inevitable thoughts that would flood my brain as I tried to go to bed that night. So there I lay, with my stomach still cooled by the homemade ice cream we had that night and my mind relentlessly haunted by Nicole's image. I closed my eyes in a vain effort to sleep, but the only thing I saw was the vision of her, laughing, talking to her friends in the department store.

Why didn't I talk to her? Would she have talked to me if she had seen me? Surely, she would have at least said, "Hi." After all, she was one of the only girls that had shown any interest in talking to me at all before I got my contacts.

I stared into the darkness and sighed. *Why is she such a roadblock to me? Roger's right. I really should ask Amanda out. Maybe Amy.* But I still liked Nicole. A lot. I had never asked her out, not in five years of knowing her. Now here I am, sixteen years old, without a single date under my belt just because I can't get the guts up to ask this one girl out. *Geez, she could say 'yes' for all I know.*

I moaned in frustration into my pillow and pulled it over my head.

How could I possibly tell her how I felt now? I can't just come out and say it. My feelings have gotten way too out of hand for that. And of course there was no chance I would call her.

So there in the dark that night, I made a decision: I had to do *something* about Nicole Ellis if I was ever going to get on with my life. Slowly, I swung my legs over the side of the bed and sat up. A knot of nervous energy formed right below my breastbone as I ran all ten fingers through my hair. Suddenly an old idea, one that I had contemplated and dismissed on so many other nights just like this, hit me with a new and resolute force.

I sprung up and clicked on my reading lamp. I grabbed a spiral from my bookcase. At the top of the first page I wrote, "*Dear Nicole . . .*"

The prose, already imprinted in my mind over the years of these lonely, wishful nights, flowed from my pen with ease. With the only light in the room shining directly on the note pad, I sat with my legs crossed under my notebook. I was naked except for a pair of cotton gym shorts. With my contacts out, I had to lean my back over drastically to see what I was writing. My ears reached out in the silence, but the only sound was the scratching of my pen and an occasional creak as I shifted my weight on the bed.

The right side of my mouth curled up in a grin as I scribbled there in the dark. Shakespeare should have been so romantic. I told her how I was smitten with her from the first time I saw her the first day of school in the sixth grade. (A seventh-grader knocked off my glasses in the lunch line. She picked them up and the first sight I saw as my eyes came back into focus was her smile.) I explained how, over the last year, I had grown to care for her more deeply as I became more acquainted with her beautiful personality as well. Finally, I proposed an outing that was sure to be enjoyable, regardless of whether we decided to be any more than just friends.

When I was done, I opened a brand new pack of white paper and copied the letter in my best handwriting, signing the bottom of the page with the most elegant signature of my life. I then tiptoed out of my room and into the dark, silent hallway. I walked into Roger's room, which served as our study when he was off at school, clicked on the desk lamp there, and pulled out an envelope and the phonebook.

I decided not to put a name on the return address, only the number, street, and city. *Better for her not to have any preconceived notions before she reads the letter.*

I dug around in the drawer for a stamp. The sound seemed to echo through the silent house. Roger started turning in his bed. Fighting the darkness and my own myopia, I struggled to read Nicole's address and copy it to the envelope. Roger began to move even more in his bed, so I squinted hard, copied the address, shut off the lamp, and quickly pawed my way out of the study and back down the hallway.

Back in my room, I lay down for a fitful night's sleep. I was determined to get up and mail the letter before I had a chance to think too much and chicken out.

Morning came and I grabbed the letter, pulled on a shirt and some sandals, and walked downstairs. I never stopped my determined march until I walked down the street to the mailbox, slipped the letter through the slot, walked back home, and flopped down on the couch in the living room. After a few minutes of TV, I passed out in satisfied slumber.

By the time Roger woke me up, it was almost noon. The sun came through the family room window at a steep angle, shining light on the sandals that were still on my feet.

"Sorry to wake you up, Jay, but I was making sandwiches. Do you want one?"

"Sure." When I sat up, it felt like wet cement was shifting around in my head. The emotional excitement of the night before was a faint picture obscured by a groggy mess.

I was barely coherent through the meal with my brother. After shoving the last bit of sandwich into my mouth, I trudged upstairs to my own bed, still drained from my restless night.

As I crawled into bed, my open spiral notebook caught my eye. Near the bottom of the page, I saw my name, signed "Jay C. McGee." I paused. The first clear thought of the afternoon shot through my mind: *Did I really sign my name using my INITIAL?!*

The fog began to dissipate quickly as I remembered what I had done. I remembered being so proud of it, but I struggled to remember exactly what I had written. My stomach dropped and my hands shook as I reached for the notebook and began to read.

The first time I saw you was in the sixth grade. I bumped into you in the lunch line and you looked back at me and smiled. I was hooked.

Hooked? I cringed, my heart throbbing in my chest. *That's exactly what you want to do, Jay, set yourself up as a deranged, addicted psychopath in the very first sentence.*

My eyes frantically skimmed down the page to the next section of the letter. I could feel every follicle on the top of my head, and a tingle crawled down the back of my neck. Another sentence caught my eye.

I have learned that you are just as beautiful on the inside as you are on the outside.

I gasped for air. I could feel my sandwich threatening to come back up my throat. *Now you're a psychopath who writes like you were fired from Hallmark.* I could see my infant social life flashing before my eyes.

I read the next sentence.

I've got an idea for a day that will be fun for us both no matter what.

NO MATTER WHAT?!! I threw the notebook across the room.

"FffsshhjyaaAAA!!" I screamed, in too much anguish to manage intelligible profanity. I buried my face in my pillow. "What have I *done*?"

Tears were in my eyes when I raised my head from my pillow. But through the tears—and out the window of my bedroom—I could make out the shape of the mail truck driving by my house.

I tripped over my own legs as I leapt from my bed and out the door of my bedroom. I skipped the last half of the staircase, landing hard on the foyer tile before nearly breaking the front screen door as I burst through.

Now in my neighborhood, the mailboxes were not at individual houses but in a group of boxes for each block. I was racing to reach the truck before it finished at the next block and left the neighborhood.

As I sprinted down the block, the strap of one of my sandals broke, propelling the shoe end over end onto a neighbor's lawn. But I kept my eyes fixed on the mail truck, driving slowly down the street ahead of me. And despite the burning on the bottom of my bare left foot, I was gaining on it.

Finally, the truck pulled to a stop at the mailbox for the next block. I caught up to it just as the mailman was stepping out of the door. As I stood there, doubling over and gasping for breath, he scowled at me. Wisps of red hair escaped from all sides of his U.S. Postal Service hat. His cheeks were cratered with acne scars. When he opened his mouth to speak, I could see a full half-inch gap between his two front teeth. "So what do you want, kid?" he grumbled.

"I need . . ." I swallowed hard to regain my breath. "Can I get a letter back?"

"Nope."

I couldn't help but whine. "But it's my letter and I don't want to send it anymore."

"I can't do it," the postal worker said flatly. "I could get into trouble."

As I gasped for air, I couldn't help but despise the man. He was built like a bean bag chair. I closed my eyes, forcing myself to stay polite.

Slowly and quietly, I lowered my voice and stated, "You don't understand, sir, how important it is that I get this letter back. Could you please help me out?"

The mail carrier pulled at his stubbly second chin as he stared back at me as I pleaded with my eyes. "I'll give you a second to look in there and find it, but I do need to see some ID from you."

"Why?"

"To match it to the name on the return address, of course. You did have a return address, didn't you?"

The long walk back to the house felt like a death march. I opened the front door slowly. Roger was there waiting for me. I just walked past him and started up the stairs.

"What was that all about?" Roger called behind me as I moped up the stairs. "Hey, who died?"

"Me."

"What? Jay! Why were you chasing a mail truck? Did you do something stupid last night?"

"I gotta get ready." I closed the door behind me and picked up my summer basketball jersey. My weekly game started in two hours.

That game was the only public appearance I could muster that week. As the days passed and I became more and more certain Nicole Ellis had read the letter, the sickness in my stomach grew.

I only decided at the last minute to even go to my next game. But when I walked into that gym and that smell of rubber and lingering sweat hit my nose, I knew I was ready to play.

On rested legs and newfound energy, I cut through, stepped around, and shot over the defense with deadly accuracy. The clammy self-consciousness that had covered my body all week melted away under the warmth of my sweat and hot shooting touch.

With nine seconds left in the game, I took the ball with my team up by two. I was fouled quickly and went to the foul line with the chance to put the game on ice. Cool and collected, I stared down and nailed the first free throw. The next one would seal the game.

After spending way too much time of my summer league games with one eye in the bleachers, I focused completely on the rim. I had tunnel vision. Nothing could break my concentration now. Nothing . . . except Nicole Ellis walking across the baseline. She had just entered through the door near the left corner of the floor and was walking over to join people sitting in the right bleachers. The ball bounced off the left side of the rim.

I didn't hear a word of what Coach Mike said during the timeout. The self-conscious feeling came back, now aided by my perspiration to make me feel cold and slimy all over.

When the other team's desperation three-pointer bounced off the back iron and the game ended, I just stood at midcourt. For the first time all summer, I longed for the hour-long postgame meeting that would follow a regular season game. Instead, all I got from Coach Mike after the game as a pat on the back and a "Nice game, McGee."

I lingered as long as I could at midcourt and around the bench, making small talk with my teammates and helping the equipment manager pick up water bottles. I made sure to keep my eyes away from the doom that awaited me in the stands.

Eventually, all the water bottles were put up and all the towels were gathered, and I finally turned to face the bleachers. They were empty. I turned my head wildly, scanning the gym, but she was nowhere to be seen. I jogged out to the parking lot in time to see her drive by with two other girls. She smiled and waved. I waved back and watched her drive away.

As I drove home, my head pounded with confusion. She had to have gotten the letter by now. It had been a week. My thoughts flooded on the way home . . .

Why didn't she say anything?

Maybe she was just being nice.

Maybe she gets so many love letters she just throws them out without reading them like junk mail.

No, that's stupid.

She must have read it.

But she acted the same as she would have otherwise.

Maybe she decided to ignore it.

"She probably already knew," I said out loud as I searched for the key to unlock the door to the house. I stopped and smiled. She had to already know I liked her. I wasn't exactly smooth or subtle. *That's* why she acted like nothing was different.

A lightness came over my body as I felt the freedom of my revelation. She knew I liked her all along. She was nice to me anyway. Why would that change now? But I had taken my shot. I could finally shut the door on Nicole Ellis.

I practically skipped into the kitchen.

Roger was there, smirking and holding a stack of mail.

His smirk building to a laugh, he tossed something onto the table. A familiar white envelope skidded across the table toward me.

"You might want to wear your glasses the next time you try to read in the dark, you near-sighted dork," Roger laughed.

I held my breath as I flipped over the envelope. On top of the handwritten words "Nicole Ellis" was a stamp from the post office. It was a red stamp of a pointing hand with a message printed below.

RETURN TO SENDER. NO SUCH ADDRESS.

Chapter 3

BACK TO SCHOOL

The rest of the summer always flew by after my dad's birthday. Before long, it was a week before the start of my junior year, and I was back-to-school shopping with my mom—which was just as embarrassing as it sounds. I was actually never the type to be embarrassed to be seen with my parents or family, though. I love my mom, and, besides, am I supposed to be embarrassed I have *parents*? That being said, there's nothing that makes you feel more like a "little boy" than going in and out of a dressing room so your mom can see how your clothes fit, and you don't exactly want kids from school seeing you do a model turn for your mother.

I had the reputation in my family as the "fashion-conscious" one, which would have been hilarious to anyone who actually saw me dress as a teenager. (There was this dude my sophomore year who looked me over disdainfully one day and said, "I can't believe you can throw those clothes on in the morning and think you're ready for school.")

My family reputation dated back to when I was about ten or eleven years old. In those days (from my preteen through my junior high years), back-to-school time was the only time I got to get a haircut from the salon at the strip mall rather than Mom cutting my hair herself. One year, I picked a style out of one of those books, and all the mousse in the store couldn't make my hair lie down and behave. I ended up with a spike, which I suddenly decided was cool. So I became the first male in my family to want gel for his hair. My concern for my hairstyle, along with my insistence on high-top shoes that year (even if they were "Winner's Choice" from Wal-Mart), made me a fashionista by the standards of my house, and I never really lived it down.

My "high standards" when it came to fashion caused Mom to try to keep an eye out for affordable fashion trends. One year she had seen a morning show or something that had said all the cool kids would be wearing layers of brightly colored three-button t-shirts, with the outer shirt open and the inner shirt buttoned, and the sleeves rolled up to reveal the second color. So we filled my closet with three-button t-shirts of every color, and I made the middle school scene on the cutting edge of rolled-up-sleeve fashion—it was rad, man. So rad that this particular fashion never made it to our part of southeast Texas. All it took was one kid asking, "Why do you always wear two shirts?" and I was back to basketball t-shirts and jeans.

By the time of my junior year, Mom had discovered outlet malls (brand names for less!). I was trying on different combinations of Bugle Boy apparel, going in and out of the dressing room, hoping Mom wouldn't say anything embarrassing about the fit of my jeans.

As I was coming out of the dressing room one time, I caught a glimpse through the window of a couple of girls walking by that I recognized. I quickly retreated back into the dressing room, and they bypassed the store. These sightings happened once or twice more—it was kind of like those scenes in *Jurassic Park* when the raptors would dart by a window in the background—but I still felt safely undetected.

But just as I thought we were safely on our way to the car, I heard a high-pitched, "Oh, *hi*, Elaine!" My mom had been spotted by Donna Benson from church, and behind her, coming out of the Sunglass Hut outlet, were her twin daughters Hailey and Bailey Benson. Crap.

The Benson twins were perfectly nice people—don't get me wrong. And I didn't really care that they saw me out with my mom. It was just that they were from our new church and were supposed to be my new friends, because not only were they in the youth group with me but Mom and Dad had already become pals with their parents. But we weren't friends yet, and our relationship consisted entirely of the awkward small-talk that I am terrible at.

"Hi, Jay . . ." said Bailey (I think). *Which one is it? I think it's the nose that's different . . .*

"What's up?" I said, trying to talk to both of them. *Don't stare at their noses . . .*

"Just, you know, shopping with Mom," she said, her stare drifting past me.

"Yeah, me too . . ." This scintillating conversation carried on in vague questions about school activities, unmade sunglass purchases, and similar topics, answered by shrugs, *umms*, and sentence fragments. Finally, after a few moments of awkward silence, our mothers separated, and I hopped in the van to head back home for the last few days of summer vacation.

It was a representative sample of what my whole experience at our new church was like. Calvary was quite a bit bigger than any church we had been part of before, where Roger and I used to make up almost half of our age group. Now I had not only lost Roger's coattails (sometimes it seemed my nickname at church was "where's-your-brother") but I was now in a church that also had a private Christian school, whose students made up a large majority of our youth group.

These were nice kids. They didn't exclude me on purpose. They really did try to be friendly, but I was an outsider, someone they only saw once or twice a week, who they had never known before.

Making friends has never come easy to me, and I had no clue how to make a new friend *unless* it came naturally. And trying to make friends with these kids was a cross-cultural experience.

I was a church kid, through and through. By the time my junior year rolled around, I had probably missed fewer Sundays in my entire life than the number of school days I missed in fourth grade alone (which was the year I learned to manifest my dread of school into visible physical ailments). I knew the Bible stories and the answers in Sunday school better than any kid I knew, including all these Christian school kids.

Despite all that, I was new to the Christian teen subculture. There weren't enough of us in our old church or in my high school to maintain any subculture at all, but at Calvary, it was in full force.

These kids had closets full of Christian t-shirts—the ones with catchy bumper-sticker slogans like, "Eternity: Smoking or Non-Smoking?" and altered brand-logo t-shirts, like the one where "Jesus Christ" is written out in "Coca-Cola" font ("He's the Real Thing"). I had no idea where these things were even sold.

While I was trying not to pick up profanity from my teammates and classmates at school, they had mastered the sincere "Oh, heavens!"

They had the entire Michael W. Smith catalogue, knew Amy Grant songs by heart, and a few even listened to some "edgier" Christian rock songs like "To Hell With the Devil." I liked Weird Al.

So even though I looked at Hailey and Bailey and thought of them as the kind of girls I ought to be interested in—pretty, Christian girls who shared my values—I always felt like an unwashed public school kid around them. And I never picked up any vibe that they were interested in me, either—too worldly to be one of them and too churchy to be a "bad boy."

And then there was the money thing. We were by no means poor, but we had faced some tough times through the years and were still trying to catch up. I had no concept of or taste for designer *anything*. We were on the cutting edge of nothing. These kids were different, wearing their Christian t-shirts with jeans that cost more than all the clothes we walked out of the Bugle Boy outlet with that day, combined. They talked about Super Nintendos and CD players with enhanced stereo speakers. They spent spring break skiing and had summer vacations to Florida, California, or even cruise ships. Their families had boats docked at the marina. They knew which restaurants were "cheap" and which were "nice"—to me the standard for a nice restaurant was if it had menus and waitresses at all.

These things might have kept me on the margins of a few conversations, but these disparities were nothing compared to the difference in transportation. Kids at our church had used BMWs and Mercedes, brand-new Mazdas and Toyotas, or full custom pickups and SUVs. I drove (when I could get it) my dad's brown 1983 Oldsmobile. Most of the time, I went around like a beggar, asking people for rides.

I didn't have to beg for rides from my youth group much, because I was usually with my parents, but it was an everyday struggle at school. Basketball was the last period of the day, and we never got out in time to catch the bus, so I was stuck without a way to get home. No one wanted to commit to driving me home on a daily basis, so every afternoon contained the humiliating quest to find a willing friend to take me home.

On the last day of summer, I found myself in the passenger's seat again—this time with Dad on the way home from the store.

"It sucks, Dad," I was already dreading going back to the everyday search for a ride home. "I know there's nothing we can do about it, but I feel like an idiot every day."

I was trying hard not to sound like I was whining about not having a car. It was just the reality of the situation, and that was fine with me. But if there was one thing I loathed the thought of doing, it was to bother someone with "me"—to subject someone to my presence when they'd rather I just go away. The worst part about the ride thing was that people would help me out of pity, and so I could never know who really didn't mind bringing me home and who was secretly annoyed by the imposition.

"I guess that's why I can't call people," I said, "It's sort of the same thing. How do I know whether they really want to talk or if they're sitting on the other end, waving the phone around, silently begging me to shut up and let them go?"

Dad thought for a moment, then cracked a small grin and adjusted his glasses. "By 'calling people,' do you mean 'calling girls'?" he asked.

I stuttered for a moment before I answered. Dad didn't usually so boldly charge into the subject of girls like that. "No, I really mean everyone, Dad. But especially girls, I guess."

Dad laughed a little. "I know it's tough to talk to girls. Give yourself time."

I shifted in my seat to turn toward him. "You know, it's not that hard at school. I don't know why. Maybe it's because there's always something going on around us to talk about or make a joke about or something. Maybe it's just that I can see their real reaction. I don't know. It's more natural."

"You know, you don't have to pressure yourself to do anything more than that," he said. "You're a long way from being ready to look for a wife."

"Come on, Dad, I'm sixteen years old, and I've never even been on a date! I feel like a loser."

"You don't have to prove yourself to anybody, son, and if you start dating a girl just to prove something to yourself, you're doing it for the wrong reasons."

I wanted to object, but Dad wasn't direct like this very often, so I sat there and listened in a sort of a stunned silence.

"And you'll be looking for the wrong things. It'll make you feel good about yourself if you can get a girl that everyone thinks is beautiful to go out with you, but then your relationship is about how pretty she is. She's going to be worried about how she looks all the time, and she'll always be looking for you to tell her how beautiful she is. You don't want 'the prettiest girl in school' as your girlfriend."

But it didn't matter what my dad told me. I *did* want the prettiest girl in school as my girlfriend, because there was nothing I wanted more than to be around Nicole Ellis as much as possible.

Chapter 4

A NEW YEAR

The school year kicked off with homeroom, just alphabetical groupings for state testing and getting schedules. This year, I was anxious to see how my schedule would shake out. I knew basketball would end my day, but the rest was a gamble—nobody wanted a tough class first period before waking up.

But mostly I was worried about how my mix of classes would shape my day. Most subjects offered "regular" or "advanced" tracks. Teachers pushed me for all advanced, but I picked what I liked or found easy, avoiding extra projects and papers in tedious subjects.

Last year, I shared a mix of advanced and regular classes with Nicole, plus Spanish and our varsity sports period (basketball for me, cheerleading for her). We had a lot of classes together, so I nudged her last spring to stick with Spanish II and advanced math for junior year—partly for her, mostly to share classes.

So as I looked at my schedule that morning, I silently hoped that I would have every class with her until we parted ways for our sports.

I arrived in first period (advanced history), and, alas, it was not to be. I ended up sitting behind another cheerleader named Shannon, who was the girlfriend of one of my teammates, but was friendly and fun to be around, too.

Second period came, and there was Nicole, with an open seat next to her. She made eye contact and smiled, seeming to invite me to come sit by her.

"Hi, Jay!" She already had her markers out, decorating her name in bubbly letters on her English book cover. Her skin had a deep tan, no doubt from lots of time in Galveston over the summer.

I sat down next to her and leaned in. "Longmire, huh? I was hoping for Coach LaSalle again." She giggled. Our sophomore English teacher assigned us movies to learn our novels and had us act out the Shakespeare in class. It was sort of a joke—but it was fun.

I wasn't nervous around her at school anymore. In this setting, we were friends—good friends, even. But as class began, my heart started to ache. The words of the Letter started running through my mind again. It hadn't reached her—thank God—but I still meant what I wrote. It didn't matter now, though. All I could do was sit and smile and keep burying it all as deep as I could inside of me.

By the time the weekend arrived, my thoughts shifted from the first week of school to Roger's return to college. It was my last weekend with him before he left for the fall semester, and we ended up hanging out in his room like always.

Even as he was preparing for the pressure of his junior year of college, he more than anyone knew the pressure I faced in my junior year of high school. That was the year that Roger got cut from the basketball team. When I mentioned something about Nicole and Spanish class, Roger saw an opportunity.

"So how many classes do you have with her?" Roger asked me. He was gathering his stuff to leave in the morning. I had been telling him about how Nicole and I had been laughing together in Spanish class about our teacher.

"Only two." My synchronized schedule plot had failed, but we did sit next to each other in both classes.

"Let me ask you something . . ." Roger's voice became softer and he looked straight at me. I dreaded what was coming. He hadn't mentioned the Letter since he skidded the envelope across the table to me the day it was returned. "What was in that letter you wrote to her, anyway?"

"It was just a really stupid love letter," I mumbled. "God saved my life when he made me write down the wrong address."

"What did it say?" He threw a large duffle bag on his bed to start packing.

I was a little annoyed. *Why did Roger need to know*? But I never hid much from my brother. I wanted to make a joke about it, but I couldn't come up with anything funny to say. Finally, with a sigh and a shrug, I said, "I guess I told her how I feel about her and asked her out."

He stopped packing and sat down. "What did you say about that?"

I grabbed his basketball and spun it in my hands. "I said we could go to Astroworld and an Astros game."

"No . . . about how you *feel*." He leaned toward me. "What did you say in the letter?"

I tucked the ball beneath my arm. "That's the worst part. I told her that I love her. She would be totally weirded out if she . . ."

Roger hopped to his feet. "Why did you say that? You don't *love* her!"

"What do you know about it?" I bounced the ball on the floor in frustration. "How can you say I *don't* love her?"

He started throwing books into a backpack. "You don't even really know her! You've just been obsessed with . . ."

"It's different than before!" I raised my voice to interrupt him, then slumped back into his couch and stared at the ceiling, flipping the ball up and catching it, practicing my release. "I've spent a lot of time with her in class over the last year. We've talked, and . . ."

"There's a difference between making someone laugh in class and really knowing someone, for one thing," Roger turned toward me and sat back on the bed. "And there's a *huge* difference between loving someone and having the hots for her."

"But it's not just that," I said, sitting back up, staring at the ball as I talked. "I don't just have the 'hots' for her, because I don't really think of her like that . . . I mean, I *do* . . . but . . ."

Roger tossed his softball glove toward one of his bags. "What are you talking about?"

I fumbled the ball to catch the glove, then looked down. "I mean, it's not like I just *want* her, you know? I guess you could say I think she's 'hot,' but that's not *all* I feel about her. I care about her, you know? I'm attracted to her physically, but it's not like I just want to have sex with her or anything like that . . . I mean . . . the thought of *actually having sex* with anyone terrifies me. I just want to be with her, to care for her, to hold her. What is that if that's not love?"

"I don't know, man." Roger shook his head and sat down slowly. "You know how I talk about Tiffany, right? I've liked her since freshman year. At first, it was from a distance. But now, she leans on me for emotional support sometimes. She asks me to help her with things. That gives me something to give her, and it gives me hope. But Nicole hasn't let you into her life to do anything but laugh at the Spanish teacher together."

I sat up and looked at him. "I know, but I want more than that."

Roger looked at me. "Hey, I'm not saying that you don't feel something special for her. I think you do. But you don't love her. Not yet."

He paused and rubbed his fingers in his hair like he always did when he was thinking. "I've been thinking about this since I knew you wrote the letter."

As much as I hated it that anyone knew about the letter, there was a sense of relief to hear someone else give thoughts about the thing that had tortured me for weeks.

"I think when you love someone," he said, fingers still moving through his hair, "it's less about what you feel as much as it is about what you give. I can't see how she's given you a chance to give her anything she needs or wants."

I want her to want ME, I protested inwardly. *I want to give her ME.*

"I don't know if you can love somebody if you're not part of her life."

Chapter 5

99¢ BLIZZARDS

The night after I first got my driver's license (November of sophomore year) was so foggy that I could barely see the red lights at the intersections. Cars were just blobs of headlights. Dad didn't realize it was that bad when he let me take his car for my first solo driving experience. I made my way through the foggy darkness to the red glow of a Dairy Queen sign. I was meeting my best friend John Agee for 99¢ Blizzards.

Meeting for cheap Blizzards soon became a tradition because this store's "limited time special" ran in perpetuity throughout our high school years and it was a perfect fit for us, what with my love of ice cream and John's love of not spending much money. It got us out of the house and gave us a chance to sit and talk while still "doing something."

John was once the star athlete of the school. As a seventh-grader, his imposing 5'9", 180-pound frame made him a force in three sports—charging through defenses as a fullback, holding the line as a defensive end, dominating the boards as a power forward, and, in his favorite sport, commanding the field from behind the plate. As a junior, he was a smallish 5'9" and 175-pounder who no one would dream of putting on a defensive line or the front court of a basketball team. His baseball career was ongoing but stalled and frustrating.

Despite his one-time status as a star athlete, John was a bit of a dork, which is probably why we got along. John's voice had changed by the time I met him in the sixth grade, and he hardly talked, and when he did, he barely opened his mouth. Our first conversation was a series of grunts about recognizing each other from Sunday school class:

"You go to my church, huh?"

"Yeah"

He had the reputation of being sort of a curmudgeon who didn't have much tolerance for the frivolities of teenage life. He spoke a lot about habits that would serve him later in life, what would look good on a scholarship application, and preserving money for college. He always seemed to dress for school like he was going to a job interview (which, combined with the fact that he had a five o'clock shadow by sixteen, made underclassmen often mistake him for a teacher).

Still, those of us who knew him knew he could be hilarious, and there was nothing more fun than to break through the serious façade and make him laugh hard enough to snort or let out a high-pitched "tee-hee."

We talked about sports, our coaches, our teammates, sometimes God, but mostly about what you might call "theories of life." Girls fit into the latter category, but usually only in the most general of terms—what girls were thinking (as if we had any idea), what they wanted, and what we thought they ought to want.

John used to say things like, "When girls get to college and stuff and they start looking for someone to marry, they'll want someone smart and solid—like us." It was a hopeful thought, but neither of us wanted to admit we were lonely right now or that the belittling we caught from our teammates about never having a girlfriend cut deeper than we let on. Things changed quickly during our first Blizzard of our junior year.

"Kat keeps getting these *girls* to call me." (Kat was John's younger, much less socially awkward sister.)

He was acting as if the calls annoyed him, but I was sort of in awe. John was literally the only person who ever called me. I have no idea what I would have done if I had girls—*plural*—calling me!

"That's cool, isn't it?" I asked.

"I dunno," he grunted (his voice always got lower and his mouth opened even less when he talked about embarrassing things). "They giggle a lot."

He took another bite of ice cream and then suddenly looked up, straight into my eyes. I expected him to change the subject, but he didn't.

"Kat says these girls like me, but I'm not sure she's not just getting them to call me to laugh at how I don't like to talk on the phone."

"It *is* pretty funny to hear you try to talk on the phone," I cracked, but my mind flooded with questions: Could it be possible that John had multiple girls chasing him, talking to his sister about him, and calling him? How? How could multiple girls be calling John and the most I ever get is a smile or a laugh or a pat on the shoulder that I blow out of proportion and analyze to death? I tried to shake off these self-pitying thoughts and listen to my friend.

"I don't want girls to like me that I don't like. You think I can't talk to *you* on the phone, you should hear me with these girls. I can't seem to get out a sentence."

"I guess that's a good way to get them to stop liking you."

He leaned over the table with wide eyes and gritted teeth: "But all they do is giggle and *keep talking*!"

"Doesn't seem too bad to me," I laughed. "A girl has never called me at all, so . . ."

"So you don't know the experience. These are just freshman and sophomore girls that *maybe* have a crush on me because they're friends with my sister. These aren't the kinds of girls you want interested in you."

"So what kind of girl is that?" I was smirking, because I knew the question made him uncomfortable. I knew exactly what he meant, but I liked to see him squirm, and we were getting into new territory here.

"Uh, you know . . ." John barely opened his mouth at all, his voice deepening into a gravelly mumble. "I guess . . . solid."

"*Solid*?" I couldn't help the laugh or the bit of candy from my last bite of Blizzard that flew out of my mouth. "Girls wait their whole lives hoping to be called 'solid.'"

He broke a sheepish smile. "Shut up."

I chuckled for a few seconds, then took a chance at digging a little deeper. "What do you mean by 'solid' anyway?"

"You know what I mean. Someone who's not trying to get your attention all the time, who can talk without giggling. Good grades. Good values . . ."

"Good-looking?" I offered. I was still having a little fun with him, but I also knew we were opening up an area of conversation that we had stridently avoided for the past several years.

"Well, yeah," he said. "She doesn't have to be perfect or anything, but I mean, you've got to be attracted to her."

"And it's better if she doesn't have to try too hard at it," I interjected. "Girls look best when they just have jeans and a t-shirt on or something, without a lot of makeup."

"That's good for the future, too," he shot back. (John was always true to his forward-thinking nature.) "Once you're married, you'll see her without makeup all the time, and you still want to like the way she looks."

"So, John," I pressed in a little further, "who is someone at school that you consider to be 'solid'?"

"I don't know," he thought for a minute. I could tell he was deciding how much more he wanted to give away here. "I guess Shannon Roberts is like that."

I shook my head and laughed—total cop-out. He was naming the cheerleader from my history class, someone who had been going out with the same guy for years now. Way to name someone totally unavailable, dude. "If she's so solid, what's she doing with a guy like Jimmy Schroeder? He's sort of the opposite."

"I know, but this is high school. I have this theory that when girls get older, they're gonna . . ."

"I know your theory!" I didn't want to let him off the hook to get back onto the realm of the theoretical. "What's another example of the kind of girl we want to like us?"

He thought for another moment. "I really respect Rajita Patel."

I suspected John was still evading. "You respect her because she's ranked first in our class. Is she really the one you're wanting to go out with?"

"Hey, I never said I *liked* any of these girls. You asked for examples." He stopped for a second to scrape the last bit of his ice cream and sip on his water. I thought he was shutting it down, but he surprised me by looking up and saying, "OK, what do you think about Angela Baines?"

I didn't know Angela all that well. She was in the choir and she played volleyball. She was a senior, but I had a math class with her my sophomore year.

"I like Angela. It's always attractive when a girl can sing." As I said that, I recalled briefly having a thing for her last year after watching her sing in the Christmas choir show. "Isn't she also president of the FCA?"

The Fellowship of Christian Athletes was pretty weak at our school, so to be president didn't mean much more than she was at more meetings than most people. But it was still nice to know she was enough of a believer to want to go at all.

"Yeah," John said, "that's kind of why I brought her up. I thought she might be the kind of girl you would like."

We threw out and discussed a few more names, but my mind started to wander back to who I really liked. I got quiet for a few moments, then looked at John and asked, "What do you think about . . . Nicole Ellis?"

"She was my neighbor when I was in kindergarten through third grade, so I used to know her really well," John replied. "She moved to a new house with her mom after her parents got divorced and switched elementary schools. I haven't been around her much since we've been going to the same school again."

Now I had to decide whether to play her off as just another name or to reveal what I was really feeling. "Well," I stammered, "I've had a lot of classes with her the last couple of years. I think she's pretty, um . . ." I gulped. "Solid."

John stared out the window as he spoke, using the same tone he had for the last few names we brought out. "Yeah, she's smart. And I think every guy has liked her at some point. I think that she's . . ."

Our eyes finally met and he stopped. Suddenly he knew that she wasn't just another name I was tossing out. I was breaking out of theory and the hypothetical and getting real. I averted my eyes and chuckled nervously.

After a few moments of awkward silence, John grinned. "So Nicole Ellis, huh? How long has this been going on?"

"Um, to tell you the truth," I confessed, "probably most of the last five years. Especially the last year or so, since we've been in classes so much together." Even though we'd never opened up about this type of thing before, I was sort of embarrassed my best friend didn't know about something that had been weighing so heavily on my heart for so long.

John didn't seem offended, just thoughtful. "I hear she's a good girl," he said, finally nodding his head in approval. "Kat still knows her pretty well. I don't think she's a big partier. She's dated a few different guys, but she hasn't gotten too serious with any of them."

A feeling of relief came over me. Relief from getting this out to someone other than just Roger, from having John's endorsement, and, I had to admit, from hearing a report on what she was like outside of school, something I realized in that moment I knew nothing about.

Relief turned into an outpouring of words. The dam of privacy and pride had been breached, and I told John everything—the first meeting in the cafeteria line, the way her smile made me feel then and now, how she had been kind to me when I still had my glasses, and how laughing with her in class was the highlight of my day. (I stopped short of telling him about the Letter, though. I was still trying to convince myself that it never happened.)

As I finished with all this gushing, all John could do was smile, but he wasn't making fun of me. "Wow, you've really got it bad," he said, shaking his head. "I don't know what to tell you."

One thing that made John a good friend is that he would never leave me hanging. I had opened up my heart to him, and, as hard as it was for him, he wasn't going to leave me out there alone in my vulnerability. His eyebrows suddenly lowered as he looked down, deep in thought.

"Do you remember Rachel Mathis?" he asked. Sure, I remembered

Rachel. She started attending my old church, where John still went, right before my family switched.

"The soccer player? Does she still go to Memorial Baptist?" Rachel was about an inch shorter than John, well-built and athletic, with light brown hair in tight curls cut just above her shoulders. I thought she was cute when I met her, but I hadn't gotten a chance to get to know her.

"Yeah, she still goes most of the time." John was back to mumbling through his teeth. "I tutored her in math a little bit last spring. She had a boyfriend at the time, and it kind of pissed him off. Nothing was going on, but it did help me to get to know her better."

"So are you telling me you like her?"

John let out an exasperated sigh, fighting to open up and admit to me—and maybe to himself—for the first time that he really did like someone. "I mean, yeah, I guess. She works hard, stays in shape, gets good grades, and we go to church together. She smiles at me a lot, but it never seems like she's smiling about how quiet I am or anything. And, uh . . ." (for some reason this last part seemed to pain him to most to say out loud) "I like her hair."

I couldn't help but laugh. Then he started laughing, too. It was the kind of cathartic laugh that only two best friends who understood the unspoken context around a situation could have. We were awkward and we were clueless, but we knew we were safe with each other.

As we laughed, I got up to get a refill of my drink. When I got back, John started gathering trash and asked, "So, has your coach let you actually touch a ball yet this year in offseason? All we've done is run."

And so we finished the evening on more familiar ground, but our theories of life had suddenly gained new relevance and immediacy. I knew he knew about Nicole. He knew I knew about Rachel. We both went to bed that night wondering what came next.

Chapter 6

COUPONS

It would be incorrect to say that neither John nor I had experience asking a girl out. While I had never gotten past my little dance with the telephone, John had once summoned up the courage to ask a girl out face-to-face. It did not go well.

It was our sophomore year, and John was feeling big with his new driver's license and a 1979 blue Buick he had inherited from his dad. He also had a two-for-one coupon to Marble Slab Creamery that was burning a hole in his pocket. He was well aware that the star pitcher of the softball team, Gabby Carson, had a long-standing crush on him that dated back to middle school. The next "logical step," John decided, was to ask Gabby out for ice cream.

What happened next would become infamous among the baseball and softball players at the school for the rest of the year. John approached Gabby as she was leaving lunch with a group of friends, *ice cream coupon in hand.*

"So, uh, Gabby," John stuttered, mostly just staring at the glossy paper he held out sheepishly in Gabby's general direction, as if to allow her to read along. "I have this coupon for that new ice cream place, and I was wondering if you'd want to go try it out with me after school."

Seventh-grade Gabby would have been delighted. But she was now a statuesque blonde, nearly six feet tall, who had been an honorable mention for the all-state softball team as a freshman. She had college guys interested in her. Tenth-grade Gabby wasn't impressed with a JV catcher with an ice cream coupon. She glanced toward her snickering friends, then back down at John, who had to look up to meet her eyes, tossed her hair, and said, "I'm training after school. Sorry!"

There was a way that girls in my school would sort of *sing* "Soorreee" that almost communicated delight as they shot guys down. Gabby's melodic apology was pitch-perfect for making John feel three feet tall and all alone, and word quickly spread that John had tried asking Gabby Carson out with a *coupon*.

"I heard you actually tried to hand it to her! Dude!" Charlie Gonzalez groaned. Charlie had been teammates of ours in basketball and baseball and occasionally tried to coach us in our social skills. He meant well, but some seniors on the team overheard the story. By the end of the athletic period that day, John was "Johnny Coupon" with all the seniors, and some still chanted "*Cooooooup*" during John's at-bats the following spring.

I tell you that story to tell you this one.

A couple of weeks after our conversation at Dairy Queen, John found out that the Astros were offering students the chance to present a report card with all A's and B's to receive a chance for buy-one-get-one-free tickets to an upcoming game. Since we could each get a set of two tickets, I saw an opportunity.

"No way." John was not on board.

"Am I really getting resistance here from Johnny Coupon himself?" (I couldn't resist).

John was not amused. "I'm serious, man. You don't get it. It's not just the coupon thing. That whole Gabby situation . . ." He clenched his jaw, shaking his head. "That was brutal . . ."

"Well . . ." I paused, thinking of a way to overcome his reluctance. "It's more of a 'voucher' anyway."

He gave me the death stare. "There's no way that a coupon or voucher or anything else is going to be involved with the next time I ask a girl out."

"It's not like we're going to go up to them with the voucher in hand and say, 'Hey, I got good grades so I can save money. Will you go out with me?' We can just use them when we buy the tickets, then say 'I have tickets for the Astros game this Saturday.'"

He shook his head again. "We go to games all the time," John continued to protest, "we don't use coupons then."

"Those are four-dollar outfield seats. We can afford to get good tickets with this deal."

"Then let's just get the good seats and just go with our dads or something. Or we could go twice. Just guys nights, you know?" His eyes practically begged me to drop it. So I did.

But I couldn't get the idea out of my head. We get the tickets, John asks Rachel, I ask Nicole, and we all go together. I had the idea that having the tickets already in hand would put some pressure on the girls to agree to go, since we'd already laid out the money. I had even picked out a day: Saturday, September 18th against the Padres. But there was no way I would have the courage to call Nicole and ask if we weren't both invested.

At least that's what I thought. Then came English class. Nicole sat next to me, and we often found ways to laugh together in class. There was a group of four of us—Nicole, myself, Charlie Gonzalez, and another cheerleader named Hannah who got together whenever it was time to work as a group.

It was sort of a typical Tuesday that day; we were breaking into groups to read a short story and answer a few questions. Our group finished quickly and started talking about different things. Hannah started bringing up a recent bad date. Charlie jumped in with his own thoughts, and Nicole told a story about this college guy who had taken her out a couple of times but turned out to be a real loser. It was the kind of conversation that I was seldom a part of, and the thought of the coupons and baseball tickets pressed hard into my mind as I listened.

I decided to make a casual remark about how Nicole was available for someone else now, coolly pointing to myself in a flirty, tongue-in-cheek kind of way, and then gauging her reaction. That's what my brain *decided* to do.

But my mouth blurted out, "I have tickets to the Astros game on September 18th. You want to go with me?"

Aaaaaaa! What did I just say?!?!

Nicole turned her face toward me, sort of startled.

Did I just ask Nicole Ellis out in the middle of second-period English class? Two and a half weeks ahead of time? Can it be possible she was not listening? Return to sender! Return to sender!

She smiled kindly. "Sounds like fun," she said.

Did that really happen?! I refused to even glance toward Charlie or anyone else sitting nearby. Before I could say a word in response, the teacher started speaking. "OK, people, let's all get back together and turn to page 53 . . ."

Chapter 7

COACH

It's sort of ironic that the two people who dominated my thoughts in those years both stood at five feet, three inches tall. Coach Mays, a 50-something-year-old fireball with contempt for all things that were not basketball, was the only person I was as desperate to please as Nicole—probably more so. At least Nicole would smile at me every now and then.

Coach Mays did not smile. Coach Mays glared, his eyes hidden under dark black eyebrows until he got *really* mad, and then they bulged out with bloodshot fury. There was no white or color in his eyes; they were black—with red where the white should've been. He had a black mustache that hung over his top lip, which we swore he was born with, so we only ever saw his bottom teeth—yellowed and bared in times of particular rage. He wore his hair in a flat top, always cut to the same perfection that he demanded of his players.

"*And you wonder why the heck you're on the bench! That was pitiful!*" His cheeks puffed out with air for emphasis as he spit out the p's and b's of his favorite words to describe our play—"*Pitiful! Brutal!*"—as he ran alongside his target with remarkable speed and endurance.

When practice came to a standstill, he often punctuated his contempt with a slight lift to his tiptoes, but that dainty (and somewhat amusing) posture was just his upswing before the verbal axe fell, cutting us down to a level where the diminutive coach towered over even the largest of us.

On practice days, Coach still rocked those beltless polyester short shorts that seemed to be standard issue for all coaches in the '70s and '80s. His shirt was a Wildcats basketball t-shirt that looked to be two sizes too small (boys' medium was our guess), tucked into his shorts and hugging his pecs and biceps sculpted by his daily push-ups and pull-ups routine as well as his small paunch sculpted by his daily Lone Star Beer routine. At the end of practice, all of us took a knee so that he could stand above us as his dark gaze fell on each of his targets.

"*Some of y'all think that once you're up here on the varsity—you got your letter jacket and you get to stand out here at the pep rally with the cheerleaders waving their little pom-poms—you think you're something. That's all you want. That dog won't hunt, fellas.*"

His eyes shot back and forth. We avoided eye contact, because once he settled on a certain player, his words were ruthless.

"*Benson! What the heck happened to you?*"

Eddie was an early bloomer, physically. He was one of the best couple of players on his eighth-grade team as a six-foot-five 13-year-old, but now, as a six-foot-five 17-year-old (and not the biggest kid on the court anymore), he had stagnated.

"*I had you inked in on varsity your sophomore year, and now you might still be stuck on JV as a junior. And you wonder why.*"

Eddie didn't wonder why. Eddie had been told why at least once a week for three years. And Eddie no longer cared why.

"*You used-t'could play D. You used-t'could rebound the basketball. You used-t'could get us reliable points in the paint. Now you just suck.*"

Numbed by the drumbeat of Coach's verbalized disappointment, Eddie was playing out the string of his basketball career without passion or purpose, and his interests had turned to his car and his girlfriend—and Coach had thoughts about that.

"*Look at you. You're overweight. You're weak. You play for a few minutes at a time, and you're already suckin' wind. And what are you doing to get better? Leavin' as soon as the bell rings to hop in your ol' Mustang with that little girlfriend of yours, uh, 'Mustang Sally.'*"

The problem was that Coach Mays could not imagine someone who played basketball but didn't make it the top priority in his life. He expected absolute devotion, and he demanded perfection. You'd think with all the yelling he did, we must have been a terrible team, but we weren't. We were a perennial playoff team and in a fight for the district title every year. But that wasn't enough.

"*I know y'all whine to each other about why I'm so pissed off all the time.*" He moved to his tiptoes and raised the pitch in his voice to imitate our "whining": "*We're a playoff team, Coach! We sneak into the playoffs every year, Coach! Why you so hard on us, Coach?*"

Before any of us could crack a smile, he boomed out the answer to his question: "*Because it ain't good enough! As long as we get the win and you score a couple points, you go home happy. You have to wanna be perfect!*"

Coach took a deep breath, stuck his hands in his pockets, and leaned back on his heels. He did that when he was about to get reflective; we shifted on our knees to settle in for the long haul.

"*I remember a game where I had a triple-double—twenty-seven points, twelve assists, ten steals. I shot 10-for-12 from the field, 7-of-8 at the line. I came home, and my dad lays into me about why I missed those two shots and that free throw and why I had a couple of turnovers. I was like, 'What is wrong with you?'*

"*He puts me up against the wall and says, 'You weren't perfect! You can't be satisfied till you're perfect!'*" Coach paused, widened his eyes, and softened his voice: "*And y'know what? He was right. He was right.*"

"*Do you think I played NCAA Division I basketball at my size by settling for anything less than perfect?*"

As we had heard about a thousand times, Coach Mays played his college ball for Virginia Military Institute for Coach Louis "Weenie" Miller in the early '60s, when the team went from a conference doormat to the NCAA tournament. (Most of the team didn't bother to do the research to find out that he never got off the bench.)

"*Most of y'all are twice my size and have three times my talent, and I could* ***still*** *kick your butt right now. Why? 'Cause you don't care about getting any better. You don't put the work in to be* ***perfect****. It's fine. It's fine. We'll just coast along being just good enough to squeak by against teams like Lee or Rayburn*" (he spit those names out with contempt) "*and then gettin' our butts handed to us as soon as we get to the playoffs—against teams that are outworkin' us every dang week.*"

His face flushed and his voice rose again to a bellowing roar: "*I am tired of it! I am sick of it! It's pitiful! I am done, fellas. I am done with backin' into the playoffs and gettin' our butts kicked every year, because we face a team ready to win—ready to execute—and we're just happy to be there.*"

"*If you ain't gonna put in the basketball work, you ARE gonna put in the conditionin' work. Get on the baseline. Suicides on my whistle. Go!*"

Suicides were a conditioning drill where we sprinted back and forth from the baseline to the free throw line, halfcourt, the other free throw line, and the opposite baseline. If Coach saw any of us doing anything less than a sprint, he would add to the number we had to do.

I ran the suicides in a fog of spit, sweat, snot, and rage. My guts churned with malice toward the man to whom I gave my soul but who stood in front of me day after day and yelled at me about how I didn't care. And yet the corner of my eye kept looking to the sideline to see if he saw how hard I was running.

Coach was inside my head, shaping my moods, my opinion of myself, and (even to this day) setting the tone for my inner dialogue. When I was in his presence, he was the most important person in the world to me, even when I hated him. All I had wanted since I was five was to play basketball and succeed. Coach Mays held the keys, and he hardly looked my direction, and when he did, it was to summarily dismiss my ability with a few biting words.

I protested and argued with his blunt assaults in a near constant internal monologue, yet my own self-accusations echoed his voice as I attacked myself with unforgiving brutality nearly every time I failed to meet my own hopes or expectations. I had gracious and supportive parents, a brother who could be tough but was always in my corner, but the validation I craved—and there were only two kinds I valued—could only come from Coach or from Nicole. I need to be starting on varsity and playing well, with a girlfriend—Nicole—cheering from the stands. Without those things, it was my own voice saying "You suck" day after day.

When it came to basketball, I only did a couple of things really well. I could create space off the dribble (though I wasn't great at dribble penetration all the way to the basket) and I could shoot. My best shot was the fifteen-foot jumper. It was the distance I had honed for countless hours on my driveway, and I could hit that shot as a jumper, a quick catch-and-shoot, dipping under the defender, or fading away. Those two skills combined—a quick dribble into space and BAM!—had allowed me to be the leading scorer at each level from seventh grade through JV as a sophomore.

If Coach valued either of those skills at all, he never showed it. I could score all I wanted, but as soon as someone drove past me to the basket, I would hear it.

"*Move your dadgum feet, McGee!*" he bellowed, running alongside me as we move back down the court. "*You wonder why the heck you're still sorted with the JV squad. You're terrible defensively!*"

His offense didn't really make room for midrange shots; ballhandlers who penetrated inside the three-point line were expected to drive to the basket, dish it inside to a big man, or kick it outside for a three-point attempt. So as soon as I would miss, he would pounce.

"*You wanna pass the ball one time for me, McGee? Keep your eyes up! There's more to the game than shooting the basketball, son.*"

Sometimes I wouldn't miss for a while—I usually shot about seventy percent from my favorite spots—and I would glance his direction, hoping to get a few words of approval.

"*You get that same kind of consistency from three-point range, and we might could use you. But you only want to shoot what's comfortable. That ain't gonna work at the next level.*"

He wasn't wrong. Extending my range was something I was working on, but it didn't come as easily. I had been an inside player most of my life, because I was tall (over six feet as a freshman), but by basketball standards, six-foot-two is no longer tall by tenth grade, and I needed to learn to play outside and, especially for Coach Mays's offense, to shoot threes. I had been in the gym all summer, working on my three-point shot, but I was still streaky and noticeably less accurate than I was from shorter distances.

Mays cut Roger his junior year, saying he was never going to be good enough to play on varsity. He said the same thing to three of my JV teammates when he dropped them at the end of last season. Every day, I balanced my belief that I deserved make varsity—even start—with the fear that Coach would completely write me off and cut me from the program entirely.

Coach seemed to be blind to my work or my passion. Instead of seeing the one guy on the team who was as obsessed with basketball as he was, he seemed to see me as the brainy nerd who went home and studied all the time. It was an impression that was shared by my teammates, who I never saw outside of school and basketball and had assumptions of their own.

"Hey, Charlie, who was that girl I saw you with at Shawn's place the other night?" We were lined up in groups of five for free throws at the end of the period, and the guys were turning their thoughts to other matters.

"Which one?" Charlie responded with a cocky laugh, his shot banging off the back iron.

"Can you just concentrate so we can go home?" I grumbled, almost to myself. My legs felt like they were filled with concrete, and we needed to make fifteen in a row as a group to be dismissed.

"What's the matter, Mac?" Oscar ("Big O" our senior big man) had overheard me. "You got some science-fiction show you need to get home to?"

Yes, I am a nerd, I thought, sarcastically. *I am anxious to get home and watch Star Trek and study my physics textbook for fun.* I did want to get home, but if I was going to watch TV, it was going to be SportsCenter. And I was more likely to zone out playing NBA Jam on the Nintendo than anything else.

"Oh, you'd be surprised!" Charlie interjected, a huge grin on his face. "Big Mac-Daddy knows more about this than you think! Our boy has some *game*!" My eyes widened as I remembered what had happened in second period that morning. "Guess who asked Nicole Ellis out in the middle of English class today?"

Before anyone could say anything else to mock me, I shot back the only thing I knew to say: "She said 'yes', didn't she?"

Chapter 8

MAC DADDY

Do they still use the term, "Mac Daddy"? In my high school days, when lyrics from Sir Mix-a-Lot and Kris Kross were still very much in the vernacular, it was usually a self-anointed term when a guy was feeling particularly confident in his ability to attract the interest of girls. Since my name is McGee, "Mac Daddy" was a nickname I bore ironically, to poke fun at how I was decidedly *not* a "mac daddy."

But when word started leaking out that I had asked out Nicole Ellis in English class and that, perhaps, she had even accepted, I started hearing the call every time I walked down the hallway: "MAC! DADDYYYYYY!" Guys would holler, come out of nowhere and put their arm around me, call out "MAC DADDY!" one more time, and walk off laughing.

This wasn't completely new behavior. I always identified with the poor souls trying to get copies in Rob Schneider's famous Saturday Night Live "copy guy" bit, where he would call out the person's name, what they were obviously doing ("*makin' cop-pays!*"), and spout other nonsense until they finally were able to escape his presence. It was as if Schneider had been hanging out with me in high school and witnessed what I called "Mac talk."

"Maaaac! Mac-DADDY! What is *up*?" someone would say, always with a smirk and always talking *at* me, not *to* me.

"Not much," I learned to reply.

"Daddy-Mac! Yo! What you doin'?" he continued, despite the fact that what I was doing was obvious ("Uh . . . walking to class") or I was plainly doing nothing. Maybe there was some sort of answer to this that I never figured out. It's possible that guys who approached me with "Mac talk" were being friendly in their own way, but it always felt like mocking.

I never figured out how to convert Mac talk to a real conversation. Usually, if I started to actually talk to the guy, he'd just blurt out "Maaaaac!" and walk away chuckling.

Normally, this sort of encounter happened a couple of times per day. Now it was several times in each passing period between classes, often with a clever statement like "*Mac Daddy is the Daddy Mac*!" or interjections of "*Nicole Ellis*!" and always, *always* with plenty of laughter. I got a reprieve during actual class periods, and—mercifully—no one did this in front of Nicole.

The bombardment was heavy for a couple of days and then started to die down. Up to this point, the whole thing had been a huge joke to everyone, but no one believed that I was going to go out with Nicole. And during this whole time, I was too embarrassed to even talk to Nicole, let alone bring up any sort of commitment she may or may not have made to go to an Astros game with me. I was paralyzed.

But that's what 99¢ Blizzards are for, right? I called John to meet me up at Dairy Queen. He was a little annoyed with me.

"You're on your own, man." John got right to the point. "I thought we decided to just go with our dads or go twice or something."

"But it would take the pressure off both of us, don't you think?" I was still trying to convince him to ask Rachel Mathis to go and make it a double date. "And it would probably be less awkward for Nicole if we went as a group."

"But now everyone knows you've asked her," John said. "Don't you think if I asked Rachel now, she'd think it was an afterthought or something?"

"Blame it on me. Tell her I jumped the gun."

John jammed his spoon into the Blizzard. "That's an understatement," he grumbled. "You're gonna set me up to be a joke again, just to bail you out, dadgummit. I said no more coupons."

"The plan was to buy the tickets first . . ."

"That was *your plan* . . ." he interrupted. "I knew I never should've told you about Rachel." He tried to keep the death stare on me but then chuckled and shook his head. "I don't know why you don't want to just be alone with Nicole."

We went back and forth for a while, long after the last spoonful of Blizzard had been consumed. It took me a while to make him understand why I thought it'd be easier for us if we went as a group. Finally, at about the third ice water refill, John let out a heavy sigh.

"You know I won't leave you hanging . . ."

I leaned in, smiling. "And you get to go for it with Rachel . . ."

He smirked. "Yeah . . . but we need a plan."

We formulated the plan as the booths around us filled up and emptied more than once. We would treat the first invitation in English class almost like it never happened. Instead, he would ask Rachel and I would revisit the idea with Nicole on the same day.

If one girl refused or backed out, the plan was for Kat to step in (she'd absolutely love to have a front-row view of one of us attempting to go on a date). She could pass as my date if Nicole didn't go. And she and Nicole had known each other since they were little.

John wanted us to borrow his dad's brown 1991 Oldsmobile Delta

88; it was an absolute boat of a car that I thought was not cool enough to *borrow*.

"It's nice and roomy and rides smooth," he insisted. "Girls like cars that ride smoother."

"No one has ever impressed a girl with his dad's Oldsmobile," I said, "but *your* dad's Oldsmobile is better than *my* dad's '83 Cutlass with no A/C." I was referring to the only car I could possibly offer. "I guess it's your call."

We planned to drive into Houston to buy the tickets over the weekend. Monday was Labor Day, so we chose Tuesday as the day to talk to the girls, eleven days before the day of the game.

I got back home from getting the tickets late Saturday evening. My mom was on the couch waiting when I got through the door; I saw her smirking when I turned the corner into the living room. Somehow, she'd been tipped off.

"So Jay," she said, "you and John were gone for a while." Mom had that signature twinkle in her eye that lit up the room when she smiled, even though she was suppressing a full grin.

"Yeah," I sort of grunted out. "We had to redeem the vouchers at the Astrodome box office, and, um, we wanted to get them ahead of time."

"Now why is that?" She was determined to make me tell her what was going on. I was pretty determined not to tell her about it. I could already tell that she was misinterpreting the situation.

"Me and John just wanted to make sure we got the seats we wanted." I started toward the stairs.

"I heard you were getting four tickets." Mom wasn't going to give up easily.

"Roger needs to keep his mouth shut," I grumbled. I caught Roger up on the phone the night John and I put together our plan; he had to be the leak. "Mom, it's no big deal. We're just going to see if we can get a couple more friends to go with us."

"Are these friends *girls*?" Mom's tone was starting to shift from having fun with me to a voice that let me know that she thought she had the right to know.

"I don't even know yet, Mom." I was exasperated, but I knew that Mom wasn't going to let me just drop it and escape. I grumpily flopped down at the far end of the couch but looked off into the kitchen rather than at her. "It's no big deal."

"I think your first date is a big deal," she said.

"See, you don't know what's going on, Mom." My voice was slightly raised, probably with a little more of an aggressive tone than I was even feeling and definitely more than what she deserved. I had a bad habit of turning simple conversations with Mom into arguments back then.

Mom pursed her lips. Her temper could match mine at times (we were a little too alike in this way), but this time she wasn't going to fire back. She simply said in a pleasant tone, "Then why don't you tell me what's going on, so that I do know?"

I sighed. I was ashamed of my grouchiness, but I didn't want to talk about it. I didn't really even know what was going on myself. Neither Nicole nor I had mentioned the game since that day in English class, and for all I knew, she didn't even remember. Even if she did end up going to the game with me, my hopes were not high that she would consider it an actual date.

I guess I paused too long trying to think of what to say next, because Mom was the next to speak. "What's her name?"

"I might go with this girl who I'm friends with from some of my classes."

"Whose name is . . ." *Mom, why can't you just drop it?*

"Her name is Nicole," I finally relented, then quickly added, "but it might just be John's sister or something. We don't know yet. And it's not going to be my first date or anything like that."

"I think taking a girl to a ballgame counts as a date." When Mom said it so matter-of-factly, it was hard to deny, but I was determined not to get my hopes up.

"I know she doesn't think about me that way," I said. "We just talk in class and stuff. She's like the best-looking girl in school. She just said yes to be nice."

"So you already asked her and she said yes?" *Crap. She caught that.*

"Sort of." I put my face in my hands and groaned, "Do we really need to talk about this?"

"All I hear is that you're friends from class, you asked her out, and she said yes. I don't see any reason to believe this is anything other than a date. You don't know what she's thinking."

From her perspective, I could see that what she was saying made sense. But my mom was hardly an objective outside observer. Now she *wasn't* the kind of mom who thought all her babies were perfect—especially in these years, we butted heads all the time—but she was certainly on my side and thought the best of me. It was hard for me not to be dismissive of her perspective on a situation like this.

"You know when I was in school," she said, "there was this one boy in my math class that I became friends with. We talked every day in school, and I really liked him. I kept waiting and hoping that he would ask me out, but he never did. I bet this Nicole has been the same way, waiting for you."

Now I *knew* she had no clue. Nicole was just waiting and hoping *I* would ask *her* out? I laughed out loud.

"What?" she protested. "You don't think I know about these things? I was a teenage girl once." Mom seemed a little offended; for one, because I was dismissing her perspective, and two, because I was selling myself short. Mom was fiercely loyal to me; the one person I knew was a fan of mine. When I played basketball, there was no one louder in the stands. Whenever I missed a shot, I was fouled; whenever *I* fouled, it was a clean play. And now, from her place in the bleachers, she thinks *Nicole Ellis* is the one with the secret crush on *me*. Hilarious.

"Of course you would think that," I said as I got up, still laughing a little. "I don't even know if she even wants to go. I asked her in the middle of English class in front of a bunch of people like a dork. She probably just didn't want to embarrass me."

"So you haven't talked to her about it since?"

"No," I shrugged. I was now inching my way toward the staircase for my escape. "I'm supposed to on Tuesday, and John is supposed to talk to the girl he was going to ask. I guess we'll see then." I moved toward the stairs more quickly now. "I'm going upstairs now. Good night, Mom."

Mom sighed. "All right. Good night."

Tuesday came quickly, and before I knew it, English class had come and gone without me getting the nerve to talk to Nicole about the game (but I didn't want to talk about it with Charlie close by anyway). Spanish class was going to be my last chance. Luckily, Spanish class always had a lot of down time. During our time to go through our worksheets, I cleared my throat and brought up the subject.

"So, uh . . ." I had a hard time saying Nicole's name out loud, so I usually just started talking. She turned her head toward me.

"Remember the other day in English class when I talked about that Astros game? I was, um, wondering if you still were thinking about going."

"When is it, again?" she asked. Clearly it wasn't circled with a heart on her calendar, like Mom was imagining.

"It's a week from Saturday, if you still want to go."

"Sure." She smiled. It wasn't a forced or patronizing smile, but it wasn't her dazzling smile she had when she was really excited or laughing.

"Actually, John Agee has tickets, too," I added, sort of embarrassed to change the plan. "He's going to either bring his sister or Rachel Mathis. Is that OK?"

"Yeah! That sounds like a lot of fun," she said.

I didn't know what to say next. I glanced up at the clock. Just a minute or so left in class. Good. "I think John is planning on driving. I guess I can let you know when we get all the plans together. We were thinking about getting something to eat first. Is that OK?"

The bell started to ring. Nicole bounced up and started loading her backpack. "Yeah, just let me know times and stuff."

"OK." My heart rate started to slow down, my muscles started to relax, and my stomach untwisted. It was OK. Things were still on. Suddenly, the nerves were replaced by an air of happy excitement. This was really happening!

A quick call from John after school confirmed that Rachel was on board, too. The plan was working. And the game was less than two weeks away.

Chapter 9

CLUELESS

Once concrete plans were in place, word got around. When it was just a funny story of me asking Nicole out in English class, I just got a bunch of goofy "Mac Daddy" talk that was mostly meant to poke fun at me. Once people started to believe she was actually going to a game with me, everyone wanted to give me advice. I don't know which was worse.

Charlie added to a rambling list of things to say and not to say every time I saw him. Tell her she looks nice. *I'm too scared to comment on her appearance.* Don't talk about Star Trek. *I don't watch Star Trek.* Talk about what she likes to do. *Sure.* Don't talk too much about basketball . . . or church . . . or baseball . . . or English class . . . *I know. I'm not that interesting . . .*

Since Jimmy Schroeder had spent time with her while dating Shannon Roberts, he told me all his supposed insights into things that she hated about other dudes she'd gone out with. Other guys on the basketball team gave advice that ranged from disgusting (mainly just to watch me react to it) to little details about how to greet her mom when I picked her up. Whatever they said, it was unsolicited and it was exhausting.

I was now down to less than a week before. That Monday, I walked into history class, and there was Shannon with a huge smile on her face.

"Soooo . . . . Saturday!" she was practically singing. "Are you excited?"

"I guess Jimmy told you," I mumbled, averting my eyes as I sat down at my desk. I trusted that Shannon wasn't trying to make fun of me, but I really didn't want to talk about it. "Yeah, it's this Saturday."

"Come on . . . tell me about it!" she sat side-saddle in her chair, leaning over the back of her chair toward me. Maybe Shannon's reaction was telling me that Nicole was not denying it in front of her friends.

"Did Nicole talk about it at all?"

"Oh, just that y'all are going to the Astros game this Saturday with John and Rachel. I think that's really cool."

"Well, that's all there is to it, I guess." I sort of wanted to know what Shannon was told. I sort of wanted to qualify what I said with a "*I know we're just friends*" disclaimer—with the faint hope that maybe Shannon could contradict that—but I was already feeling too exposed here. So I decided to make fun of myself instead. "Yeah, I asked her in the middle of English class, like a dork."

"Oh, don't worry about that," she said. "She said 'yes,' didn't she?"

Now she was sounding like my mom. Just when it started to occur to me that she had a point, the bell rang and history class started.

In the pizza line at lunch, I found myself standing next to this senior on the baseball team named Tom who I only sort of knew from a chemistry class the previous year. With barely a greeting, this preppy rich kid started rambling on with advice about where to take her to dinner, what clothes to wear—generally suggestions I couldn't afford. As we were about to take our pizza and part ways, he sheepishly added, "So how did you get her to go out with you, anyway?"

"I don't know," I shrugged. "I guess I finally just asked."

All the last-minute advice was overwhelming and a bit superfluous. John and I already had our plan. A good way to hide that you are clueless is to speak with confidence and authority. John and I were well-schooled in this manner of speaking, especially to one another. I think we could see through each other's crap, but it didn't stop us from piling it on.

It started with John's insistence that the girls would be impressed with the "smooth ride" of his dad's Oldsmobile. Later, we started talking about the other details.

"Where are we going to eat?" John asked.

"It's best to let the girls decide." I was sure that was the gentlemanly thing to do. "We can eat anything, and we don't know them that well."

"If we're going to get there early enough to both drive downtown and have dinner, we're going to have to leave pretty early," John added. "5:00 is too early to have dinner. They won't be hungry."

"It will be after six by the time we get downtown," I said. "Let's just find something close to the Astrodome."

"That's a good idea," he said. "I'm going to drive, so that puts you in the back seat with Nicole and me and Rachel in the front."

We went back and forth giving each other advice on how to act and what to talk about; I mostly parroted Charlie's advice, but with an authoritative air to match John's bravado. John cautioned me that the girls probably won't know much about baseball, so we should treat it like we were taking them to their first game.

John's statement made me think of a game I saw that Saturday. "I saw this game where Bob Costas was talking about when his dad took him to his first ballgame," I said. "He talked about how he bought him a coke and some peanuts and taught him how to keep score. It was one of his favorite memories."

John was inspired. "That's a great idea. We should teach them to keep score!"

I laughed out loud. "That's obviously not what I meant."

"Why not? It would help them understand the game! Keep them engaged!"

I couldn't picture how that could possibly work for our benefit, but John was insistent. Finally he paused, and his voice devolved into his self-conscious mumble, yet he was firm in what he said: "Think about it, Jay. To learn how to do it, they'll have to, uh, *lean in* close to see." I was convinced.

So the plan was in place: I would pick up Nicole and bring her to John's where we'd all leave together in the Oldsmobile. We'd drive close to the Astrodome and find something to eat, leaving enough money for a snack and a couple of scorecards at the game.

Friday night arrived. The football team was playing an away game that night, so I sat with nothing to do but watch TV with Mom. We had reached the *M*A*S*H* re-runs that always aired after the 10 o'clock news, which did nothing to occupy my mind as I shifted nervously on the couch. Dad sat with his chin sunk to his chest, asleep. Mom was waiting me out. Finally she spoke.

"So you've got your date tomorrow night. You look nervous."

"It's not a date!" I groaned, burying my face between my hands. "I wish everyone would just leave me alone about it!" I was growling with exasperation, but Mom wasn't scared away so easily.

"I don't know why you keep saying that," she said, trying to take the edge off of her own annoyance in her tone. "Can you tell me why it's not a date?"

"Because I'm a dork, Mom," I said, throwing my shoulders back on the couch. Dad shifted a little and snorted, so I lowered my voice, speaking slowly and emphatically. "You don't know that. You're my mom. You don't see it. I've been the biggest joke in the school for weeks."

"I think you're just self-conscious," she said. "Look at yourself from the outside. You're an honors student. Smart, talented—and an athlete! You're the kind of guy that girls have always chased after."

"There's no way Nicole likes me, Mom. Not like that."

"Why not? My friends at church are always telling me what handsome boys I have. '*They must have the girls lined up*,' they say."

I rolled my eyes. "Awesome. Middle-aged moms think we're hot. They should ask their daughters what they think. I think the votes are in on that one."

"How does it make sense that she'd go out with you if she didn't like you?" This piece of evidence was a lot more meaningful to her than to me.

"Mom, we're friends from class. She's always been nice to me. She doesn't want to embarrass me." This is how I explained it to myself every night.

"So she likes you in class," Mom said, holding out her arms like she always did when she thought she was making a good point. "Why won't she like you at dinner? Why won't she like you at a baseball game?"

I exhaled heavily and closed my eyes. I could see Nicole saying "sure." I could see the mocking smiles of the guys. I could hear the laughter. "You just don't know how it is to be me, Mom," I said softly. "She's in a different league. Roger could tell you."

"Roger has the same problem you do," she said. "He had it first, and now he's convinced you, too. Who made these 'leagues' anyway?"

"Everyone did, Mom."

"No," she said, shaking her head. "I think they're your own invention. You and Roger are smart, but you don't know everything, and you certainly can't see inside the hearts and minds of girls. You're clueless."

I cracked a smile. She was at least right about that. "Mom, I appreciate that. I do. But I've been trying really hard not to get my hopes up. I think we're just going to go to the game and then that will be that."

She leaned forward. "Jay," she said, "I know you don't want to get your hopes up and get hurt, and maybe you're right and she's just going with you as a friend. But there's nothing wrong with hope. Hope is what dating is all about. If you give up before you start, what's the point?"

My mind went to all the plotting I had been doing with John. We weren't really treating it like a hopeless exercise. "Well, Mom," I said, getting up from the couch. "You can be sure that we're giving it our best shot anyway."

Mom smiled with that little Mom-sparkle in her eye. "So now you're just going to escape upstairs, then?"

"You got it!" I headed up to my room, the familiar helicopter sounds and "Suicide Is Painless" droning over the end credits of *M*A*S*H* as I made my way upstairs.

I lay in the darkness that night, my mind shuffling through the details of the next night. I went through the plan. I rehearsed things to say. But my thoughts kept returning to what Mom was saying, what Shannon said, and even that rich kid Tom.

Am I the only one treating this as a pity date? Would it be so dumb to hope that Nicole is giving me a real shot here?

Chapter 10

THE DATE

I hardly ate all day as the hours crawled by. I tried shooting some in the driveway and going to the store with Dad, but nothing resolved the tangle of nerves in the pit of my stomach. Nothing helped.

Today is the day. I can't believe this is happening.

At 3:30, I got in the shower and took my time, scrubbing in crevices I usually just assumed the water would handle. When I got out, I went ahead and shaved. Unlike John, there wasn't much to worry about, but the little wispy mustache that I could grow wasn't a good look. I put on the cologne my aunt got me for Christmas last year—Gravity for Men. *Was that too much?*

I wasn't about to get dressed up. This is a baseball game. I pulled on my caricature t-shirt of Doug Drabek and Greg Swindell, the Astros' big free-agent signings. Drabek was on the mound that night, so it felt right. I thought about wearing my Astros cap but decided to gel my hair instead. Mom would approve of that call.

I was still ready too early. I sat through a re-run of *Simon & Simon* with Mom, my foot tapping nonstop. When it was finally time, I grabbed my keys and headed out the door.

I stuck my keys in the ignition and a feeling of nerves grabbed hold of my stomach. I could hardly breathe. My hands shook as I started the car and backed out of the driveway.

I already knew the way to Nicole's house. Shamefully, I had known it since the day The Letter came back marked Return to Sender. Her address had been seared into my brain, and in moments of weakness, I had driven by once or twice—just to see where she lived.

Now, I was actually pulling into her driveway.

Nicole answered the door herself. *Relief.* She was dressed in a plain orange t-shirt, jeans shorts, and white sneakers—pretty close to what she looked like on a typical school day, nothing that screamed "date." Then again, aside from the cologne, I wasn't exactly dressed differently either.

"Hi," she said cheerfully. She turned and locked the door behind her. I opened the heavy brown passenger door and she climbed in. As I started the car, I sent up a silent prayer that the Cutlass would behave for the short drive.

"You, uh, look good." The words barely made it out of my mouth. Maybe I didn't even say "good" out loud.

"What?"

"Never mind. We're here."

Rachel and John were outside when we pulled up.

Oh crap. *John's mom was taking pictures*! I turned and looked at Nicole. Her eyes widened a bit. We would not be posing for any pictures. We got out and stood on the other side of the car. John's mom started to motion with her hands. I was trying to figure out how to politely decline when Kat came out and saw the panic in my eyes.

"Hey!" she sang out as she ran over to Nicole. They greeted and hugged and Kat occupied her until John convinced his mom that it was time to get on the road. *Ah, Kat to the rescue.*

Once we were in the car, Rachel and Nicole started chatting immediately, catching up on random topics like old friends. About ten minutes into the ride, John cleared his throat, trying to wedge himself into the conversation.

"We, uh, were gonna stop for dinner." He was practically grunting the words. John was reverting to his worst habits of speaking through his teeth. "We're passing a bunch of places now, but we thought it might be good to wait till we're closer to the Dome. Is that ok with y'all?"

"It's all good," Rachel said easily.

I decided to chime in. "What kind of place do you guys want to eat at? We were going to let you choose."

Nicole shrugged. "I don't know what's out there." And the girls picked up right where they left off.

Things took a turn when Nicole asked Rachel how long she had known John.

"I've known John since kindergarten," Nicole said with a teasing smile.

Rachel's eyes lit up. "Oh, so you've got *stories*! I've got to hear what John was like when he was little. I picture this tiny little adult walking around first grade."

Nicole laughed. "He was quiet but still kind of a show-off . . . John, do you remember when you got sent to the principal in third grade?"

"*YOU* got in trouble, John?" I had never heard this story.

John cracked a smile. "The wall-ball incident!"

Wall-ball was a game where you threw a tennis ball against the school wall at recess, and other players had to field the ricochet. If you bobbled the ball, you had to sprint to the wall before someone else scooped it up and fired it back. John had fielded a ball that had kicked off of another kid and was rolling past the teachers. Too far for most kids to have any hope of throwing him out. But John had the best arm in the school, and he wanted to show it.

"I grabbed the ball with my right hand, and with one motion tried to side-arm it back to the wall. But Ms. Daniels was, uh, *in the way.*"

"He threw it right off of her face!" Nicole squealed. "She stumbled back; her glasses went flying."

Rachel howled with laughter. I could hardly breathe.

"And she was really pissed off!" John said. "It took three teachers and the vice principal to convince her it was an accident. She was the one teacher I ever had that really didn't like me."

After that, everything flowed naturally. No more forced small talk—just all four of us joking around. It felt easy. It felt fun.

Then we hit traffic.

As the congestion thickened, the conversation faded. It dawned on us that we had gotten distracted and never actually picked a place to eat. Now, dinner time was creeping up, and we weren't in the best part of town to be pulling over.

I started scanning the businesses beside the freeway, looking for a possible place to stop and eat. Here in Houston, we had reached the area of town where you want to stay on the freeway: strip clubs, adult bookstores, "*abogados,*" and small-scale industrial buildings. Then I spotted a sign for "Sandvik" (an engineering firm).

"Maybe we could go to *Sandvik,*" I piped up. "You think that's some sort of *Svedish sandvik* shop?" I think they pretended not to hear that one.

I shut my eyes in embarrassment. *Pull it together, Jay. Now is not the time for your dad's humor to come out.*

I could feel the tension start to build for John as we moved past the slow-down and made the turn onto the loop toward the stadium. He scanned the exits, but nothing seemed to be the right place. The mall at the intersection was notoriously sketchy. Every other sign was for a gas station or a payday loan place.

"We should just pass this up and drive around," I suggested as we neared the stadium gates. "There's gotta be something around here somewhere."

We kept driving. Fast food. A bar. And then, we turned a corner and saw . . . a Sizzler. "How about Sizzler?" John asked with some relief. The girls agreed, and we pulled in.

Only it wasn't a Sizzler. It was a Western Sizzlin'—a wannabe Sizzler. It was Saturday night in Houston, and there were three cars in the lot. When we stepped out, the smell of stale water hit our noses. Maybe it was just the puddles in the potholes . . . maybe not.

I realized when I sat down that I had barely eaten all day, and it had finally caught up to me. I was starving. And with the traffic slowdown, we had less than an hour before the first pitch. The hostess sat us down with four waters. The buffet was closed for some reason, but there was a salad bar.

Despite the restaurant being nearly empty, five minutes passed before a waitress appeared. John and I spent that time nervously checking the clock and finishing off both our water and ice. The girls visited the bathroom together and after returning to the table scanned over the menu. No one talked much.

When the waitress finally came by, she got our drink orders and disappeared for another five minutes. I could see the tension building in John's jawline as his eyes darted between his watch and the door to the back of the restaurant where we had last seen our waitress. Providing the ideal ballpark experience for our escorts did not involve missing the first pitch.

The waitress finally reappeared. John cut her off before she could finish her greeting. "Do you have anything that will come out quickly?

We are trying to make it to the Astros game, and all of us are real hungry right now."

"We do have a special tonight," the waitress said. "Spaghetti with meat sauce. Comes with a salad bar, and you can get that right away."

John looked at each of us and said, "That sounds good, right?" Then facing the waitress he said decisively, "That's what I'll have."

Rachel hesitated. "Sure."

Nicole shrugged. I had budgeted for steak but didn't want to be difficult: "I guess it's four specials then," I said. "Are there plates at the salad bar? Do we just go now?" Whatever it was, I was ready to eat.

All four of us went to the salad bar. The lettuce was too wet, almost floating on the water at the bottom of the bowl. Most of the rest of the vegetables were either too dry or obviously straight out of a can. The ranch dressing, at least, looked pretty normal. I built my salad first, mostly just with soggy lettuce, croutons, Bac-Os, and those weird crunchy noodles I only saw at salad bars. As I went to cover it all with ranch, I looked back and saw the others being much more hesitant.

John started with some lettuce, but when he leaned over to reach the tomatoes, a trickle of translucent water trickled off his plate onto the offering of rubbery chickpeas. That was enough for the girls.

"I think I'm just going to skip the salad bar," Rachel said, putting her plate back onto the stack. Nicole did the same. John, now holding a plate of undressed lettuce and several packets of saltines, followed them back to the table.

Meanwhile, I had a mountain of salad and a growing awareness that I was the only one actually eating, so my solution was to shovel the salad down as quickly as possible, trying not to let ranch drip down my chin or onto my shorts.

John tried to fill the gaps by offering saltines to the girls while rattling off baseball trivia. "It's the first domed stadium, you know . . . the

Astros were renamed when they moved there; they used to be called the Colt .45s . . . Jeff Bagwell won Rookie of the Year a couple of years ago, but he broke his hand getting hit by a pitch, so he won't play tonight . . ."

Then the spaghetti arrived. Each plate had a generous portion of spaghetti and a very chunky meat sauce, but something was just . . . *off.* After a couple of cautious bites, Nicole was the first to speak up.

"Does y'all's meat have sort of a weird texture?" she said, breaking up the chunks of meat with the fork. "It's almost like meatballs but not."

"Yeah, it's chunky, but it's sort of soft," said Rachel.

"It's almost like . . ." I said as I chewed. I was trying to pinpoint the texture, and then it hit me. "Meatloaf! It's like they turned *meatloaf* into spaghetti sauce."

Nicole and Rachel laughed, but John nodded thoughtfully. "I've heard that they run specials to use up ingredients. I wonder if they made too much meatloaf yesterday . . ."

I don't know if John meant it as a joke, but we all stared at our plates, picturing yesterday's dinner mashed into today's sauce. Everyone stopped eating. Well, everyone except me—I mean, I paused for a moment, but I was just used to eating whatever someone put in front of me.

After a few moments where I was the only one still eating, Nicole asked, "Are you going to keep eating that?"

I looked down at the plate. I was already two-thirds through it. I paused, feeling stupid if I suddenly quit and stupid if I kept going. "Well, I guess I figured we're paying for it and I was pretty hungry . . ." My voice started trailing off. "I think I'm about done."

I ate a couple more tentative bites then put down my fork with still some of my dinner left on my plate, and John started hunting down the waitress to get the check so we could pay and leave.

John shook his head as we walked to the car. "Sorry about that place," he said.

"Oh, the garlic bread was pretty good," Rachel said with a playful smile.

John laughed. "And the cracker packets weren't bad."

Once we got in and John turned the key, his head snapped to the clock on the dash: 6:55 p.m. "We, um, gotta get going," he mumbled, then whipped the Oldsmobile out of the parking spot and onto the street. After a couple of minutes, he grumbled, "This isn't right!"

Nicole leaned over the middle seat. "Didn't we take a right into the restaurant? I think you took a right when we left."

John hit the brakes and swerved right onto the next street. Nicole fell backward into her seat.

"Don't worry about it, John," Rachel said. But I knew John. His ears and neck were red. He was embarrassed at being late, and embarrassed that he cared that we were late. He took three deep breaths, but his head still turned sharply from left to right, trying to decide what was the best way back to the stadium.

Meanwhile, with every turn and U-turn, Nicole and I were swung back and forth in the back seat. I could feel the meatloaf spaghetti rebelling in my belly. Finally, we were in line to get in and park. As we sat there, it was getting sort of stuffy. I was nervous because I was sweating a little. I looked over at Nicole. She was sweating . . . a lot.

We pulled into a parking space. Everyone was happy to get out of the car. Rachel looked at Nicole, and they started speaking together in quiet voices. Rachel looked concerned; Nicole seemed to be reassuring her about something. But I noticed Nicole's hand was on her stomach.

John pulled my attention to our own private conversation. He had the tickets, and he wanted to discuss our seating order. Should we sit next to each other with the girls at the end? Or have the girls sit next to each other? We let the girls walk ahead of us as we walked behind. Rachel had her hand on Nicole's shoulder. Rachel started laughing. Nicole was shaking her head and smiling.

John nudged me with his elbow. "They're having a good time," he said proudly. We followed them to the gate, as the girls walked arm in arm, Rachel laughing and Nicole alternately waving her hand at Rachel and covering her mouth. *Suddenly they're best friends*, I thought.

Once we got into the stadium, we could hear the Padres taking their first at-bats. John wandered over toward the seats, craning his neck to see what was going on. The rest of us went into the bathroom. I came back out, and John was shaking his head.

"Padres have already scored," he said. "Drabek just doesn't have it this year."

"You've got to chill out and concentrate on the girls," I said. "We missed the first pitch. It's no big deal. Let's just stick to the rest of the plan."

"Yeah, I already got the scorecards," John said, handing me one with a pencil. "I've got the first inning filled in. You can copy what I have."

I was copying the events of the top of the first onto my scorecard when Rachel came out of the bathroom. "Nicole got sick," she said, "but she says she's going to be OK. She's in there washing up."

Oh, great. I knew she didn't look very good in that back seat. So much for John's "smooth ride." Everything is ruined. In no world is puking part of a good date.

A few moments later, Nicole came out. She had an embarrassed smile. "I'm OK," she said. "I think I just need something to eat now."

I hesitated. *What do I say to this? Should I apologize? Bust on John's driving?* Instead of thinking of anything, I just nodded and led her toward the concessions.

She looked things over, and I looked over my shoulder to John and Rachel. He was at one of the rolling stands, dropping cash on—of course—peanuts and Cracker Jack. Nicole picked out some fries and a drink, and I got some nachos.

We got good seats—about five rows from the field down the first base line, close to the bullpens that were in foul territory. It was a good view of the outfield, but not much better for seeing the pitcher and batter than our normal general admission seats in center field. John went in first, then Rachel and Nicole, and I sat on the aisle.

I sat down, trying to balance my nachos and scorecard on my lap and put my drink in between my legs under the seat. The seats were an awkward fit for my long legs, especially since I needed to turn my body slightly to the left to watch the game. I was trying to figure out how to make sure that my legs weren't invading Nicole's space while also not staring down at her legs.

Meanwhile, I tried to execute the plan with the scorecard. I dutifully kept score through a couple of uneventful innings without any notice from Nicole. It wasn't until I spilled cheese all over the card getting up to cheer during the Astros' four-run third inning that she saw the scorecard at all.

"Can I get one of your napkins?" I asked. "I got cheese on my scorecard."

"Sure," she said. "What is that for, anyway?"

I started explaining, showing her how I colored in the diamonds when the Astros scored. But there was no "leaning." No spark of interest at all. And with everyone turned away from me toward home plate, conversation was awkward at best.

At least keeping score kept my mind busy—kept me from overanalyzing every second, from constantly wondering if she was having a good time, from worrying about what she thought of me. John, on the other hand, seemed completely in his element, pointing things out around the stadium, filling any silence with baseball talk.

About halfway through the game, John asked the girls if they had any favorite players on the Astros.

Rachel smirked. "I kind of like Steve Finley." She shot Nicole a look.

"Yeah, he's pretty good in center," John said, "but I wish he'd hit more."

Nicole grinned. "He's got *other* talents, though . . ." Rachel giggled.

John was oblivious. "Well, he can steal some bases, too . . . I mean, he's a good player, for sure."

I groaned. "They're not talking about baseball, John!"

Suddenly, Steve Finley was my *least* favorite Astro, especially when Rachel and Nicole started yelling out together "*Steeeeve! Steeeeve!*" when he ran back our direction as he headed toward the dugout between innings.

The game was mostly uneventful. The only home run was by the Padres, and even with the Astros' bats quiet, the game never seemed in doubt. Without anything happening on the field, I had nothing to talk about. Nicole and Rachel chatted, their bodies turned away from me, making it impossible to join in. I mostly sat in silence, checking in with Nicole every so often to make sure she was still feeling okay.

After the sixth inning, I gave up on my scorecard.

At the seventh-inning stretch, we all got up, but I was too afraid to sing "Take Me Out to the Ballgame" out loud, like I usually did. As we shuffled around, Nicole stepped on my abandoned scorecard.

"I'm sorry," she said.

"Don't worry about it." *Why do I even have a scorecard?*

"Don't you need this to keep writing things down?" she asked.

Writing things down.

I could feel guys back at school laughing at me. Of all the nerdy things that my teammates imagined me doing, never once did they even imagine me sitting there *taking notes* while I was on a date. *Where was that on your list of don'ts, Charlie?*

I was ready to leave right then, but the game was close enough that John would never let us leave before the last out. We stood for the last inning as Doug Drabek struck out the side for a complete game victory.

Leaving the stadium, several people pointed to my t-shirt and gave me a thumbs up. Even Nicole noticed how my t-shirt matched the occasion. She poked Drabek's caricature on my chest and smiled: "Your guy did good."

She broke the touch barrier one last time when I held the car door open for her, giving my shoulder a quick pat. "That was fun."

The trip home was quiet. Before I could blow those brief moments of physical contact out of proportion, Nicole had curled up against the door and fallen asleep. No one else said much either, and John drove straight to Nicole's house to drop her off.

As we pulled into her neighborhood, she stirred, stretching as she opened her door before I could get out to help.

"Thanks, y'all," she said, her voice groggy. "Sorry I fell asleep. I don't know why I was so tired." She yawned again and looked at me. "I'll see you at school, OK? Thanks again, Jay!"

And with that, it was over. I rode back to John's, got in Dad's car, and went home. That night in bed, I stared up into the darkness. If I ever had a chance, I don't anymore. I don't know how John did, but I blew it.

Chapter 11

NERD

Move your dadgum feet, Jay.

I muttered to myself as I grabbed the ball to throw in the in-bounds pass. I had let my man by me again. Monday's intrasquad scrimmage during basketball period was not going well.

The ball came to me on the left side. My man came right up on me, guarding against a three. I pump-faked and got a little space to the right—unconscious movements from the thousands of other times I'd received a pass in that same spot. I had space to shoot but hesitated for a moment. As my window closed, I bounced a pass around the defender toward Eddie Benson who I saw cut toward the block. Intercepted. Fast break. Another easy basket.

Get your head out of your butt, I growled.

Coach Mays blew his whistle furiously. "Get your head out of your butt, McGee!" He ran out into the middle of the court. "Everybody to the bench!"

As we jogged over to the bench, Coach stayed right behind me. When I sat down, he was inches from my face: "*We can't improve our varsity if you're playin' like a middle schooler! Sit your butt down.*" He called in a sophomore guard to take my place and blew his whistle for the scrimmage to start again.

You pretend you're good enough to run with the varsity squad, and you can't even get your crap together enough to practice against them. Pitiful. Now it was my own voice chewing me out. *Get your head together. What is wrong with you?*

Days like this threw me into a panic. I thought I was one of the best two or three scorers in the school, but I was a junior, and I hardly ever practiced with the seniors and the other returning lettermen. I was mostly grouped with the sophomores—clearly headed for junior varsity. Surely Coach wouldn't cut me after I led the team in scoring last year, but if I kept playing like this . . . well, Coach did cut Roger when he was a junior. *What if he decides he can never use me?*

This whole thing with Nicole was just stupid. I never had a shot with her. What a joke. ***I'm a joke****. And now I'm so much up in my own head about girls that I can't even play basketball. Why am I thinking about this again? Watch the practice!*

"*Where the heck is your brain, McGee!*" Coach was yelling at me again. "*Pay attention! I said get back out there for Gonzalez! Do you wanna play today or not?*"

It had been a weird day. I was dreading coming to school, because I assumed I would be bombarded with questions on how the date went with Nicole, but I wasn't. (It turns out that, most of the time, people aren't thinking about you as much as you imagine that they are, especially in high school.) But I did get a few questions. My answer to how it went was either "OK, I guess" or the more truthful answer of "I don't know."

When the bell finally—mercifully—rang, I packed up my things and went out to the parking lot for my daily routine of searching for a ride home. I was asking around when Charlie came up to me.

"Hey, Mac Daddy," he said, waving me over. "You still need a ride? Come on." I climbed into the car.

Charlie had been as close as anyone to the situation the whole time. He witnessed me inviting Nicole to the game during English class, and he was the one who asked Nicole how things went right in front of me that morning in that same class.

When he asked the question, he looked my direction with a smile that told me he was having some fun at my expense. I could feel my face flush as I turned to Nicole to see what her response would be.

She looked me straight in the eye with a charitable smile. "We had a good time," she said. No mention of puking, scorekeeping, or meatloaf spaghetti.

But on the ride home, Charlie seemed to be much more well-informed. He had gotten to John during 4th-period Physics.

"Did she really throw up, man?" Charlie didn't have that huge smile he got when he was having fun at my expense, but his smirk was enough for me not to want to talk to him.

"I should have walked home," I grumbled. Then I let out a little chuckle. "I don't know if it was the Western Sizzlin' or John's driving."

Charlie wasn't laughing. His smirk was gone. "You should've taken her home after she puked, Mac." He glanced over at me and shook his head.

I felt ashamed but then got defensive. "How was I supposed to do that?" I snapped. "John and Rachel were there, too. And it was John's car."

I wasn't sure if I was convincing myself or not. I added quietly, "I guess I had enough time to drive her home and come back before the end of the game . . ." I paused for a moment. "But she really did say she felt OK after she got out of the bathroom."

Charlie thought for a minute. "Yeah, I guess so." Then he started laughing—a slow chuckle and then a louder and fuller laugh. "Did you . . ." He had to work to catch his breath now. "Did you write stuff down or something?"

My face flushed with embarrassment. I can't believe someone knew about that. "That was John's idea! And then I don't think he even did it."

"What were you even doing?" He was laughing so hard I was afraid he couldn't even see to drive.

"Watch the road!" I grumbled at him, then added sheepishly, "I was, um, keeping score."

"Holy crap, you're a nerd!" Charlie howled. "I told you a lot of things to do and not to do. I didn't think I'd have to tell you not to *keep stats* during the game instead of talking to Nicole!"

Charlie wasn't trying to be cruel, but his words were a dagger to my gut. I didn't know what to say. Charlie was right; I had tried, but I failed miserably. I had blown any chance I had, because I couldn't get out of my own way. And now everybody knew for a fact what I already suspected; I am a hopeless nerd.

That night, I couldn't sleep. I stared up into the darkness thinking about Nicole, just as I had done countless nights before, but this time it was different. There was a pit in my stomach, but it wasn't the longing or the nerves that characterized that feeling so many other times. It was . . . *what?*

I tried to place the feeling. It was true that I was embarrassed and a little angry. Who told Charlie about me keeping score? I didn't want to know the answer. If it was John, I would be pissed, because he's the baseball guy and it was his idea that he bailed on. If it was Nicole . . . I shuddered as I thought about it. *What a dork.* But that feeling in my gut that night wasn't embarrassment or anger—at myself or anyone else. It was . . . *grief*—a sense of loss. Whatever hope I had allowed myself to feel in the past few weeks was dead. The dream of the past five years was dead.

Tears filled my eyes as I turned my head to bury my face and my tears in my pillow. My heart turned toward God in prayer—a wordless prayer, begging him to give me another chance with Nicole. There was no answer, no assurance that he would help me. Just silence in the darkness of my bedroom. My mind reached out toward heaven desperately until exhaustion took me and I fell asleep.

I went through the week feeling like every conversation I passed in the hallway was about how badly I had blown my chance with Nicole. I told myself that it was ridiculous that anyone would be talking about me—but I couldn't shake the idea that I was the butt of everyone's joke.

My parents noticed my moping. Dad asked me to go to the store with him. He did that when he wanted to talk. We talked through the grocery aisles together, but I tried to dodge any serious conversation.

Finally, we pulled up into the driveway. Dad put the van in park and looked at me. "Jay, I know that the date last week didn't go like you hoped. You haven't talked about it, but it's obvious."

"I don't want to talk about it, Dad," I groaned.

"I'm not looking for the details," he said. "I just want you to know that there will be other girls. I'm proud of you for trying and putting yourself out there. That's a hard thing to do."

"It's not that, Dad." I sighed. I wanted to talk, but I also really, really didn't want to talk about it. And I wasn't sure what to say. "I'm . . . it's just that . . . I just hate it. I hate it." I found myself unable to stop repeating myself, "I hate it. I hate it. I hate it . . ."

"Jay!" Dad interrupted. "You hate what?"

"Being a nerd!" I shouted. "I hate being a nerd."

Dad shook his head. "What's a nerd, anyway?"

I rolled my eyes. He knew exactly what I meant. "You know what a nerd is, Dad."

"I know what the word means, sure," Dad said, then paused and added, "but I want you to think about it more."

"Think about what, Dad?"

"Whether it's so bad to be a nerd."

I rolled my eyes. "Gimme a break, Dad!"

"I'm serious." His voice lowered and he turned in his car seat toward me. "One definition of 'nerd' is the kids who get good grades . . . the smart kids. It's not bad to be smart and to do well. These kids who make fun of nerds are going to end up working for one when they grow up."

"It's not that, Dad! There are lots of people who get good grades that aren't nerds. I just have no game at all. I'm not cool."

"Cool? Think about that word, too." Dad was getting going now. "Cool is neither hot nor cold. Think about pictures of what it means to be 'cool.' It's people who don't care about anything. Nothing fazes them, because they don't care, and because of that, they can stay 'cool.' And then you become a 'nerd,' because you *do* care. You care about your grades, you care about basketball, you care enough about other sports to watch and follow closely, and you obviously care about this girl. If you were 'cool,' no one would know you cared about any of that stuff. But let me tell you, it's good to care. It's good to care about your education, about your team, about your success, about your relationship with God, and to care about people. It's good not to be 'cool' about those things."

I sat and thought about what he was saying for a little bit. He was right; most of the time people made fun of me, it was because they could tell I cared about something more than they thought was cool. My nerves got the best of me sometimes, because I really, really cared. It made me look like a spazz.

"But Dad," I looked down, trying not to let my voice crack, "nobody respects me. I'm this big joke to everyone. '*Mac Daddy*' the dork who can't get a date, who they think goes home and studies and watches science fiction every night, who's stuck on JV . . . and the girls just think I'm a nice, harmless guy to help get them answers in class. That's all I am."

Dad reached out and grabbed my shoulder. "That's not all you are. That's not all you are to me. That's not all you are to your mom or to Roger or to John . . ."

I interrupted, "I'm not talking about you guys, Dad!"

". . . and that's not all you are to God."

I sighed heavily, slightly pulling away. My thoughts ran hot through my mind. *I'm not talking about God, Dad! I'm not talking about my mommy and daddy and brother and best friend. Big deal if they respect or love me . . . what does that prove?*

Dad looked at me intently, seeming to read my thoughts. "I know that you want to win the respect and love of other people, Jay. But if you keep ignoring what the people who love you—and know you best—see in you and say about you, and only take seriously the opinions of people who *don't* know you well, *don't* understand you, or *don't* love you . . . Jay, you're going to make yourself miserable *and* you're going to miss the truth. I'm your dad, and I know you. I love you and I'm proud of you and I believe in you. Your mom . . . your brother . . . and I know John, too—they all feel the same way. We know the truth about who you are, and we love you. *We* respect you."

I stared out my window at my reflection in the sideview mirror. Dad's words made sense, but they couldn't penetrate what I was feeling. I didn't like the person I saw in that mirror. I didn't respect him. I was a nerd, and I hated it.

"And God knows you best," Dad continued, "and he loves you most. That's true and it matters. You have to let him define you, not the people who don't know you or care about you. You may not be ready to hear this right now, but it's true."

I got out of the car and walked into the house. Dad was right about one thing: I wasn't ready to hear any of that.

Chapter 12

SOUNDS LIKE A SQUIRREL TO ME

My high school Sunday school teacher loved telling this joke: A class of five- and six-year-olds had a little boy named Billy. He quickly learned that if he answered "Jesus!" to every question, the teacher would smile and say, "That's right, Billy!"

Then one day, the teacher was introducing a lesson, and she asked the question, "What is a small furry animal that lives in a tree and has a bushy tail?"

Billy tentatively raised his hand. "I know the answer's Jesus," he said, "but it sounds like a squirrel to me."

The first time I instinctively answered "Jesus" in Gary's class, his eye twinkled and he quickly added, ". . . *but it sounds like a squirrel to me, right?*" As time went on, I heard him repeat the joke (or just the punchline) countless times.

Sunday school is like that. We know the answers. Trust God, do the right thing, love others . . . all that stuff. It's not hard. We know the answer's Jesus. But sometimes, life is pretty squirrely.

Time passed, and the embarrassment of the Nicole date was getting further behind me. I was back to just joking around with Nicole in class, hitting my shots (and not constantly turning the ball over) in basketball workouts, and everything in general seemed to be getting back to normal.

But late at night, the thoughts came back. Every question I asked into the darkness, I knew the answer, just like it was Sunday school. When will I get a girlfriend? *Just be patient and trust God.* What do I do with all this sexual tension in the meantime? *God wants me to wait until marriage.* Why do I have to feel so different all the time? *Christians are supposed to live differently from the rest of the world.* Why can't I get Coach Mays or any girl to notice me? *It's okay, because God sees me and notices me.* Why do I feel so rejected? *Jesus loves me, this I know, for the Bible tells me so.*

My head told me the answer was "Jesus," but it sure felt like the answer was making varsity or getting a girlfriend (even if it wasn't Nicole). So I lay awake deep into the night, replaying shots I made and shots I missed, thinking about what Coach said or didn't say, comparing myself to guys sorted with the varsity or to guys who walked down the hallway with a girl on their arms. I thought about conversations and possibilities, who might like me, and what I said that made Nicole laugh today and what that might have meant. My mind circled between basketball and girls and then back to basketball, sometimes for hours before I could manage to get to sleep.

October brought one of the biggest events of the year for the church: the city-wide youth conference, held in downtown Houston at the Summit, where the Rockets played. It was a huge event with teens from all over southeast Texas gathered for Friday night and all day Saturday for music and teaching. Everyone looked forward to it—not just for good music and funny speakers, but because of the thrill of staying in hotel rooms, swimming in hotel pools, and hanging out with thousands of other teenagers.

I tried to convince John to come with our church group, but he wanted to stay home and watch the World Series, and I knew there was no talking him out of that.

Without him, I was stuck with the private school kids from my church, and despite seeing them a couple of times a week for months now, we still hadn't bonded yet. So when it was time to pile in the vans—about twenty-five of us caravanning to Houston in three vehicles—everyone jumped in next to their friends, and that left me in the front seat of a van next to my Sunday school teacher, Gary, who was also my roommate for the weekend.

With his youngest of four kids now a senior, Gary had been a "youth group dad" for a long time, and he knew how to talk to us. I felt a lot more at ease with Gary than I did with the other youth group kids, so it was fun just to take the long car ride with him, talking about basketball and other things that popped to mind.

Looking in the rearview mirror, our van was actually full of who I thought of as my "church friends," the people I talked to when I went to church or went on outings but with no interactions away from church. In the second row were Hailey and Bailey Benson, who spoke in low tones and would pause whenever my eyes turned to them. They always seemed to be afraid I might ask one of them out. With them was Gary's daughter Jamie, a senior who was friendly like her dad, but she was sort of the queen of the group, which meant if you were talking to her, there were always three or four other people in the conversation. Whenever she spoke on the ride, all eyes and ears turned to her.

Looking to the back row, there was Chris Herrington. I used to play Little League with him, but his family was the kind that didn't own a TV, so we didn't have many common interests anymore. And curled up in the back corner was Will Parkman. Will had been homeschooled for a long time before his current rocky tenure at the Christian school, and now was mostly in open rebellion against his strict parents. He had a sharp, sarcastic sense of humor that was funny, but more and more, he just sat in the corner on mute.

When we arrived at the conference, the music service had already started. On stage was a man who resembled Uncle Joey from *Full House* playing a synthesizer piano, wearing a Hawaiian shirt and leading the crowd in a raucous rendition of "Pharaoh, Pharaoh." This was a "motions song," where specific dramatic hand motions went with every phrase. In today's youth conferences, they go directly into the hands-in-the-air-eyes-closed portion of the worship, but '90s youth music usually started with these meaningless "fun songs" to engage everyone up front.

Our group joined in cautiously, glancing sideways to see with what level of enthusiasm the others threw up their arms in a big "O" or yelled out "Let my people go! Yeah, yeah, yeah, yeah!" It wasn't long before everyone but Will Parkman, who just slumped in his chair, was laughing and doing the motions. I did my best to be a good sport through the silly songs and to sing along during the more serious ones, too.

As "Uncle Joey" closed the worship session in prayer with his synthesizer providing the mood, the weekend speaker took the stage. As the sound of thousands of teens taking their seats filled the arena, we got our first look at him on the Jumbotron. He was a short, skinny guy in his mid-40s with a receding hairline and a bushy mustache—not immediately the kind of guy who you'd think could get teenagers to engage for an entire weekend. But his opening bit about the different types of kids you'd see at the conference that weekend had everyone laughing and pointing at one another.

As the talk went on, I sat with the conference book in my lap, trying to follow along with the lesson, but I kept looking around at the other kids in my group . . . *Hailey and Bailey are laughing . . . Jamie is staring off into space . . . Chris is locked in, taking notes . . . Will is checked out, drawing graffiti in his book . . .*

My eyes also shifted to other groups . . . *I think that's the small forward from Lake . . . Is he a believer, too? That girl looks cute, but I can't really see her face . . . maybe if I tilted my head . . . Ah! She caught me looking! Look away*!

"Some of you," the speaker's words reached my ears again, "are looking around at everyone else to see who you are and whether you matter."

He got me.

"Stop doing that!" His voice reverberated through the arena. "This weekend, pay attention to God like he pays attention to you. Here in Psalm 139, it says that God's thoughts about you outnumber the grains of sand. I know it's hard, but I challenge you—just for this weekend at least—to look to God to answer those questions, and not anyone else."

My eyes locked back into my conference book as I considered his words. He was right. I hated always looking at everyone else. As the speaker led us in a closing prayer, I joined him in asking God to help me. I continued to think through the closing song, and then the first night of the conference was over. As we dismissed, I scanned my group and saw everyone huddled in clusters of conversation, and I trailed behind them in silence as we walked to the van.

Back at the hotel, Gary didn't have much left, barely saying goodnight before crawling into bed and beginning to snore. I just lay down and tried to sleep, staring at the ceiling and listening to the sounds of other teenagers laughing and running down the halls lasting well into the night.

The question of where the church kids got all those Christian t-shirts was answered the next morning as we arrived at the conference. As we walked into the concourse, merch tables crowded every entrance to the seating area—CDs and cassette tapes, books, jewelry and other wearables, and table after table of Christian t-shirts, with teens crowding around to spend the money their parents had sent with them.

I was looking at a cassette for last night's musician when I saw a girl looking at me. When she saw me looking, she smiled and waved . . . and then started moving quickly in my direction. *Um . . . what*?

"Jay!" she called out, her pace quickening as she weaved through the crowd toward me. *Who is this?* Then as she got closer, it hit me. *From the church I went to with John. Her name is . . .*

"It's me, Carol. Remember?!" She was right in my face now, eyes sparkling. I was frozen from embarrassment that she noticed that I didn't recognize her right away and not having a clue what to say. I just nodded quickly, trying to reassure her that I remembered her.

I did remember Carol. The last time I saw her, she was about 14 years old, but she looked eleven and acted thirty-three. She was an only child who grew up around adults, and her gestures as she talked and her mannerisms always made her seem like a mom trapped in a kid's body.

She reached out and touched me on the shoulder, her manicured nails reminding me of Hailey and Bailey's mom. "I saw you across the room and I was like, 'No way!' How are you? You look great! No more glasses, huh?"

I sputtered out, "Things are, uh, good . . . I got contacts now" *Did she say I look great?*

As for her, she sure didn't look eleven anymore. She was tall, maybe only four inches shorter than me, and her shape was definitely more mature. She was . . . *pretty, I guess*? But as she talked about her high school and her new church, I hated that my brain got stuck on two things: her neck was really long, and she still dressed more like a mom than a teenager.

Then I noticed she wasn't talking anymore, just standing there with a big smile on her face. She was waiting for me to respond to . . . something. *What did she just ask me?*

"Sorry, what?" I finally spit out.

"I said, is John here with you?"

"No . . . he still goes to Memorial Baptist."

She smiled again. "Oh my gosh! I can't believe it's you!" She touched me again on the chest. "You have to come find me at lunch time, OK?" I nodded.

Suddenly, she moved in toward me, arms reaching for a hug. I quickly turned sideways, and our hips bumped together like a couple of grocery carts. She reached one arm around and leaned her head on my shoulder as I lightly patted her back a couple of times like I was touching a hot stove until she let go. The music was starting for the morning session, so we each left for our own groups.

As the lights came up and the speaker stepped onto the platform, it was time to follow through with what I prayed last night and give God my full attention. "God knows what you're thinking. Did you know that?" he began. "O LORD, you have searched me and you know me. You know when I sit and when I rise; you perceive my thoughts from afar."

He knows I can't concentrate on him for ten minutes without thinking about basketball or scanning the room for girls . . . Even as I scolded myself, I found my eyes searching the area again. *There's that girl from yesterday . . . She's not that special, now that I can see her face . . .*

Another girl caught me looking a couple of sections away, shook her head slightly and looked away. *What a loser. Just listen.* My eyes moved back to the conference book, but as I looked down, I got a whiff of Carol's perfume that was still on my shirt. *Why did she wear that old lady stuff?*

My eyes went up. *Why can't I just like someone who likes me? There's no good reason not to like Carol. But why does she like me anyway? Has she been thinking about me for three years? Where is she anyway?* My eyes searched and I saw her, because her face was already turned toward me. She was searching, too. She was almost a hundred yards away, but I could see her, and she could see me.

"God sees you," the speaker's voice was reaching a crescendo. "It doesn't matter how far you run from him, doesn't matter how much you hide from him, he sees you. He knows you. He loves you."

She doesn't even know me.

"God knows you the best, and you know what? He loves you the most."

I wrote down that last line in my book, but all I could think of during the closing prayer were the pair of eyes watching me. I didn't want to hurt anyone's feelings, so I was hoping to get lost in the crowd going out to lunch and dodge Carol for the rest of the conference.

I hurried up the stairs and into the concourse. I weaved through the crowd, but I got stuck behind another cluster bunched around a t-shirt table. Then I heard it. *Clomp, clomp, clomp, clomp . . .* The unmistakable sound of someone running. Fast. I started walking again, but someone grabbed me. Manicured nails dug into my shoulder. I spun around and saw Carol. She was trying to hide her heavy breathing behind a smile.

"You almost got away from me!"

"Sorry . . . I didn't want to lose sight of my youth leader . . . but they're all here buying shirts and stuff."

So I was stuck there making small talk. The kind I'm really bad at making. *Maybe this terrible conversation will help her lose interest.*

I spotted Gary moving toward the doors. "I've got to catch my van to lunch," I said.

"Where are y'all going?"

I had no idea. It wasn't like I was the one deciding. "I think just the mall."

She smiled. "That's where we're going! Maybe I'll see you there."

I made my escape, riding shotgun with Gary again. My gut turned at the idea I was going to hurt Carol's feelings if I had to talk to her again. I didn't want to lead her on, and I didn't want the discomfort of being direct. There was only one option. I'd like to say it was an accident, but I definitely talked Gary into going to Pancho's instead of the mall.

After lunch and some hang-out time back at the hotel, we were back at the Summit for the final session. As we started to sing and I started going through the motions of the songs, my eyes were back to scanning. *Did the Lake guy do the motions, too? I owned that guy freshman year . . . Here he is wearing a letter jacket, and I'm still practicing with the JV . . . And he's got that girl right there next to him . . . I've got nothing but a bunch of church friends who don't care if I am here or not . . .*

One person did care that I was there, and I tried hard not to see her. My mind swam with a chorus of repeated thoughts: *I have got to make varsity this year . . . I don't want to deal with this Carol thing that's come out of nowhere, but I can't hurt her feelings . . . Why is it never a girl I like who likes me?*

The thoughts were so invasive that the music and the start of the final talk just sort of glided over my head. I was sitting, staring into space when my foot knocked my book into the row in front of me.

Gary was sitting there, and he opened it up to the right page and handed it to me.

There was the Bible text in front of me: "Search me, O God, and know my heart; test me and know my anxious thoughts. See if there is any offensive way in me, and lead me in the way everlasting."

God knows all these anxious thoughts.

"Turn those anxieties and give them to God," the speaker was nearing his final point. "God promises to lead you."

The reason I'm so anxious is because I don't put God first. I am too obsessed with basketball. I'm too twisted up over girls. I need to put him first.

We stood to sing the final song together. My heart lifted to God in a prayer.

I hate living like this. God, help me put you first.

As I prayed, I felt like something had been lifted off my shoulders. I sang the rest of the song with a full voice, as my heartbeat quickened inside my chest.

Somehow, the rest of the night went smoothly. I still had some dread that Carol would run me down on the way out, but when we saw each other from a distance, we just waved as we were carried in different directions by the flow of the crowd. I had *fun* with my group at dinner and, for once, actually talked with everyone in the van on the way home.

I lay in my bed that night with a sense of thankfulness. I gave my anxieties to God, and he took them, at least for one night.

And now that I'm putting God first, maybe now he'll give me a girlfriend.

Chapter 13

THE LIST

It was easy to put God first that Sunday, but when Monday morning hit, thoughts of basketball overwhelmed my mind from the moment I woke up. It's the last week of practice before Coach splits the varsity from the JV squad, and I still have no idea where I'm going to end up.

Coach usually carried ten players on varsity, maybe eleven if there was a senior that he never intended to put in the game. There were six returning lettermen, plus a senior who was on JV last year. That left—at most—four spots for juniors or sophomores coming up from sub-varsity teams.

I had reason to believe I was going to be one of them. I led JV in scoring last year, and things had been going well in practice in recent weeks. I hit six three-pointers one day, and I blocked three shots and had two steals another day in the intrasquads last week. Defense and three-point shooting were the things Coach was always yelling at me about.

My teammates seemed to be respecting me more. With all the varsity players there, Big O picked me second when we were picking teams at the last open gym before the season started. When Coach divided us for the three-point contest, there were guys taunting the other group, "We got Mac!"

Coach Mays was harder to read. As the season drew closer, he stopped yelling at me as much—he hardly looked my direction at all. He mixed me in with the returning lettermen some, but I still logged plenty of time with the sophomores, too. I lost a lot of sleep trying to decode it all—even as I did my best to "give it to God" (whatever that meant).

When I dressed out and hit the gym that Monday, the sight of the large, glowering figure next to Coach Mays made my stomach drop. Coach Ward was at today's practice. Coach Ward was the coach of the JV team, and when he finally took time from his football coaching duties to show up to basketball practice, it meant that decision time was near.

Coach Ward had been my coach for two years now. He was the coach of my freshman team, and then he moved up to JV when yet another assistant basketball coach had grown tired of Coach Mays's overbearing ways and left for another school. Coach Ward didn't care that Coach Mays was overbearing; he'd rather be on the football field anyway.

I watched from the corner of my eye as Ward leaned in, nodding as Coach pointed to players. *Who are they talking about?* I knew Coach Mays would take the guys he wanted, and Ward would be left with the rest. I assumed Coach was talking to him about who would be on Ward's JV roster, so I didn't want them talking about me.

Ward ran Coach's plays and implemented his game plans. Other than looking the part—he towered a full foot over Coach Mays—there was no indication in anything Ward said or did that he knew or cared anything about basketball at all. He just stood there, stone-faced. Coach Bored.

My hands felt jittery as my eyes kept darting to the coaches and their conversation. I received a pass and launched a three. Off-target. The ball ricocheted from the rim off Eddie's hands and bounced so that Ward had to dodge to keep from getting hit in the face. He threw the ball back in, growling, "Geez, Benson, can you grab a rebound for once?"

Ward's coaching was mostly made up of exasperated statements like, "You gotta make those shots" or "Stop turning the ball over." Unless Coach Mays showed up to berate us, the postgame meetings with Coach Ward lasted less than five minutes. Today, he put in about half an hour of practice before he'd had enough. With a nod to Coach Mays, he strode out of the gym—back to the field where he wanted to be.

The night before the rosters were going to be posted, I was back at Dairy Queen with John. I was a wreck, sitting there poking at my Blizzard because my stomach was too twisted to even want it. I wasn't saying anything.

"I don't know why you're so nervous." John finally broke the silence. "I went to a bunch of your games last year. You were the best on the team."

"But what *you* think doesn't matter," I shot back. "There are only three or four slots. Tee is coming up as the new starting point guard, and Jimmy and Charlie have been practicing with varsity all year. If he takes another one of us at all, there's still a chance he takes Darryl or even Eddie."

John scowled. "Charlie? Jimmy? Really? Why?"

"Charlie's a better athlete than me—faster, better hops, defends better. And Jimmy's always chucking up threes like Coach wants."

John rolled his eyes. "How does that help if he misses all the time?"

I shrugged, staring down into my ice cream. "I think Coach just *sees* them as varsity guys. They fit in . . . they look the part."

John shook his head. “That’s dumb . . . but coaches get stuck on their own way of thinking sometimes. Like Coach Thomas. He’s always telling me to swing more—doesn’t care that I walk more than anyone on the team. In fall league, I hit .222 but had a home run and three doubles—and with my walks, I was on base as much as anyone . . .”

I knew the story. “And he said, ‘Since when are you a .220 hitter?’ and started messing with your swing. I remember.”

John nodded. “All he cared about was batting average. Never mind that I had the best on-base percentage on the team. It sucks when the thing you’re good at is the exact thing your coach undervalues.”

I jammed my spoon into the cup. “And it’s gonna put me be on frickin’ JV again!” I grumbled, falling backward in my chair in frustration.

I grabbed my cup and ate a few bites as I stared off into space, my body tense as I stewed over the idea of my name on the JV list.

John decided to change the subject. “You know how you stopped going to FCA?” Fellowship of Christian Athletes at my school wasn’t all that Christian and didn’t have anything to do with being an athlete. I had gotten tired of the trite devotionals and silly games.

“Yeah,” I cracked a smile, glad to be thinking about something new. “That ‘Honey-if-you-love-me-you’ll-smile’ game was the last straw.” It was a game where girls would sit in a guy’s lap and say “Honey, if you love me, you’ll smile.” If he smiled, he was eliminated. Having a girl in my lap didn’t seem appropriate for Bible study and was extremely dangerous for a *particular* form of embarrassment. I never returned after that.

“Well . . .” his voice lowered to a mumble as he shifted in his seat. “Do you know that sophomore girl Ashley Lansford? She’s an athletic trainer.”

“Yeah. She sometimes works basketball practice. Why?”

John looked down. “She’s been coming to FCA. What do you think of her?”

I smirked. “I think we’re talking about what *you* think of her.”

“I was, uh, thinking about asking her out.”

I cocked an eyebrow. “Really? Are you giving up on Rachel Mathis already? Didn’t she say, ‘Let’s do this again sometime’ after the game?”

“You know she’s always been busy every time I’ve called her since then. She even skipped a couple of Wednesdays at church.”

“How do you know it’s not just soccer stuff or something?”

John shook his head. “Kat says that girls say they’re busy when they just want to let a guy down easy.”

I thought for a second. I would never have known that. “Hmm. I’d rather they just say ‘no’ so I could move on.”

John leaned in. “Me too!” He sat back and shrugged. “I think I want to move on to Ashley anyway. It’s good not to get too hung up on one girl when you’re in high school anyway. Not many people marry someone from high school, you know.”

We talked for a while about his ideas for his next steps with Ashley before John said, “Nicole has come to a couple of FCA meetings recently.”

Talk about being hung up on one person. “I don’t want to talk about Nicole right now. I’m not getting anywhere with that.”

John raised an eyebrow. “Then it might interest you that I know someone who likes you.”

I sat up straight and leaned in. “Who?”

“Remember that girl Carol who used to go to our church? Rachel is still friends with her and she told me on Sunday that Carol . . .”

“I know about that.” I slumped back down. “I’m really not interested.”

“Why not?”

I didn’t know how to explain it to John without nitpicking and tearing Carol down behind her back, so I decided to just say nothing.

"It's just . . . I just need to concentrate on basketball right now." Mentioning basketball flooded my mind again with thoughts about Coach posting the roster tomorrow morning. "It's time for me to get going."

We got up, and I drove home. I couldn't sleep for more than an hour or two at a time all night, my stomach almost painfully churning. *God, I just want to be on varsity . . . I've been trying to do things your way . . . and it's not like I'm not good enough . . . I deserve this, don't I?*

I gave up trying to sleep just before 5 a.m. I showered, tried to eat, tried to read my Bible. I shot some free throws in the driveway as the sun came up. Nothing eased the tension or the nausea. But slowly, the minutes passed, and I got in the car. It was finally time.

Dad was trying to give me a pep talk on the way to school, but the words just passed over my head as my leg shook in the passenger's seat. When we got to the school, I jumped out.

Dad stopped me. "Look at me, Jay." His eyes met mine as I leaned back into the car. "Either way, it's going to be OK, son. I'm proud of you."

I nodded quickly. "Sure, Dad . . . Bye!" I stood and shut the door and walked as fast as I could, while trying to keep a cool exterior. I reached the door of the locker room, where the list was posted.

VARSITY . . . eleven names . . . alphabetical order . . . Anderson . . . Davis . . . Eason . . . Gonzalez . . . Harris . . . Jackson . . . *Nicholson* . . . I read it four times.

Then I turned to the JV roster. There it was. "McGee"—right in the middle of a list of sophomores and a freshman. On the whole team, the only juniors were Eddie Benson and me. My teeth clenched. I knew this was coming but still somehow couldn't believe it.

A surge of rage filled my body. I threw my backpack, nearly knocking a freshman over as it slid down the hallway. I picked it back up, mumbling an apology to him as I escaped into the bathroom.

I thought I was going to throw up, but I didn't. I picked up the pay phone to call my mom to come get me—but then I stopped. I was a zombie on the outside through my day of classes as my mind and my insides churned.

Sometimes I was angry. *I don't need this bullcrap. I'll just quit and play baseball or something* . . . I silently cursed Coach Mays with every profanity I knew. Sometimes I just fought back tears. *What do I have to do? I've done everything I can think of, and it's not enough.* Other times, I plotted my comeback. *I'll just have to score thirty points a game. He'll feel stupid then . . .*

At no point did I think about history, English, trigonometry, or Spanish.

At practice, I played with unhinged rage. I threw up threes at every opportunity. I stuck with every man I guarded with reckless tenacity. After a particularly hard foul, I found Coach Mays in my face.

His face was red, spittle flying from his lips into my face. "You wonder why the heck you're on the JV roster," he screamed. "You can't play a lick of D without hacking! *That dog won't hunt*!"

I matched his glare, but tears filled my eyes.

"Glaring at me ain't gonna get you anywhere, son. I know you think you're smarter than me, but this ain't math class."

I looked away, a tear slipping from my eye. I cursed it as it splashed on the hardwood. *Don't cry, moron.*

"You can cry or cuss or do whatever you want. McGee. I'm gonna coach my team. If you don't like where you are, *grow some hair on your nuts and go and prove me wrong*." And he stormed off.

My jaw clenched. *You are wrong, Coach. And I'll make sure everyone sees it.*

Chapter 14

CORY

As infuriating and embarrassing as being on JV as a junior was, there was one place in my life where I felt popular and confident: Spanish class. Nicole and I sat together, quickly breezing through assignments and generally just having fun together. The people around us seemed to always be looking to *us*—for answers, for laughs, for direction on how class would go that day.

Most of the fun centered around our frumpy, perpetually confused teacher, Mrs. Navarro. Her English was broken, and her Spanish was often a little off, too. She told us she failed English four times. She got basic conjugations wrong, mispronounced words, and sometimes would stop in mid-sentence and just stare into space.

Some of her lines became legendary. An office aide just walked into her room once to get the attendance, even though the door was closed. She glared at the aid until she left.

"You don't just go through closed doors without knocking." She spoke with a serious, concerned tone. "What if that was someone's house? You could find naked people."

She also verbally called attendance every single day, long after every other teacher glanced at the seating chart to mark absences. She called every name, even though one kid never showed up to class all year. Every time a classmate attempted a Mrs. Navarro impression, it was a thick accent and a high-pitched "*Martín? Martín?*" (Nicole liked mine the best.)

When we weren't joking about our teacher, Nicole used the down time to write notes. Before texting and social media, a lot of teenage girls passed notes folded a certain way they must have taught in middle-school-girl class. Nicole liked to decorate hers with an artistic rendering of the person's name.

One of my life's ambitions was for Nicole to draw my name on a note. I watched her decorate so many names—usually just other girls she was friends with, but I noted with envy every guy's name she drew.

I had been seeing a name I didn't recognize for a while now—always carefully crafted by Nicole in multicolored bubble letters. At first, I ignored it. But eventually, my curiosity got the better of me. "Who's Cory?"

Her face flushed as her hand moved casually over the name. "Oh, um . . . Cory Jacobs. I don't know if you know him. He's a sophomore."

Hollywood portrays high school "popular" kids as a caste made up of plastic beauties and dumb jocks, who enforce their status through bullying. But usually, popular kids exemplify the true definition of the word—well-known and well-liked. Nicole was like that. So were Shannon Roberts and Charlie Gonzalez.

Sure, there were some hangers-on who put others down to protect their place, but these people were not truly *popular*. So I had never heard of Cory Jacobs.

Popular kids are respected. People enjoy watching them perform or cheering for them as they play their sports. They admire their intelligence or athleticism or humor or artistic talent.

Cory had no discernible skills. When he was finally pointed out to me, I saw he looked vaguely athletic—he was tall and well-built—but he didn't play any sports. He wasn't musical, artistic, or academically gifted. He did have a truck—a brand-new Chevy Silverado that he revved loudly in the parking lot—but no mechanical skills.

Kids who are *popular*? Almost everyone actually likes them. Maybe it's because they are secure in their status, but they lift others up more than tearing them down. So people enjoy hanging out with them. Cory spoke with a cocky arrogance that made the girls he flirted with giggle but belittled everyone else around him.

The more I heard about him, the more I couldn't figure it out. *Why is Nicole sending this loser all these notes? What is she thinking?* I wasn't so much envious as . . . disappointed.

I pointed Cory out to John at the final football game of the season. Our team was undersized and terrible, so we spent most of the time at the games people-watching. John was watching Ashley Lansford pass out water and wrap ankles. I was watching Cory lean over the railing, trying to talk to the cheerleaders. Every so often, Nicole and one or two other cheerleaders would run over to him, laugh about something, then dash back to the rest of the squad.

Our ritual after the game was to drive around like we were suddenly going to be invited to go somewhere or try something different (we went bowling once), but then we'd just wind up at Chili's sharing a plate of nachos and tearing through about a dozen baskets of chips and salsa and twenty Dr Pepper refills between us.

I wasn't in the mood for ranting about Coach Mays, so our talk centered around girls. John and Ashley were going to the movies on Saturday.

"Movies are a good no-pressure first date," John explained with all the authority of someone who'd never been on a movie date before.

"Not too much pressure to talk—and there's always ice cream or something after the movie, if you feel like it."

I laughed. "You still have that Marble Slab coupon?"

"Shut up." He set aside his empty glass for the waitress to refill it.

We exchanged theories on first dates for a few minutes. John talked about borrowing his dad's Oldsmobile again, and that brought Cory to mind.

"Man, you're thinking too much . . ." I shook my head. "You just need your daddy to buy you a brand-new Chevy, and then you don't have to think about it at all." I rolled my eyes. "Apparently, anyway."

John shot back. "You just don't like Cory because he's got Nicole's attention."

"Maybe so." My voice softened. "I just never figured Nicole would go for some random putz, just because he has a nice truck."

"You don't know anything about that guy. You didn't even know he existed, like what? A week ago? You've never even talked to him."

I shook my head. "Yeah, but did you watch him today? He's a complete tool."

John thought for a second. "Remember that guy last year who was jealous that Nicole and Shannon talked to you in Spanish and so he put down how you dressed? He seemed to think you were a putz, too."

"I probably am." I laughed, then realized I had hijacked an important conversation. "Sorry . . . tell me more about this Ashley situation. Is this a see-how-it-goes thing or do you think you're headed toward having a girlfriend here?"

John looked past me and talked through his teeth. "Uh . . . well . . . she already asked me to winter formal."

"How could I not know this already?!" I slapped the table and jumped up, both from this revelation and the fact that seven Dr

Peppers had me in desperate need of the restroom. I pointed to him as I dashed away. "You're telling me everything when I get back!"

I came back to re-stocked chips and salsa, and John explained the situation. Winter formal was a dance in early December where, by school tradition, the girls asked the guys. Ashley and a group of friends were planning to go together, and she invited John at the most recent FCA meeting.

As we counted out cash for our check, John paused thoughtfully, then spoke up. "You know, Jay, you could go with us . . ."

"Without a date? No way."

John smiled mischievously. "I have a feeling someone might ask you."

I groaned. Another secret. "I hate when you do this. Is it someone I'd actually want to go with?"

John started toward the car. "I promised not to tell . . . but I did give her your phone number."

John could stonewall with the best of them, so once he decided not to tell, there was no way to get it out of him. I went to bed scrolling names through my mind.

By Saturday morning, I was running through every possibility in my head. And then, just after noon—the phone rang. I wasn't expecting a call so soon, but I still got to the phone before my mom. "Hello?"

"Hi . . . Jay?" I didn't recognize the voice.

"Yeah." My voice shook a bit. "That's me."

"It's . . . Carol . . . I saw you at the conference?" Her voice told me she was a lot less confident on the phone than she was the last time I saw her. "From Memorial?"

I pursed my lips. Carol? Seriously? I *told* John I wasn't interested. "Oh. Hi, Carol. What's up?"

"John gave me your number. I hope you don't mind?"

I wanted to reassure her. *Don't be a jerk, Jay.* "No, it's fine."

"Well, you know the winter formal? I was wondering if you had a date yet."

I winced. "No." I'm no good at lying, even if I wanted to.

"Super . . ." She exhaled. "I mean . . . would you want to go with me?"

My brain searched for something to say that could let her down with kindness, but all I could think to say was, "Sure."

"Super!" she repeated. "So we'll make plans later, then?"

My mind went to John's plans. "John is going with a big group, so we could all go together . . . you know, *as friends.*"

Carol paused for a moment. "Yes . . . exactly. As friends. That's what I was thinking . . . We'll have a good time."

I smiled. "Good . . . well, I guess call me in a couple weeks and we'll iron out all the details, okay?"

"Sounds good." And with that, we said our good-byes and hung up. I sighed. *At least no one can make fun of me for not having a date.* But the dance was more than a month away, and I had just punted my chance for someone more interesting to ask me.

A little more than a week later—a Monday morning where gossip was high but energy was very low after Halloween weekend—I walked the halls into English class hearing lots of talk about winter formal. As class went on, Nicole and Hannah talked together in low tones, and I thought I noticed them glancing my way several times. I tried to shake it off, but . . . *what's going on?*

As we were leaving class, I found out. Hannah was smirking. "Hey, Jay . . . we have a question for you." I turned to them as my heart started racing.

Nicole stood from her desk in front of me. "Do you have a date to winter formal?"

Oh, crap. What is happening? My mind swam with the absurdity of turning down Nicole Ellis for *Carol.* I wanted to go back and throttle the guy who said "sure" to Carol instead of waiting. My heart sank—*too late now.* And since I still didn't know what was going on, I just told the truth.

"Yeah. I'm going in a group with John and some of his date's friends."

Nicole smiled. "Sounds like fun. I'll see you there, then." And with that, she and Hannah walked out into the hall together.

The rest of my day was ruined, of course.

I beat myself up. *I'm such a moron. Why say 'OK' five weeks ahead of time? To a girl I don't even like? I'm just going to end up hurting Carol's feelings and feeling bad about that, too. Idiot.*

Then my mind turned on John. *None of this would've happened if John had listened. I said I wasn't interested. He gave her my number. He always thinks he knows what's best, but he's just as clueless as I am.*

But mostly I just tried to figure out what actually happened. I played out the scene over and over. *What were Nicole's exact words? Did I see any disappointment when I said I had plans? What kind of smile was that?*

Nicole gave me no more clues in Spanish class. Just a joke about how Mrs. Navarro pronounced my name "*Yay*"—no different from usual. Most of the class was taken up by a vocabulary test.

I got through basketball practice and went home, but my mind kept swirling. *Why was Hannah involved at all? Wait . . . was Nicole asking me if I had a date for Hannah's sake? Was it Hannah that wanted to go with me?*

I tried to watch TV, but by about 7:30, I had enough. "This is stupid. I gotta find out something."

I grabbed the phone. I had Nicole's number memorized, even though I had never dialed it. Before I could chicken out, I punched in the numbers. My hand was weak and shaky as I tried to hold the phone to my ear. I couldn't breathe—the air stuck in my chest—as I heard the rings . . . *one . . . two . . .*

"Hello?" It was Nicole's voice.

"Hi . . ." As I spoke, all the breath I had been holding came out all at once. *Don't breathe into the phone, idiot.* "It's, um, Jay . . . McGee . . ." I held my breath again.

"Oh, hi, Jay." Her voice was casual, like I called her all the time. "What's up?"

I tilted the phone to exhale away from the receiver, then tried to speak. "I just wanted to call you and ask you about something."

I don't know what my plan was. At this point, I think I had decided that if Nicole was about to ask me to the dance, I was going to go with her and deal with the fallout. But mainly I just wanted answers.

She was cheery. "Ok, sure."

My mouth was completely dry. My heart was beating like we were in the middle of a set of suicides. "You know when you asked me about winter formal in English today?"

"Yeah."

"I was, um . . . wondering why you asked."

"Oh." She paused—I could almost hear the realization hitting her that I could have misinterpreted her question. "Hannah and I just thought it was cute that you were actually going. Kat told me you got a date."

"So . . ." I couldn't hang up without knowing. I had to ask. "You have a date already, then?"

I heard a soft, sympathetic sigh. Then in a quiet—almost apologetic—tone, "Yeah . . . I'm going with my boyfriend . . ."

I shook my head. *Boyfriend . . . of course . . . oblivious as always, Jay.*

"You know . . . Cory."

Chapter 15

SUPER!

The start of the JV basketball season brought familiar sights—teams running around in last decade's varsity uniforms, Coach Bored hunched over, glancing between the court and the printout from Coach Mays in his hand that told him the game plan, and the freshman cheerleading squad leading half-hearted cheers toward mostly empty bleachers.

I usually had a cheering section—or at least a few people there to support me. Mom was there every game, squealing with delight with every sunk basket and complaining loudly to whoever would listen whenever calls didn't go my way. Dad was at her side when he could be there, usually just quietly observing. Less frequent—Roger came when he was in town, John went to most home games, and occasionally Gary would turn up, as well. This year, there was a new addition.

For the first three games of the season, there she was, wearing something like a hand-painted t-shirt or sweater with shoulder pads along with high-waisted pleated jeans. Carol was my number one fan. She sat near John at the home game but all by herself at the two road games. Each time she noticed that I spotted her, she gave a little wave with her manicured nails.

The morning after the third game, I was walking to English class when Hannah came up next to me. She had that same playful smirk on her face that she had the day she and Nicole had asked me about winter formal.

"Are you dating *Carol Young*? I remember her from 8th grade!" She poked me. "Does Jay McGee finally have a *girlfriend*?" It annoyed me how cute she thought this whole thing was.

"No!" I said, escaping through the doorway as we arrived at class. "We're going to the winter formal together, but we're just going as friends."

Hannah smiled and shrugged. "I don't know if *she* knows that. I hear she's been bragging to a bunch of people that y'all are going out."

I was in a bad mood already. *Ugh. I only scored nine points last game, and now I have to deal with this, too.* The more apparent it became that Carol was hoping this dance would lead to something, the more desperate I was to shut it down, but, well, *how did Nicole treat me*? She's never embarrassed me or made me look ridiculous to people, and I didn't want to do that to Carol, either. *Treat others as you want to be treated*, as Jesus said. Still, I had to say something.

Unfortunately, Carol called first.

"Hi, Jay . . . It's Carol." Her voice was stronger this time, with a sense of determination.

I had no idea what to say. "Hey, Carol. Um . . . how're you doing?"

"Fine."

Silence. Awkward. *Think of something to say.*

Carol spoke again. "I have been thinking about the dance, and, well, we haven't really hung out since middle school . . . So I was thinking that it might make the dance less awkward if we went out together before then."

And that was how, instead of having a direct conversation about how we were NOT dating, I ended up going on a movie date with Carol that weekend.

Carol had moved to another school district after eighth grade. I didn't think it was that far—maybe fifteen miles—but as I made my way through an endless gauntlet of stoplights driving from one suburb to the next, I realized the effort she put into getting to my games. After nearly forty minutes of driving, I got there ten minutes late.

She stepped onto the porch wearing a form-fitting mock turtleneck tucked into khaki slacks that rode high over her waist, fastened with a black, four-pronged belt, at least four inches wide and lined with chrome accents all around. Over the turtleneck was a sequined cardigan buttoned only in the middle. As she clicked beside me toward my car, her high heels and high hair made her seem taller than me.

When she got in, I immediately saw we had a problem. The ceiling liner in Dad's car had come unstuck, sagging worse than my teammates' jeans. It rubbed against her hair, and I had a sudden vision of hairspray and static sparking a fire. I shoved the cloth back up, trying to smooth it out.

"Sorry. My dad's car sucks."

She slumped lower in her seat as I pulled out of the driveway. The heavy scent of her perfume filled the car, triggering memories of the scent that always lingered in the house after my mom hosted ladies' Bible studies.

It's never a great idea to just show up at the movie theater and then decide what to see from whatever is playing—especially in the doldrums before the Christmas season. A quick call to Moviefone—or at least a glance at the newspaper—would have helped a lot, but I was about to pay for my lack of effort.

The big release that weekend was *The Three Musketeers*, but we were 40 minutes late—or 90 minutes early. If it were John or Roger, we just would have waited, but I didn't want to kill an hour and a half with Carol.

I turned to her. "So it looks like our options are down to *Look Who's Talking Now* . . . or I'd be willing to watch *Rudy* again."

She shook her head, looking over the board. "You've already seen Rudy. We should pick something new . . . What about that *Piano* movie? I know it's rated R, but Siskel and Ebert liked it."

Hmm. Still a 25-minute wait, and it would be embarrassing if I got carded, since I was still a couple of weeks from turning seventeen. But Danny Devito voicing the thoughts of a dog wasn't something to fight for, so we got the tickets and sat down on a bench to pass the time.

She sat down first and I sat beside her, leaving "plenty of room for the Holy Spirit" (a saying from youth group). We sat there for a few seconds, watching people walk by. Then she turned to me, all smiles, and restarted the conversation loop we'd been stuck in since I picked her up.

She asks a question. "So . . . what do you have coming up in basketball?"

I give an answer. "We have a tournament coming up next week. I get to get out of school on Friday."

"That's cool."

I attempt a follow-up. "Um . . . How about you? Anything coming up?"

"Not really."

I don't know if it was nerves or she just didn't have anything to say, but despite the obvious attention she put into getting ready and her constant smiles in my direction, she struggled to respond with anything more than "That's cool . . ." or "Super!" over and over.

After a couple of those loops, I had enough. "Let's just go in. I'll get us some popcorn and Milk Duds or whatever."

She jumped up and reached for my arm. "Super!" I stiffened but allowed her to hold my arm as we walked into the theater.

We grabbed some popcorn, candy, and cokes and settled into the dark theater. I braced myself—my first taste of arthouse cinema. I was forced to watch *Citizen Kane* once and kind of liked it. *Maybe this will be okay.*

From the opening title cards, I knew *The Piano* wasn't my kind of movie—soft music, period costumes, a mute woman forced into a loveless marriage. I thought I would just be bored . . . *and then the clothes started to come off* . . . I looked down, suddenly imagining Miss Anne, our old Sunday school teacher, shaking her head in disapproval from across the room.

Well, I guess that's why it's rated R. An artsy moment of 'authenticity' for the Oscar voters. Whatever. It's over now.

But every time I thought I could relax, the clothes would come off again, the sex scenes getting more explicit. Then a rape. And a cut-off finger.

I shifted. I went to the bathroom. But I never got the courage to ask Carol if she wanted to leave. I was too embarrassed even to look her direction. Besides, I paid for this movie—might as well finish it.

We walked out in silence until we reached the car.

I shook my head as I started the car. "That Siskel's into some weird crap!"

The first laugh of the night. It was fun—until her laughing stretched too long, turning breathy and high-pitched.

Then she touched my knee, just a quick brush with her nails.

"You're so *funny*, Jay!"

I glanced at her with a closed-lip smile and put my eyes back on the road.

About halfway back to her house, as we approached a strip mall, Carol said, "I wonder if TCBY is still open . . ."

I shrugged. "Huh. Didn't know TCBY was still around." And I kept driving.

When I got into her driveway, she stayed in her slumped position under the sagging ceiling liner. She turned to me.

"You know, the dance is still three weeks away. Maybe we should . . ."

I cut her off. "Carol, I . . ." Eyes in my lap, I forced the words out. "I thought we agreed we were just going to the dance as friends."

I could see her arms fold out of the corner of my eye. Her voice dropped to almost a whisper. "Yes, I know that. I just thought . . ."

I shook my head. "No . . . you haven't been acting like you know . . . You've been telling people we're dating . . ."

She gasped. "No . . . I didn't say . . ."

"Whatever. It's okay . . . I just wanted us to be—you know—*clear* about things . . ." I glanced over at her, hoping she'd see the apology in my eyes.

That was all I had to say, and there wasn't anything else for her to say either. Slowly, she got up out of the car. "Good night, Jay. Thanks."

I drove the long road home. Every stoplight, I caught my reflection in the rearview mirror and shook my head. *I'm a jerk.*

The next Tuesday brought a home game—with the notable absence of Carol in the bleachers. From that game through the weekend tournament, I was just a little off—not hitting my threes, missing more free throws than usual, and never getting into any of those grooves that brought the big scoring numbers.

So it was a good mental break when Thanksgiving hit.

After dinner, Roger and I sat in his room, bellies stuffed, the Cowboys-Dolphins game on mute, trying to catch up. Roger flipped a basketball in the air while I ranted about *The Piano* for half an hour. Eventually, I ran out of steam and just lay there, staring at the ceiling.

"I don't know," I sighed. "I don't feel good about how I've treated Carol, but I don't know what else I should have done."

"Are you still going to the dance with her?"

"I think . . ." I paused. *Have I even seen or spoken to her since the movie?* "I mean, I'm not trying to bail on her."

Roger laid back, flipping the ball in the air again as he thought. "There's a difference between being nice and being passive, you know."

"I know," I muttered. "I just don't like saying 'no' if it makes people feel bad."

Roger caught the ball and sat up. "Yeah, but if you don't, you just let things sort of *happen* to you . . . it feels worse, but I think it's nicer to say 'no' early."

"I tried . . ."

Roger jumped back in. "No, I know . . . I'm saying you DID do it early with Carol. You saw where it was headed and you cut it off. That's a lot better than what Tiffany has done to me."

Tiffany had kept Roger in her bullpen since the third week of freshman year. She'd let Roger do all sorts of things for her—and that gave him hope—but every time he thought things were headed in the right direction, she'd start a relationship with a different guy.

I chuckled. "Man, if I had held on longer, I could've had Carol hauling a sofa-bed to my third-floor apartment . . ."

He threw the ball at me. We laughed and then settled in as the game caught our eye again—this was the infamous snowy game where

Leon Lett fumbled the game away for the Cowboys after a blocked field goal.

After the game, we started passing the ball between us casually.

"Dad says you're not off to the greatest start this year," Roger said. "You're not letting all this girl stuff get in your head, are you?"

I held the ball for a second. "No . . . I don't think so. It's been weird. My shot is just off this year."

"Why do you think that is?"

I thought back to our first practices after the varsity cuts. I had been shooting the ball with a lot of confidence—maybe too much. I wasn't really looking for my teammates.

Ward—who never says anything—points to me after a practice and says, "You come in here all cocky, like, '*yeah, I'm a pretty good shooter*.' You think you're too good to be here. But you're still a JV player, aren't you?"

I scoffed at the time, but the words stuck. I felt that accusation every time I went up for a shot—like I had to justify in midair if I should really be taking it.

Roger laughed. "I've heard you called many things, but '*cocky*' is not one of them. Ward just didn't want to be there that day and took it out on you."

I turned to Roger. "I don't know . . . it's like since then, I'm not sure whether to go out there and score as much as possible or to stop and look to pass. I'm questioning every shot, even as I go up with it."

Roger shook his head. "One thing's for sure. You can't go through life second-guessing every shot you take."

Chapter 16

WINTER FORMAL

It always felt a little empty when my brother left for school again. Roger stuck around for my 17th birthday on Friday—Mr. Gatti's pizza buffet with my family and John and back home for cake and ice cream and presents. Wild as ever. When Roger pulled out of the driveway on Saturday morning to head back, I went up to his room, flopped on his couch and flipped through the channels to pass the time.

I didn't have to kill a whole lot of time, because John came by that afternoon to bring me along as he got fitted for a tuxedo for the winter formal. I perched on a stool as the guy from Men's Wearhouse took his measurements.

John flinched when the guy measured his inseam. "You're really not renting a tux?"

I smiled. "Oh, yeah . . . looks like a lot of fun."

He shot me a look. "I'm serious. The girls are paying for everything else. I can't believe you're not springing for a tux."

My jaw clenched. John had been lecturing about my attitude toward this dance ever since he shoved Carol at me. "You know I don't have the money for that."

That was mostly true. I didn't ask my parents for money for anything that wasn't school or church—and even then, only when absolutely necessary. My birthday money meant I technically had enough, but I didn't want to wipe myself out for this dance. I had a black suit my parents got me for my grandma's funeral sophomore year, and I figured that was good enough.

John eventually guilted me into buying a new white dress shirt. I had finally called Carol and confirmed we were still going, and I didn't want to be a bad date. My plan was to go, try to have fun with John, and do my duty as Carol's date—open doors, pose for pictures, maybe even dance with her a couple of times.

On the night of the dance, I found myself posing for pictures on a front lawn I had never been on before, surrounded by unfamiliar faces. We were going in a group of ten, organized by Ashley and her best friend Heather, someone I just met that night. She introduced me to her boyfriend. I immediately forgot his name.

A short, curly-haired senior from Heather's theater class introduced herself and her date—*was it Monica and Hector? Something like that.* She brought along her best friend —*Erica? Elaine?* — whose escort was her cousin from another school. His name was Doug.

Unlike some groups, we drove cars into Houston instead of renting a limo. Our first destination was a mid-range steakhouse near downtown. Scattered throughout the restaurant were other clusters of tuxedoed teens and sequined gowns among the more casually dressed patrons. We sat at a long table set for ten—I sat at the end, across from Carol and next to John.

Carol's hair was teased high, her makeup thick. Her red velvet gown had a high neckline and long sleeves, made with rhinestone-studded lace. It made me itchy just looking at it. I wore a red tie to match.

I shed my jacket, fidgeting with my tie to avoid dipping it in food while slurping Dr Pepper to spare my white shirt.

Maybe because we were both so uncomfortable or maybe because there were no expectations, but I found it much easier to talk to her. At our end of the table, I even started to have a little fun. Sure, sometimes I'd see Carol staring off silently and realize I was in a side conversation with John, but I'd always try to correct that and include her again.

Shortly after the entrees arrived, I went to the restroom. I found myself at the sink next to Doug. He was fairly short—maybe 5'7"—with broad shoulders, a long chin, and curly hair that he kept short on the sides but which went a little longer on top and in back—not quite a mullet, but close.

As he was washing his hands, he gave me a sideways glance. "You having fun, dude?" His tone was sharp—almost accusatory.

I hesitated. "Well . . . yeah. Sure."

Doug dried his hands with two quick shakes. "You might have more fun if you talked to your date." And then he was gone.

I froze in front of the mirror, looking at myself. My body tingled with self-consciousness and shame. *Am I still being a jerk to Carol? Am I that oblivious?*

As I went back to the table, I saw Carol and Ashley laughing together as John smiled with a mouthful of food. *Everybody's having fun. What's that guy's problem?*

As we ate, I kept seeing Doug glance to the end of the table—toward me or toward Carol, I couldn't tell. My shoulders tensed more and more as the meal went on.

Once we got back to the car, I opened the door for Carol and went around to the other side and sat next to her.

"You having fun?"

She smiled. "Sure. I'm looking forward to the dance. The older girls back at Memorial said they had a good time at these."

I gulped. Ugh. Dancing. "That's cool." I could feel the nerves rising in my gut as I thought about where we were going—dinner was the easy part.

We rode silently for a couple of minutes as John and Ashley talked in the front seat. I leaned in toward Carol and mumbled. "Um, are you OK? I mean, I know you only know me and John."

She shrugged. "No, it's fine. This is fun. Doug actually goes to my school, though. He's in my physics class this year. We had English last year, too. But I don't really know him."

"Huh. You know more people than I do, then."

We drove into the parking garage of the Galleria-area hotel. Our fancy shoes echoed in the concrete garage as we made our way to the elevator. We stepped off the elevator. Noise. Color. Music. People. So many people. My eyes darted back and forth—tuxes and sparkly gowns—familiar faces out of context. I struggled to recognize anyone.

My group followed the crowd to an area where they were staging photos. The girls slipped off to the bathroom while the guys saved our spots in line. We stood as people bumped us or crowded by, trying to straighten our collars and ties. John wandered off toward a mirror.

Doug looked me up and down. "Nice tux, dude."

I started looking around. *Am I the only one without a tux?* I spotted several others—even some in boots, jeans, and a sports jacket.

Doug rolled his eyes. "Five guys. Four in tuxes—Carol's the only girl whose date didn't bother."

I looked again at my suit, fidgeting with my tie and buttons. "I mean . . . I didn't really have money for a tux . . . and we're just going as friends."

He smoothed the lapel on his jacket. "I'm here with my frickin' cousin, dude."

Then the girls came out again. As I posed for my picture with Carol, I watched her eyes for any clue that she was embarrassed by me. I tried to remember what she looked like when we first picked her up. It was *all* awkward, but is it the situation or is it just me?

As we made our way closer to the ballroom, the music kept getting louder. It was loud, thumping music. My heart started thumping, too. I felt a clammy sweat forming on the back of my neck. My vision tunneled to the dark, pulsating room as the first members of our group disappeared into the darkness.

I turned around. "Sorry, Carol," I stuttered. "I need to go to the bathroom again."

I raced away with my head down, bumping and weaving my way back to the bathroom. I closed the door to the stall. I didn't really need to go, but I didn't want people to see me pacing in a bathroom stall, so I pulled down my pants and sat down.

My heart was racing now. My skin felt cold even as sweat dripped from my forehead down my nose. My right leg shook as I tried to take some breaths.

Pull it together . . . what is wrong with you?

All day, I had prepared to go to the dance, sit around and talk and eat some of the snacks, dance a slow dance or two with Carol—to try to have as much fun as I could with her without changing her expectations.

I don't know what I thought the dance would look like—maybe like on TV shows where it's a table with a punch bowl in a dimly lit gym. I expected to rock back and forth with our hands outstretched on each other's shoulders. *I didn't prepare for this. I'm not ready for this.*

The stall walls pressed against me. The air was too thick to breathe. I spotted a hook on the door in front of me. I took off my jacket and hung it up. My back sweat made me shiver as I sat back down, but my face felt like it was on fire.

My head was overwhelmed with images of that dark room, those flashing lights, the club atmosphere. The thought that people expected me to go in there and *dance* made my heart race. I couldn't move.

I closed my eyes and put my hands on the back of my head, elbows on my knees. I tried to breathe. *Oh God help me.* When I opened my eyes, I saw a drip of sweat fall from my nose to my crumpled pants at my feet. I exhaled slowly. I still felt nauseated and gassy and clammy and gross, but I could get up.

My heart rate slowed as I pulled up my pants, worrying that they were wrinkled and ruined. I brushed myself off and opened the stall. My temperature seemed to regulate as I wet my hands and my face, running my fingers through my hair to put it back into place. I wiped my face with a paper towel and met my eyes in the mirror. *You can't hide in here forever. Here we go.*

With a nod to my reflection, I pulled my jacket back on and took a big step toward the door. I stopped there, steadying my breath one more time, then I shoved through the bathroom doors, weaved through the crowd, and dove into the ballroom.

I could feel the pounding music from my toes to the hair on my head. As my eyes adjusted, I saw John and the others gathered around one of the tables that surrounded the dance floor. My eyes darted back and forth as I made my way toward them. Dancing bodies gyrating under flashing lights—bumping and grinding, fast and close. My breath started to catch again.

I spotted Carol and greeted her with a smile and a nod and sat down, trying to slow my breaths. Seeing Carol gave me some comfort.

There's nothing to worry about. Carol won't want to dance to this stuff. We'll just wait for something slower while I sit here and pull it together.

Before these thoughts could pass through my mind, Heather came back from the dance floor. "Oh, Jay's here!" She grabbed Carol's hand. "Let's go!"

Carol stood. She ran her nails on my shoulder, beckoning me toward the dance floor. I froze, the muscles in my neck tensed. I shook my head stiffly.

"Not now," I stuttered. "You . . . y'all go ahead. Not now."

Left alone at the table, I buried my face in my hands. The pulsating music pounded in my chest. My heart doubled its pace. I tried to focus on taking breaths as the room seemed to close in around me.

One song and then another passed. My breaths were quick and short. My eyes could not focus, shifting wildly around the room. I could feel drops of sweat forming on my forehead and along my temples. My face felt cold, my body hot.

"You OK?" It was John's voice. He had sat down next to me.

I swallowed, forcing a casual tone. "Yeah. Just not ready to dance or anything yet, you know?"

The first chords of a slow country melody came over the speakers. John got up with Ashley. "You sure?"

I nodded. "Yeah." But when Carol looked my direction, I averted my eyes. I just . . . couldn't. But I had enough feeling back in my legs to get up and get some punch to bring back to us. We sat next to each other staring in silence in the same direction. My jaw clenched. *Carol spent a lot of money on this, and I'm ruining her night.*

I was beginning to psych myself up to ask Carol for a dance when the music started thumping again. My body immediately seized up, breath shortening, sweat forming again as the blood drained from my face.

I looked down. When I lifted my eyes again, there was Shannon

Roberts, a bright smile on her face. "Jay! Look at you! So cool to see you here!"

I forced a smile, moving my tongue in my mouth to try to get some moisture. "Hi." My eyes felt unfocused, my limbs heavy.

She leaned in, looking at my face. "Are you *drunk*?" She turned to John. "Is he drunk?" Her voice was sharper as she turned to one of the other guys at our table. "*What did you give to him*?"

I shook my head stiffly, forcing a dry laugh as a drop of sweat trickled down the side of my face. "I'm fine. Really."

Jimmy Schroeder came up from behind her, taking her hand to lead her back to the dance floor. She touched my shoulder. "Save a dance for me, OK?"

There's no way I'm going to be able to do that. I buried my hands in my lap and hunched over, pinning my chin against my chest. My tie hung between my knees, sweat dripping again onto the floor as I tried to control my breath.

Carol leaned over. "Jay . . . I think I'm gonna head back out, okay?"

I didn't look up. "Yeah. Don't let me ruin this for you. I'm fine." I lifted my head. "Hey . . . I'll get out there eventually . . . I promise."

John came back with Ashley from the food table. He slid a plate of cheese and crackers in front of me and patted me on the back and gave a sympathetic, tight-lipped grin, then turned back to speak in Ashley's ear. It was hard to hear anything over the *thump-thump-thump* of "Everybody Dance Now."

I watched Carol on the edge of the dance floor. Heather and the other girls were doing a good job of including her, but she never met these people before tonight. It was my job to make sure she had a good time tonight. She knew coming in that it wasn't going to be a night of romance, but all I've done is hide in the bathroom or sit paralyzed in this chair all night.

But one fast song after another pulsated in the room—club music, hip-hop, disco. *Come on . . . are they never going to play anything slow?*

I could see people talking around me, but the music drowned out their voices. Suddenly, the music dropped out, and one voice continued loudly for all to hear. "Gotta feel sorry for Carol."

The voice was Doug's. With a flash of embarrassment and anger, I whipped my head around and looked at him.

Doug rolled his eyes as the music started up again. "What? All you've done is sit there and eat cheese all night."

The music was the first chords of George Strait's "Cross My Heart." I pushed away from the table. My stomach churned in annoyance that Doug thought he might be the reason I finally got up, but I was running out of time.

I met Carol at the edge of the dance floor. "You wanna dance to this one?"

"Sure." And with that, I took her hand and walked out to the middle of the floor. While some people two-stepped around us, we just swayed back and forth with our hands on each other's hips.

My hands shook just a little to begin with, but with every rock, I could feel the tension leaving my chest and legs. I struggled where to put my eyes, glancing from her face to forehead to shoulder to my hands and feet, but eventually my nerves settled.

And as the dance went on, I waited for the normal pangs of guilt or discomfort, but they never came. There wasn't that worry gnawed at me every time I was with her—the fear that if I encouraged her too much, she'd get attached and I'd hurt her. There wasn't the unbearable awkwardness of the movie date, either. It was just . . . *dull.* As I glanced in her eyes, I could see she was feeling the same thing.

As the final chords resolved, I lifted my arm for her to do a spin, which went into a side hug that was reminiscent of when I first saw her at the youth conference. We exchanged polite smiles. And then another song started.

Na-na-nana-na-na-na, na-na-nana-na-na-na, Na! Na! Na! Na! Clap! Clap! Clap! Clap!

"The chicken dance!" I heard someone squeal and everyone rushed to the dance floor, forming a circle around the edge. I pushed my way off the floor, then stood and watched as everyone flapped their elbows, wiggled their rears, and clapped in unison. *This was just like a youth group song!*

I had done enough "Pharaoh, Pharaoh" in my day that I knew I could keep up. *Hey, why not?* I squeezed back onto the dance floor next to John, where he was trying to follow along, just a half-beat behind everyone else. Before long, we were laughing and moving along with the crowd. As we spun around the floor, I looked at the big smiles on the faces of John and Ashley—and Carol, too. I realized that I was smiling, as well.

When the song was over, I stayed out on the floor for "Cotton-Eyed Joe" and even the Madonna song that followed. I stood in a circle with my group—John, Ashley, Carol, Heather and the rest—just sort of vaguely keeping time with the movements of my feet, the bends of my knees, and my hands. As the song went on, my movements got bolder. At one point my foot came off the ground as I dipped down and did something with my hands that was like "the twist"—but not. I realized I was biting my lip. *Time to quit while I'm ahead.* I walked off the floor.

I shook my head at my terrible dance move on my way back to the table, but the surge of anxiety stayed away. I sat down, just feeling exhausted.

After a couple more songs, the rest of the group joined me at the table, each of us sipping on the dregs of the remaining punch. Jackets were hung on the back of the chairs, high heels were stored under the table, and bowties lay on top. We were all a sweaty mess.

A familiar song faded up through the speakers— "The Dance" by Garth Brooks. I turned back toward Carol, but she wasn't there. I looked toward the dance floor, where I saw Doug leading her by that hand. I rolled my eyes. *Doug to the rescue.*

That left Doug's cousin sitting there alone for what was sure to be the last dance of the night. I smiled at her and extended my hand. One more dance.

As we politely rocked back and forth to the music, my eyes scanned the ballroom. It didn't seem nearly as dark as before. I saw my classmates all around. Shannon and Jimmy. Eddie and Mustang Sally. Charlie and his date. Hannah and hers. John and Ashley.

Then I spotted Nicole. I hadn't seen her all night. She wasn't on the dance floor—she was by the double doors where we all came in. Towering over her was Cory. Her finger was in his face, her face red. Did I see tears? He grabbed her arm, and she tore it away.

I craned my neck to watch as anger burned in my belly. Visions of kicking the crap out of this guy flashed in my mind as he grabbed her by the shoulders and shook her slightly.

Does no one else see this? Someone's got to do something . . .

Just as I shifted to go to her rescue, she broke free and exploded through the doors and out of the ballroom. Cory kicked the door but didn't follow.

Yes, our lives are better left to chance. I could've missed the pain. But I'd have had to miss the dance.

And then the lights came up. The dance was over.

Chapter 17

TOO EASY

I would have pushed him off her, slammed him up against the wall. He takes a swing at me . . . Duck under it, then an uppercut to his gut . . . he doubles over—a knee to his face . . .

Three weeks later, and I still sometimes ran through the woulda-been confrontation with Cory in my mind. And here in the car on the way back from Christmas with Grandma in Missouri, my brain had thirteen hours to wander in every direction—basketball, Coach Mays, and Coach Bored. John and Ashley. Carol. Doug. Nicole and Cory. Nicole and the baseball game. Nicole and the letter. I fumed. I smiled. I cringed. I shook my head in shame.

But mostly, as the fields and hills passed by my window and Dad's barbershop tapes repeated over the car stereo, I just felt alone. I was the public school kid at church, the white and nerdy honors student in the basketball program—completely uninteresting to my coaches and to the opposite sex and weird to the people who should've been my peers. Alone—everywhere I went.

I tried talking myself out of my feelings. *I've got John. I've got Roger and Mom and Dad. It doesn't matter if I fit in at church—I have my relationship with God.* I was exhausted from always thinking about what other people thought about me. *It just doesn't matter, Jay.*

Except that the thing I wanted most—to play and succeed on varsity—depended entirely on what one man—Coach Mays—thought about me. Whenever he berated the varsity—"*We can't win games if we can't score the basketball!*"—I stood there, hoping he'd look my direction and see a solution.

Winter break provided time for extended practices. We got enough time off around Christmas day for me to take my family trip, but once we got back, it was four-hour practices Monday through Wednesday and a tournament Thursday through Saturday.

This last set of games before the new semester was a chance to convince Coach to bring me up for the league games that really mattered—he was known to sometimes make a roster adjustment going into district play. But the season had been frustrating so far. I led the team in scoring my sophomore year, just over eighteen points per game. This year, my average was barely above fourteen.

I was basically trading two made two-pointers for two missed three-pointers. I knew Coach wanted his outside shooters to mostly shoot from outside the arc, so I was trying to show him that I could. But every time I went up for a three-pointer, it was like an alarm went off in my brain: *This is your shot at varsity!* And it took me out of the game and into my head.

In the New Year's tournament, though, something clicked. In our first game, I was seeing more openings near the lanes, driving in close, hitting fadeaways and drawing fouls. I had five of those old-fashioned three-point plays, three more buckets, a three-pointer, and four more free throws—a season-high 28 points. We won by twenty.

We breezed through the second game, too, on Friday, a 12-point victory. I led the scoring again, this time with 22 points. I was still getting fouled a lot (9-for-10 on free throws) and I shot fifty percent (3-for-6) on threes.

The Saturday morning game, I was hot from the field again, but without many free throws. I had 18 points going into the last few seconds. We were down by two with twelve seconds remaining.

Coach Ward looked at his printout: "We're going to have Dee run the pick-and-roll off the left elbow, but Eddie kicks it to Mac for the three." He nodded making sure he understood it right himself. "Be ready for a rebound."

I was 0-for-2 from three-point land that day, but I had been sinking almost everything else. I felt good. The play went off just as it was drawn up—Dee to Eddie to me. I caught it, set my toes behind the line and released . . . *clang*. Just a little long. The rebound bounced off Eddie's fingers and into enemy hands. We lost.

Every detail of that shot seared into my mind—the feel of the ball in my hands, the position of my feet, the breeze from the defender diving toward me, how the ball came off my fingers. I knew the exact place on the rim where it hit, where it ricocheted off the other side and where it finally spilled back over the edge. There's no telling how many times I re-shot that game-winner in my mind when I should have been sleeping.

But no time for that now. The losers' bracket game started in twenty minutes. We hustled to the next court. Ward pulled out another printout—the losers' bracket game plan from Coach Mays.

The offense we ran in this game strictly mirrored the varsity playbook. And the only role for the shooting guard was to pass and shoot threes. I made my first one—then missed my last three. I scored only six total points, and we were eliminated.

Varsity got bounced from their tournament in three games. We paid for it Monday. Practice wasn't practice; it was running. Lots of it. We ran in the gym, ran out on the track, and then ran around the fieldhouse exterior.

"*You're gonna run till I get tired,*" Coach Mays spat. He never got tired, even though half the time he was running right alongside someone, screaming in his ear.

Big O bent over to puke. Coach saw it as opportunity to get at eye-level with his big man. "*We can't win in the paint if we ain't tough!*" Coach's snuff flew out of his mouth, mixing with the mess in the grass. "*Y'all don't have a lick of mental toughness.*"

We ran as Coach spouted off all the ways the varsity wilted during the weekend tournament. I had almost tuned out when I heard. "*And on the JV, McGee is out there clanking threes when the game's on the line! Can score any time except when it matters!*"

It hurt, but I was glad to hear my name. *Well, at least he remembers I exist.*

After practice, I waited by Charlie's car, hoping for a ride home. He came out with a couple of other guys. I could tell they were talking about parties and whatever it was people did that wasn't school or basketball.

I heard my teammates talk all the time like this. It was the language of inside jokes, first names and nicknames that I didn't know, and events I never heard about. They were living in a world I knew nothing about and was never invited to join. They never talked specifics around me. I knew there was a world of drinking, parties, sex, and all that—but I never knew who was doing what or how much.

Like always, they quieted down as they approached me. Charlie smiled and nodded in my direction. "Hey Mac, need a ride?"

Once we were in the car, his smile faded. "I've had about enough of Coach Mays's BS, man . . ." Charlie's name had come up several times during Coach's tirades. He was ready to quit.

The fun stuff is too much for my virgin ears, but I do get to hear about all his problems. What am I, the team dad?

After spending a few minutes in my driveway trying to talk Charlie down from dropping basketball, I trudged with weary legs up the stairs and into my room. Winter break was over; the spring semester—and district play—was about to begin.

When I was in the thick of basketball season, the school day was just a prelude to what was really on my mind. I did my work, listened enough to learn what I needed to know, and joked around with my friends. But there was always game film running in the back of my mind and a fire in my bones to get to the end of the day and play.

The first game was a road game—a 45-minute bus ride. Hymns in my head for calm—I would sing them silently or even a little out loud. As the calm came to me, I could relax my mind—think through the game, even doze off. I stirred as we pulled up to the campus, with one vision in mind: stick to the shots you know.

First pass I received on the right wing, I faked the three and ducked under—two dribbles and BAM. Two points.

It came easy that day. I was hitting from the left and the right, the baseline and the elbow. I effectively used the three-point threat as a decoy, creating openings to slip by for quick jumpers or passes to the interior. Sixteen points, nine assists through three quarters—we were up by 14.

Coach Ward grabbed me by the jersey as we headed out for the fourth quarter. "Time to take some chances out there now, Mac."

I didn't pass up the threes in the fourth quarter—missed all three. We still won by ten.

Varsity won their district opener, too, but it was an ugly low-scoring battle, so that ruined any chance that Coach would be in a good mood. He drilled us again and again in his offense, running the same plays over and over.

"*That pass was late, Tee!*" Coach hollered. "*Your timing ain't perfect. We work till it's perfect! Run it again!*"

The JV mostly ran defense, but once we got on offense, I wanted to show what I had been doing the first game—fake the three, quick step inside . . . nothing but net.

I turned to see Coach Mays striding toward me, red-faced. "*You wanna run my offense, McGee?!*"

I opened my mouth—just to say "yes, sir"—but he cut me off.

"You come bouncing in here thinking you're big because you scored a few points on JV again." He waved his arms. "As long as you can put a good number in your spreadsheet, you're just as happy as you could be." He whipped back around, turning his back to me.

I shook my head and looked down. *I guess that means he's not thinking about calling me up.*

He whipped back around, as if he were reading my thoughts, shouting up into my face. "*You only think of your dadgum self, McGee!*"

I skipped youth group that night to hang out with Roger, who was in his last week at home before spring semester. We shot hoops in the driveway by the glow of the moon and the porch light.

Roger listened as I told him about practice that day. He shook his head and scoffed, his breath visible in the night air. "Mays is a moron. He'd rather score 45 points a game his way than adjust to the player he has."

I shook my head and sank a shot, the ball bouncing right back to my hands. "It does me no good to think of Coach as an idiot. He's the only one who can make it happen for me. But I just don't understand it."

I knew Roger was still bitter toward Coach Mays. After Mays cut him, Roger earned his letter jacket as a third-string safety on the football team. But Roger was the one who taught me to love basketball, in the driveway just like this.

We alternated shots in silence for a while, our fingers growing numb as the temperature continued to drop. Then Roger paused, lost in thought.

"You remember that suitcase you got for your 13th birthday?"

I laughed. The infamous suitcase. My first birthday as a teenager, I saw this huge present waiting to be opened—and it was a *suitcase*, something I had not asked for, thought about, or wanted. I was devastated.

"You hated that suitcase, but Mom knew you needed one."

"Yeah . . . I just used it on our Christmas trip."

"You . . ." Roger took a shot, "are like a present Coach Mays didn't ask for. Maybe one day he'll quit pouting that you're not something else and actually use you."

"Or . . ." I took a step back and launched a longer shot. "I could make myself into what he wants me to be." *Swish.*

Roger was in the stands in the next game. I tried to run Coach's offense. When the three wasn't there, I passed instead of taking the 15-foot jumper. When the ball was kicked out to me from inside, I took the three.

I sunk my second one, but I just couldn't get any rhythm after that, especially since the opposing coach stuck his best defender on me. I misfired four straight times in the second quarter from behind the arc, so in the second half, I looked to pass more. I scored a couple of times on a press break and two free throws in the third, but I missed my only shot—another three-pointer—in the fourth quarter. I ended up with just nine points, and we lost by seven.

I braced myself for another brutal takedown from Coach at

Saturday morning practice, but he hardly looked my direction. Varsity won their Friday game, and he was working on a full-court press he wanted to implement against Tuesday's opponent.

After practice, I pulled on my sweatshirt and went out to the parking lot. On Saturdays, I had my dad's car, so I wasn't begging for a ride.

Maybe that's why Charlie's guard was down. As I was putting my key in the door, I heard his voice over my shoulder.

"There were a bunch of hotties there, man . . . I thought for sure I was going to get some from somewhere, but I ended up shut down, man. I mean, there was Nicole, but . . ."

I froze, keeping my back turned.

Tee's voice: "Nicole Ellis? What's wrong with you, man? She's hot!"

"Nah . . . but that's *too easy.*"

I spun around. *What did he just say?*

Tee laughed. "Careful! Mac Daddy is gonna fight you!"

Charlie's eyes met mine, then looked away. He shrugged and softly said, "Mac . . . I'm sorry, man."

I quickly got in my car, started it up, and pulled away. My mind raced.

"Too easy"?

Chapter 18

OFF-TARGET

Too easy. It didn't make sense. Solid girl, sometimes at FCA—John said so, and Kat's one of her friends. And isn't she with Cory? What's she doing going after Charlie last weekend? The questions ran through my mind all night.

I never know anything about anyone unless it happens right in front of my face in class. If she's changed recently, I missed it. She seems like the same old Nicole whenever I see her. *What business of mine is it, anyway? Why is this bothering me so much?*

All this was still pressing on my mind when I got to English class that Monday, where Nicole smiled at me as I sat down next to her. My stomach clenched, like I was back to middle school, when I froze up with nerves every time I was near her.

My thoughts spun as I tried to understand what I was feeling. Finally, it hit me. I thought I knew Nicole. She might have been my best friend out of all the girls I knew. And now I realize I don't know her at all. And it made me sick to my stomach.

Unfortunately, my nervous, sick stomach was making me very gassy. I could feel bubbles moving around in my gut as I tried desperately to hold it in. But when I shifted to pull my textbook out, it happened—no audible sound, but I could smell it. And it was bad.

I started sniffing—carefully, quietly inhaling through my nose—first to assess the problem, then with the absurd thought that if I inhaled it enough, the odor wouldn't travel beyond my seat. Wishful thinking.

I saw Nicole's nose wrinkle. *Oh jeez, she smells it. That means Charlie will smell it . . . and Hannah . . . This is going to kill me.*

I lowered my head and kept inhaling. Out of the corner of my eye, I could see her writing something with a marker on her textbook cover as the teacher droned on. She held up the book toward me.

"Something smells," written in her bubbly lettering. My face flushed.

But just before I imploded from embarrassment, I caught her expression. She was sharing a joke with me, not accusing me. She bit her lip in amusement and tilted her head in the direction of the guy who sat in front of her.

She thinks it's Nate. All my inhales reversed into a breathy chuckle of relief. I wrinkled my nose and smirked, playing along. I felt a little sorry for Nate, who probably was smelling it too, but I didn't mind someone else taking the fall.

The nerves settled after that—no more churning and, thankfully, no more gas. But I was ashamed. I was secure enough with Nicole that I could fart next to her and she'd assume it was someone else. But one cryptic comment from Charlie, and my whole image of her is up in the air.

Charlie was ashamed, too. "I shouldn't have said that, Mac." He was taking me home after practice that evening.

I looked at him, confused. I knew what I had been thinking about for two straight days, *but Charlie*? "What are you talking about?"

"About Nicole. It wasn't right."

I turned my head toward the window. "Just forget it. It's none of my business anyway."

"No, I mean it wasn't right!" His voice was more emphatic this time. "Nicole's not easy. She's just messed up right now. Cory got her so twisted up that she's been throwing herself at other guys left and right . . . I just wasn't about to take advantage of that."

I felt a pang in my chest. "You mean they broke up?"

"Cory's a tool, man," Charlie scoffed. "He keeps trying to keep her on a string. They're constantly on and off—it's a mess. And when they're off . . . Mac, she's all screwed up."

A fire burned in my chest. Fantasies of beating the crap out of Cory filled my mind again. "How can she let a guy like that twist her up so bad?"

Charlie shook his head. "Dude, I don't know. I really don't."

I wanted to ask more questions, but we were already pulling up into my driveway. I took a deep breath, grabbed my stuff, and hopped out. *Talking about her doesn't help Nicole anyway.*

"Thanks, man. See you tomorrow." And he drove away.

There was buzz the next morning among the JV players. Report cards were out, and we had lost a player to "no pass, no play"—Kevin Peters, one of the sophomores who'd been cycling through the small forward spot all season. We were wondering if Coach would fill his roster spot at all, and if he did, who it would be.

It turned out that he brought up a freshman—Chris Jackson, who had been leading the freshman team in scoring from the point guard position. His older brother Ty was a senior, varsity's starting power forward. Chris was a lot shorter than his brother—5'11" in his shoes—but he was quicker and more athletic.

"Chris is not on this team to sit and watch," Coach Ward told us when he made the announcement. “He’s been having a great season so far, so we’re going to make room for him to play here.”

I went through my regular routine on the bus, picturing Chris taking most of the minutes at point guard from Dee, who had only been scoring about five points per game. I figured Chris would be more aggressive driving inside, so I would need to be ready for kick-outs and more open threes.

After layups drills, we huddled around Ward for the game plan. He pulled out his printout. “Here’s how we’re going to start. Thompson at center . . . Travis and Benson at 3 and 4 . . . Dee at the point . . . and Jackson, you’re the shooting guard.”

My jaw and stomach dropped. I’d started every game since sixth grade. I was still the only one on the team averaging more than ten points per game. Coach Ward met my eyes, almost daring me to complain. I patted Chris on the back and put my hand in for the pregame break.

Once I sat on the bench, though, the shock slowly morphed into anger, then rage. *I’m being shoved aside for this shrimpy kid who has never even practiced at this position.* I wanted to cheer for my teammates, but I also had to admit that I wanted to see Chris fall flat on his face.

He didn’t. When he got passes on the wing, he faked the three but instead of pulling up for a 15-foot jumper like I would, he drove all the way to the basket. He was a blur getting to the baseline. His only weakness was that when he drew a foul on those drives, he usually missed one of his free throws.

Toward the end of the first quarter, Ward finally called my name to go in for Dee, pushing Chris to point guard. Running point, Chris was a slasher, driving inside and forcing up shots or dishing to the big men. I was mostly a spectator for about five minutes on the court, then back to the bench.

I got two more five-minute stretches at the end of the half and late in the third quarter. I got one chance when Chris kicked it out to me in the third quarter for a three. I missed it, and I was back on the bench a few seconds later.

With two minutes left, we were down by seven when the other team was called for a technical foul. Coach called me off the bench to shoot the shots. I made both and stayed in the game the rest of the way. Late in the game, I made a shot after grabbing a long rebound. I finished with four points. We lost by eight.

I spent the bus ride home trying to figure out what to do. I didn't understand it. Chris was a point guard. Our point guard's the one struggling, but then he replaces me instead. But if Coach Mays wants him at shooting guard, Ward is just going to roll over and do what he wants. But we still had a hole at small forward, especially now that Peters is ineligible.

I approached Coach Ward early the next practice, while other guys were still getting dressed. He stood up and folded his arms as I walked up.

"Coach, can I ask you something?"

He barely suppressed an eye roll. "Sure, Mac. What is it?"

"I was, um, wondering about Chris playing shooting guard."

He cut me off. "I told y'all he was up on the JV to play."

"I know." I gulped. "I was thinking that if he was going to play the two if I could get a chance to play some small forward. You know I was a forward as a freshman . . ."

Ward narrowed his eyes. "We'll see, OK? You go warm up."

I went and grabbed a ball, not knowing whether that little talk did any good or not. I put my head down and practiced hard the rest of the day.

The next day, we were practicing with varsity again. Coach Mays was running a full scrimmage, running subs for both teams. He started me on the JV side at small forward—I was stunned, but then I went to work.

I was outsized by Kelvin Davis, varsity's starting small forward—he had three inches and 25 pounds on me—but he was no quicker than I was, so that masked my biggest defensive weakness. I got three chances from three-point land. I hit one of them.

After practice, Coach had us kneel down in front of him. He started going down the line, tearing into one guy after the next. Guys looked down, as if they could hide by not looking his direction. His gaze hit Kelvin.

"Davis!" he boomed. "You refuse to work! You can't get open enough to even get the ball, let alone get an open shot." He rose onto his toes. "YOU GOTTA MOVE WITHOUT THE BALL, SON!"

Coach shook his head and spit into his coke can. He waved his hand in my direction. "You had the worst defender in the program on you today, and you couldn't get open! *BRUTAL!*"

His black eyes met mine, and his lips moved into something like a smile. "McGee . . . you got to play a little forward today, son? You think you can handle forward on the varsity, do you? So you go talk to Coach Ward. You got something to say to me?"

I looked down, forcing the words out. "I . . . I just want to play, Coach."

His fingers came together in the dainty pose he made when he mocked our manhood. His voice was soft. "You're offended that you didn't start the other day. You're offended that you're a junior on the JV . . ."

I tried to shake my head. *No . . . that's not it . . .*

He threw his hands back down as fists at his side. "*WE'RE OFFENDED THAT YOU'RE ONE-FOR-ELEVEN ON THREES IN DISTRICT PLAY!*"

I hung my head, and he moved on to his next target. There was only one thing to do. No more wild shots, no more defensive lapses. I need to be perfect. Leave him nothing to criticize—nothing to mock or yell about. *Perfect.*

Once per season, we did the JV and varsity games as a double-header home game. It was the one time per season that JV players got a small taste of the varsity atmosphere—bigger crowds, varsity cheerleaders, and pep band. A lot of the crowd didn't show up until the varsity game, of course, but by the end of the game, the arena was always buzzing.

Last year, I had my best game in this atmosphere. Spurred on by Nicole and the cheerleading squad on the sidelines, I scored 32 points, including five three-pointers. When I sank a three to ice the game in the last minute, the roar of the crowd was one of the thrills of my life.

I got the starting nod this game at small forward. Offensively, it wasn't much different from playing shooting guard—both roles worked the wings in Coach's system. But on defense, I was battling bigger bodies down low. I remembered my years as a big man, using my body to create leverage to stick with my man and block out for rebounds. Perfect.

I sprinted down to my wing, executed my cuts, and fixed my eyes on the ball—except for glances toward Coach Mays to see if he was watching. No mistakes.

Back on defense, I grabbed a rebound and heaved a long pass to Chris streaking down the sideline. He caught it and flew to the rim for a fast break layup. The next time on offense, Chris drove and kicked it to me for a three—catch, shoot, *swish.*

Time out. Ward patted my back as I ran by. "Good one, Mac. Sit down for a bit." I hated to come out when I was in a groove, but my mouth was dry and it felt good to get some water.

As I sat and watched the crowd get bigger, I nodded my head confidently. This was my chance to show in front of everyone where I belonged. Everyone would be saying after the game, "Why is this guy still on JV?"

But there wasn't much chance to stand out the rest of the first half. Chris ran the point in the second quarter, and he didn't give up the ball unless he had to. We fell behind as the freshman threw up contested layups and turned the ball over, trying to force passes at the last second.

Things got worse to start the second half—three turnovers in a row led to a fifteen-point deficit. When Chris flopped on the bench in frustration at the end of the third quarter, the game was out of reach.

Dee was back at point and I was back at the two for the fourth quarter. The plan was quick scores to try to get back in the game. We started with my familiar shots—two, four, six points in three possessions. Within twelve, but time was running short. It was time to start chancing the threes.

Dee hit the first one. Chris—back in the game now—missed the next one. We traded fouls and free throws, then on the next trip down, I landed on my spot and called "ball!" Dee kicked it to me. Catch and shoot . . . three more points.

We put up five more points to draw within seven. Time out, and we went to the bench. Wiping the sweat from my face, I took in the atmosphere—the growing crowd and familiar faces. Mom screaming. Dad wringing his hands. John yelling alongside the baseball guys. The cheerleaders. Shannon. Hannah . . . *where's Nicole*? I couldn't believe I hadn't noticed the freshman taking her spot in line all night.

I saw Coach Mays prowling the area outside the home locker room. His stare was fixed on Ward, watching as the coach stared at the printouts. Then it moved down the bench. He met my eyes. *Time to show him.*

We came out in a full-court press. Dee and Chris trapped the ball along the sidelines. The desperate pass came out. I intercepted it, then passed to Chris streaking back toward the hoop. Down to five points.

After another defensive stop, Dee pushed the ball into the lane, then kicked it to me beyond the arc. I pump-faked, but instead of taking a step in, I went sideways. *Bam.* Three-point shot, two-point deficit, and I was still perfect. Six-for-six.

We traded baskets for the next minute, until it came down to the last possession. I was ready for my chance to take that last shot again, but they double-teamed me. The ball went to Chris instead. He drove to the basket . . . and lost control of the ball. I cussed under my breath as it bounced harmlessly out of bounds as the buzzer sounded.

I was frustrated, but as I jogged to the sidelines, another storyline ran through my mind. *We almost came back from fifteen down. I shot 100% from the floor, including three three-pointers.* A smile cracked the corner of my mouth.

As the varsity warmed up, Coach Mays took a few minutes to address our team. “That was a good comeback, but you put yourself in that position with dumb mistakes. Jackson, you’ve got to play within yourself. Those turnovers cost us the game . . .”

When Coach was in pregame mode, he was a little gentler—no castrating put-downs right before he goes out to coach his team. But as he went on, he never mentioned my name once. Talking about the comeback, “Dee and Chris, you ran that press just like we practiced. When we practice well, we can execute in the game.” No mention of my steal or nine fourth-quarter points.

So much for being perfect.

Coach led us back out of the locker room, where we turned to watch from the bleachers while he headed to the sideline. The varsity game was another nailbiter. Up by three with a few seconds left, Charlie blocked a three-point attempt from the corner, sealing the game for the home team.

Coach called both teams back to the locker room for the postgame meeting. After a brief rundown of the game and the mistakes they made to make it so close, Coach got quiet for a moment. He shot a look at Ward and shifted his feet. He stuck his hands in his pockets and looked down.

"Fellas . . . gather around here." We were already there.

Ward spoke up. "Coach has something he wants to address with y'all."

We looked at each other. I heard someone whisper, "I hope he's retiring."

"I know y'all don't like me. I know some of y'all hate my guts. But I've always had your best interests in mind. Once you're out of this program, things change—players sometimes even come back and grab a beer with me."

There was a loneliness in his voice, as if he were asking for us to keep that door open to him. But I couldn't figure out where he was going with all this.

He waved his hands. "Anyway, the point is that I want all of y'all to succeed. And the choices you make now can make or break the rest of your lives—and I'm talkin' about way more than basketball here."

He looked away in thought, then lifted on his toes. "Everyone says life is short. That's bullcrap, fellas. Life is *long* . . . Whatever you end up doin' in this life, you end up doin' for a long, long time. You go around thinkin' life is short, you end up doin' stupid crap without thinking about the consequences."

My eyes went back to Coach Mays, turning over his words in

my head. *Life is long*? I'd never heard anyone say that before. But the thought struck me: Coach is thirty-something years older than us. How can a seventeen-year-old even begin to understand what that many years feels like? Let alone seventy or eighty . . .

My train of thought was broken by a loud cough from Coach Ward. He looked at his watch and shot Mays a get-to-the-point look.

Mays's black mustache curled over his bottom lip as he chose his words. Then he blurted out, "*Wrap yer stump when you hump.*"

Huh?

Oh!

Yuck!

My brain flashed from confusion to understanding to disgust within a second. I stared at the ground, blood rushing to my face. A couple guys around me snickered.

Coach's voice got more stern. "It's no joke. There's nothin' that'll derail your life faster than gettin' some girl pregnant." He relaxed back onto his heels.

Coach Ward chimed in. "And don't think pullin' out will work, either . . ."

Mays nodded stiffly and stuffed his hands in his pockets. "That's right . . . you, uh . . . *dribble before you shoot.*"

I covered my face. *What the heck is this all about?*

Coach exhaled. "I think that's it. Let's gather up." We all put our hands in, shouted "'Cats!" together and we started to disperse.

I felt like I was sleepwalking as we walked out. Somebody had to know why Coach decided to gather us up for a sex talk, but I was as clueless as ever.

As I reached my mom and dad, I thought I overheard someone say something that made no sense to me.

"I bet that was about that cheerleader."

My mom gushing over my game went over my head as we drove home. My thoughts were stuck back in the locker room, replaying every weird thing Coach said. We got home late, but I decided to chance calling John. He picked up.

"Hey man, great game."

I cut to the chase. "Yeah, but Coach was really weird after the game. He sat us down and gave us some sort of talk about our future and good decisions and not getting girls pregnant."

John groaned. "Yeah. I bet Coach Thomas does the same thing for us tomorrow. It's a shame, man."

I wanted to throw the phone. *Why does everyone know what's going on except me?* "What? Why?"

"I can't believe you haven't heard." John sighed. "Nicole's pregnant."

Chapter 19

HEATING UP

Pregnant? I held the phone in silence. I felt like there was a hole through my chest, but I couldn't understand the feelings—shock, anger, grief, even betrayal—all at once.

"Jay, you there?" John's voice startled me. I dropped the phone.

I fumbled picking it back up. "Yeah . . . just—*surprised*—I guess. How do you know it's not just a bad rumor?"

"She's told a few people." John mumbled. "She told Kat."

We hung out on the phone for a few more minutes, hardly saying anything, then fell into silence. Then we heard a click.

"Hello? John? Jay?" John's mom had picked up another extension. "It's late you two. Time to go to bed."

John growled. "*Mom!*"

"Sorry, Mrs. Agee. I think we're done anyway. Bye, John"

"Bye."

That night in bed, I couldn't sleep. I tried to process my emotions. One moment I was sure it wasn't true—it couldn't be. When I convinced myself to believe it, the rage surged. *Who was I mad at?*

Cory? Nicole? I didn't have any right to feel betrayed. I wrestled, I fumed, and I eventually dozed off.

But it wasn't long before my eyes opened again. One word pierced my mind. *Pregnant.* I squinted to look at the clock. 1:48. A new emotion flooded in. It was . . . *disappointment.* I wanted Nicole to be better than this. Then I wanted to blame this all on Cory, just to protect my image of her. But I knew I'd be lying to myself.

But just as I could feel my heart trying to condemn her, something caught inside of me. Her fault or not, she must be scared. She needs help. *But what am **I** going to do? Rescue her?* I groaned helplessly.

Then I closed my eyes. *God, you can help her. Please, there's nothing I can do. But you can reach her. And if there's anything I can do, show me.*

Then my body relaxed again. I drifted back to sleep.

Nicole wasn't at school all week. I didn't see Cory either, except once—laughing with his friends like nothing had happened. No one brought it up to me directly, but the whispers were everywhere.

By Friday night, I was back on the court. Time to focus on what I can control. Time to prove myself again.

The game was against Rayburn, the worst team in the district. We built a big lead before halftime on 19 points from me and another eleven from Eddie, who was able to push around their undersized front court. In the second half, Coach just let Chris run around and do his thing while our bench players got a bunch of minutes. We won by 31 points. I scored 23.

That Sunday in Gary's class, my heart sank when we opened our lesson book. Another talk on sex. The lessons about abstinence always started with a line like, "One thing we never talk about in church is sex . . ." And yet it seemed like every third or fourth lesson in the youth curriculum was "wait until marriage."

Our class was just guys. On my left and right were Chris Herrington and Will Parkman. Chris was always there, Bible open, eager to join in the discussion. Will was always there, too, slumped in his chair and staring off toward nothing in particular. This Sunday, seated at the other end of the circle, were Adam and Tim, two guys from the Christian school who I hardly knew.

The lesson covered familiar ground using the story of Isaac and Rebekah—they were ready for each other, because they had waited for marriage. Keeping yourself "pure" until marriage, the lesson said, was a precious gift to give your wife or husband on your wedding day.

Chris opened the discussion. "My mom and dad gave me an illustration that really helped me understand."

"Ok, go ahead," Gary said.

"Well, if you knew a bunch of other people had used a toothbrush, you wouldn't want to use it, right? If I knew a girl had been with a bunch of other guys, it would be like that. I wouldn't want to marry her. That's nasty."

I had heard Chris share his parents' analogy before, but this time it just didn't sit right. I sat up and leaned forward, trying to gather my thoughts, but one of the other guys piled on first.

"Yeah," Adam said, shaking his head. "That's like having sex with all the guys she's ever been with."

Gary pushed back a little. "Guys, you're focused on the girls, but this is about you. We're talking about how you can please God before you're married." He gestured toward Chris. "You need to worry more about being the clean toothbrush *yourself* more than anything else."

Will sighed. "It's not like you can really find a completely unused toothbrush anyway, dude." He smirked. "You try to wait for a clean toothbrush, and you'll be brushing your teeth with your finger the rest of your life."

Gary flashed Will a look. "Let's get away from toothbrushes. People aren't toothbrushes. And Will actually has a point. We all need grace."

I raised my hand. "Gary, aren't some people called to marry people who did bad things in the past? I mean, Hosea was told to marry a prostitute. And Rahab was a prostitute, too, and didn't she end up marrying someone in Jesus' lineage?"

Everyone's head turned to me. I remembered a lot of stuff from Bible stories that I read as a kid that no one else seemed to remember.

Gary thought for a moment. "I *think* that's right . . ."

"But Gary," Chris interrupted, "we're not supposed to be unequally yoked. That doesn't make any sense." ("Unequally yoked" was church-speak for marrying an unbeliever).

I sat forward. "But Rahab *had* faith. That's why she was spared from Jericho. She's in that 'Hall of Faith' passage from Hebrews and everything."

Gary smiled. "I think that's right, too."

Chris wrinkled his nose. "Come on . . . Those are, like, *special cases.* Like a special calling from God or something. I wouldn't do it. I couldn't."

"But somebody needs to, don't they?" My heart raced as the words came to me. "If someone comes to Christ, they're supposed to be forgiven of everything, like their past doesn't matter anymore, right?"

"Well . . ." Tim said, "to *God . . .*"

"But if a girl sleeps around or whatever and then believes in Jesus, she's supposed to marry a Christian, isn't she? Who is she going to marry if every Christian guy acts as if she's all used up and dirty? That's not right."

Chris was still shaking his head. "I don't think you could ever trust a girl with a past like that. I wouldn't want to risk it."

I could feel my face flush. "Well, I just think that it would be hard for a girl who gets off track in high school or something to ever come to know Christ if every Christian guy treats her as used-up garbage."

Adam scoffed. "You just think that way, because that's all you see at public school. You're just trying to give yourself a pass for missionary dating—you want to date her and hope she becomes a Christian."

Will laughed. "Man, if you think the Christian school girls are that different from the public school girls, you're ignorant—absolutely clueless."

Gary stood up as he saw the temperature in the room rising. "Hey guys, this has been a great discussion, but we're about out of time. Remember, this lesson is about *you* pleasing God with *your* body, not about judging others."

He gathered us up to pray, and we all headed down the hall for the worship service. Most of the youth group sat in the first two rows. I went and sat with Mom. I tried to shift my attention to the music and sermon, but my mind continued the argument from Sunday school.

Throughout the service, I caught Mom's eyes shifting toward me. She could tell I was checked out.

Dad hit the drive-through on the way home. He liked to swing through Taco Bell on Sundays and order two of everything from their 59¢ menu.

As Mom and I lingered over the last bits of our lunch, I could tell she wanted to talk about what was on my mind, but I didn't want to talk to Mom about Sunday school . . . or Nicole.

"Jay . . ." she finally spoke up. "What's got you so quiet?"

"It's nothing, Mom." I looked down, scraping some last bits out of my Pintos-'n'-Cheese. "Just a lot of stuff on my mind."

She cracked a teasing smile. "Is it 'nothing' or 'a lot'? You've hardly said anything since we left church, and I could tell you were preoccupied during the service."

I sighed. "I'm sorry. It's probably just a distraction."

She pointed a spork at me. "I know what this is about."

"You do?"

"It's that Coach Mays," her lips pursed as she thought about him. "He can't see what's right in front of his face."

I chuckled. Mom was half-right—Coach Mays was never too far from my thoughts. "Well, Mom, I was perfect from the field two games ago and had 23 points in about 23 minutes last game, so maybe he'll see that."

"Who cares if he does?" She got up, gathering trash with one arm and waving the other in the air. "Who cares?"

"He's the coach, Mom."

Her voice got louder. "*Who cares?*"

I stood up, my voice raised to match hers. "*I DO, MOM!*" I crinkled up a few burrito and taco wrappers, slamming them into the trash can. "I want to play basketball! And if I wanna play for this school, I've got to impress him. There's no way around it!"

"Hey . . ." She put a calming hand on my shoulder. "If you want to play basketball, then just play basketball."

I flopped back down in my chair. "What is that supposed to mean?"

"I can tell you're not 'just playing' right now." She sat down across from me. "You're working. You're looking over your shoulder. You're not having fun like you used to. Tell me, what are you thinking about when you play?"

I paused, putting my head in my hands . . . then I unloaded. I told Mom everything—coaches calling me selfish, trying to take enough threes, proving that I could defend as a forward, and constantly thinking about how I compared to Jimmy or Charlie or someone else on varsity. How I looked for Mays after every made shot, and especially after every miss or defensive lapse. *Did he see*? And then, every practice after a game, I wondered if Coach would say anything—good or bad—about my performance. And always the hope—however faint—that this would be the week that Coach would pull me up for a chance on varsity.

"I can see that," Mom nodded slowly. "I can see all that from the bleachers."

"Sure, Mom," I scoffed. "You can read my mind."

"I don't know all those specifics, but I can see that you're playing to prove something instead of just playing basketball. Why do you care?"

I let out an exasperated sigh. "Why do I *care*, Mom? Really? Because it's basketball. It's the one thing I can be good at that . . ." I cut myself off.

"You're good at a lot of things, Jay."

"No one cares about any of the other stuff. People care about basketball."

Mom paused in thought. "You know, maybe you *are* playing selfish."

I groaned. "Seriously, Mom?"

"Look, you love basketball. I know you do. I love to watch you play when you're just playing for the love of it. You're so good at knowing when to score and when to pass. You make everyone around you better. This year, you just seem tense and angry and hesitant. You're playing for you—to prove yourself. I just want to see you stop caring about Coach Mays and making varsity and just remember that you love to play basketball."

I looked down, jaw clenched. Tears started to fill my eyes, which frustrated and angered me, too. *She doesn't know what it's like. I can't just go "have fun." This isn't a game. It's my life.*

Her voice was soft. "Tell me, Jay. Do you like playing basketball this year?"

I shook my head sadly. "No."

"It's more fun for me to watch when you're having fun. And I bet it'll be more fun for your coaches to watch you, too." Her voice was almost pleading. "Please forget about them and just play basketball. Just *play* . . ."

I nodded silently as a tear dripped from one eye. So much of me wanted to throw her words aside. *What does Mom know about basketball anyway?* But deep inside, something was coming awake that longed to go back to just playing the game.

Just play.

Tuesday night's game wrapped up the first half of district play, a home game against our rival school, Lake. I loved playing in these rivalry games, because they were usually evenly matched and there was a lot of emotion on both sides. Even at the JV level, we had a few more people in the stands, and it was just a little louder. As I went through the game in my mind, all the worry about what Coach thought and what I needed to do to get called up melted away. I just wanted to beat Lake. *Just play. Just compete. Win the game.*

I got the start at small forward again, with Dee Whitaker at the point, Chris Jackson on the other wing, and Eddie Benson and freshman big man LaVon Thompson inside. The starting five played the bulk of the minutes, with only Eddie—who was still a little out of shape—subbing out much. Chris was figuring out the off-guard position better, and we played with good chemistry throughout the first half. Still, the game went back and forth for three quarters.

In the fourth quarter, Chris turned the ball over on back-to-back possessions, contributing to an eight-nothing run by Lake. We were down by three going into the final minute.

Coach Ward looked at his printout. "We're running Wildcat-3. Jackson, when Dee kicks it to you, you get to the basket. Do what it takes to get to the hoop. Understand?"

Wide-eyed, the freshman nodded. I could see the tension in his body.

As we broke, I smiled at him. "This is fun, isn't it? Rivalry game . . . chance to come back and take it. And the ball in your hands."

Chris cracked a half-smile. "Yeah . . . *fun.*"

I looked him in the eye. "We're gonna do it, man. Let's go!" And we ran out together onto the court.

I threw it in to Dee and ran to my wing. Dee pushed the ball inside the top of the key, where Eddie set a pick. Dee took two steps left toward the free throw line, then threw a laser to Chris on the wing outside the arc on the right. As Chris's man ran at him to prevent the game-tying three, Chris streaked by him into the lane, and scooped a layup around their big man. The ball went off the backboard and in—and then a whistle and foul. Chris went to the line to tie the game.

Chris was usually shaky from the free-throw line, but this time, he looked toward me and smiled, like an unspoken word between us . . . *Fun*. He sank the free throw, and the game was tied. 48 seconds left.

Lake drove the ball downcourt. My man slashed toward the basket. I bodied up to him as he received the pass. He went up. I leaped, raising my hands to contest the shot. My fingers brushed the bottom of the ball, just enough to throw the shot off. It bounced off the rim, and LaVon grabbed the rebound.

The ref came in blowing his whistle and pointing at me. "Number 35, with the body, shooting two." I shook my head. *That was a clean play.*

He missed the first one, but the second one went in. We were down by one with 17 seconds remaining. We didn't have a timeout, so we just had to push the ball. Lake contested the inbounds pass but then collapsed into a half-court defense.

Dee pushed the ball across midcourt, where he was met by two defenders. He bounce-passed around them to Chris, who streaked toward the hoop. Two more defenders crashed on him as he reached the lane.

"Ball!" I cried out. Chris kicked it to me. I glanced at the hoop and the dwindling clock on the scoreboard beyond. I felt the ball spin into position in my fingers, like a natural extension of my hands.

A defender sprang toward me from my right, hands raised. I spun left, out of his way. I set my feet, locked my eyes on the hoop, and released from seventeen feet.

Swish. Buzzer. Ballgame.

My teammates mobbed me. Eddie picked me up in a slimy, sweaty bear-hug. My mom's screaming voice rose up above all the cheers in the arena. Even Coach Bored cracked a smile and shook my hand.

"Mac-Daddy!" The locker room was buzzing the next morning as I dropped off my gear. "Daddy-Mac for the win!" For once, "Mac-talk" didn't feel like mocking. I floated out of the locker room to first period.

No one else in the school was aware of the JV game. If anyone was talking about basketball at all, it was to complain about varsity's close loss in their away game against Lake. It took all my willpower not to bring up last night's game to anyone who would listen.

Going to second period, Ty Jackson, Chris's brother on varsity, gave me a respectful nod as we passed in the hall. "You the man today, Mac!" I bounced down the hall and swung into English class.

Then my breath caught in my throat.

Standing by Ms. Longmire's desk was Nicole, back in school for the first time in about two weeks. They were discussing her make-up work. I sat down and Charlie reached out, grabbing my shoulder: "I heard about last night, Mac! Ice cold! We could've used some of that in our game."

But now the words just passed me by. I looked back at Charlie and flashed a smile, but my mind was at the teacher's desk. I looked down as Nicole took her seat, then looked tentatively in her direction.

She looked no different. Same Nicole—except some of the brightness was missing from her eyes. She mouthed "Hi" while tucking a lock of hair behind her ear. Normally, she would have sat down and jumped into one of a hundred dumb conversations with me, Charlie, and Hannah. But today, nothing. Just awkward glances, half-smiles, and silence.

Spanish class was really no better. We shared a brief smile when Mrs. Navarro called "*Nee-cole*" and jumped like she'd seen a ghost when Nicole answered "here." But it was like someone had sucked all the air out of the goofiness we usually shared in that class.

The feeling lingered with me the rest of the day. Dad could tell something was weighing on me as we drove home from the store.

"You're certainly quiet tonight, Jay," Dad probed. "I thought you'd still be riding high from last night."

I cracked a smile. "Yeah, it was cool today at school." But I didn't have anything else to say about the game. My thoughts were on Nicole.

Dad could tell. "You want to tell me where your mind is, then?"

I didn't know where to start. Dad didn't know anything about Nicole—he probably didn't even know her name, let alone know her situation. I decided to start from a different angle.

"I was thinking about our Sunday school lesson last week."

Dad chuckled. "Oh really? That's not what I expected. What about it?"

"Well . . ." I fidgeted in the passenger seat, searching for the words. "We had the regular lesson on sex and waiting until marriage and all that."

Dad nodded his head. "OK . . ."

"Some of the guys started talking about girls who hadn't waited . . . like they were used toothbrushes that nobody would want. It didn't seem right."

He shook his head. "No . . . that's not the point at all. *Gary* said that?"

"No! It was a couple of the other guys—one guy said that his parents used that analogy. Gary kept trying to tell us the lesson was about what *we* did, not about girls or whatever else. But it got off track. It started to make me mad."

We pulled into the driveway, and Dad turned toward me. "Well, did you say anything?"

"I guess I pointed out things like Rahab in the Bible and that some people might be called to marry someone who had a bad past but who now has faith."

Dad smiled. "What did they say to that?"

I looked down. "One guy accused me of 'missionary dating'—that I was just saying all that as an excuse to want to date someone who . . . *you know* . . ."

Dad paused, like he was putting the pieces together. "That's not what you said, though. I know you know it's important that you find a girl who will follow Christ together with you, right from the start. We've talked about that."

I nodded. "Yeah, Dad. But I wasn't thinking about dating at all when I said that. It was just that all that they were saying about someone being all used up and nasty really made me mad."

"Why do you think that was?"

I sighed, trying to figure out how to put it into words. I pictured Nicole and the awkward silences and whispers that surrounded her. I remembered the scowls on the faces of the guys in class talking about used toothbrushes.

"I'm not trying to date her," I blurted out. "I just don't want to think of her like that. I don't like other people doing it, either."

Dad turned. "So it really is about a certain girl, then?"

I ran my fingers through my hair. "I don't know. I guess. But I don't think so at the same time. I just don't think God wants us writing people off."

Dad patted my shoulder. "I think you're right . . . what's going on?"

So I told him everything—and that it was Nicole, the one who I took to the Astros game back in the fall. He nodded his head as he got the full picture.

"She came back to school today, and everything's weird." I grabbed the back of my neck. "I guess I just don't know how to act."

Dad looked away for a moment. "Why do you think it's weird?"

"I don't know . . ." I was beginning to sweat in the parked car. "I guess it's because I thought I knew her, and now I feel like I didn't really. Maybe it's because I want to help her, but there's nothing I can do. Maybe it's because I don't really know how she feels about all this, and I don't want to make assumptions that she's ashamed or scared or even happy or whatever."

Dad opened the car door, letting some cool air slip in. "Let's get these groceries inside." We moved to the back and started grabbing bags. He stopped and leaned on the roof of the car.

"Jay, I can't tell you exactly what to do, but I don't think your instincts are too far off."

I shook my head and chuckled. "Dad, I don't have any social instincts . . . or they're all wrong."

"I'm talking about your spiritual instincts, son." Dad said as we walked toward the back door. "You're right not to pile on when someone is down, but you have to figure out how to follow through when you're around her."

I nodded my head and opened the door, rushing in to unload two armfuls of grocery bags onto the kitchen table. I felt like I released some of the mental weight, too—but only a little.

As I went to bed that night, I still felt heavy. One Dad-talk wasn't going to solve this one. After an hour of staring in the dark with a pit in my stomach, I finally went to sleep.

Chapter 20

THE CALL

I showed up to school the next day ready to treat Nicole the same as always—but Nicole *wasn't* the same. Gone was the bubbly, confident girl who was at ease with everyone from the athletes to the artists to the honors students.

In her place those next few weeks was someone whose eyes rarely met mine, whose smiles were hesitant, and whose voice was always quiet. Her chair was often empty—second period in the nurse's office, fifth period with the counselor. A freshman took her place in the cheerleading line as she sat in the bleachers next to the cheerleader with a torn ACL.

I was still watching varsity basketball from the bleachers, too. We traveled with varsity for a JV/varsity doubleheader at Lee. We kicked off the night with a win—our sixth straight. We were now in full control of the race for the junior varsity district championship.

Meanwhile, varsity was in a fight for their playoff lives. They needed to win this game over Lee, then beat both Rayburn and Lake to finish the regular season to make the playoffs.

John made the trip for this one. He crept up behind where the JV squad was sitting and leaned in. "Hey, great game, man."

"Thanks." I spoke without turning my head. We weren't supposed to be talking to anyone but teammates as we watched, but the coaches weren't watching the bleachers.

"Y'all have had a lot of momentum since the Lake game. Didn't these guys almost run you out of the gym last time?"

I nodded. Our last four wins came against the same teams who had beaten us in three of four games during the first half of district play. "We had a lot of turnovers in that one, but Chris really sliced them up today."

Chris Jackson had been taking huge strides forward, and that was big for us. He was playing with more maturity, limiting turnovers, and creating a lot of plays on offense.

John patted my shoulder. "Chris was good, but you led the team in scoring again. How many did you have this time?"

"Twenty-six, I think." I shrugged, as if I wasn't sure.

Eddie Benson interrupted. "You *think*? Dude, don't act like you ain't keeping that scorebook in your head." He wasn't wrong—I always knew how many points I had. "But if I were you, my arms would be tired."

"From what?" I asked. "From shooting too much?"

"From carrying this team!" He slapped me on the back.

I laughed and shook my head. I didn't want to think of myself carrying the team, but I was on the hottest shooting streak of my life since that Lake game. Over those four games, I shot better than sixty percent from the floor, including an even 50-50 on three-pointers. I was also a perfect 16-for-16 from the foul line.

Just then, a ball clanged off the rim and toward us in the bleachers—a missed three-point attempt from Jimmy Schroeder. Eddie caught the ball and tossed it to the ref. We looked back toward the floor, where varsity was stuck at just eighteen points halfway through the second quarter, trailing by four.

"If Mays would ever pull his head out his butt," John grumbled, pointing to our sideline. "He'd realize he could use some of *your* shooting out there." Eddie nodded in agreement.

As John pointed, it seemed like Coach Mays's eyes turned our direction. "I think I see Mays glaring at me," John said, hopping up. "I'd better get back to your parents."

With John gone, I fully turned my attention back to the game. It was only the second varsity game I'd seen all season (usually we were at home when they were on the road and vice versa), and it had my stomach in knots. I wanted us to win and get to the playoffs—Coach would go ballistic if we didn't—but the worst part was that I could see exactly how I could be helping the team, and I was stuck in the bleachers.

In the second half, Big O shut down the opposing team's big man, and Jimmy hit on four three-pointers, and our guys pulled out the win 52-50. Once again, the defense was strong, and this time, there was just enough offense. Still, Coach spent an hour making sure we knew how "*pitiful*" and "*brutal*" it was to beat Lee by only two points.

Then, almost to himself, he said something that got my mind spinning. "We ain't getting anywhere with this group the way it is."

I spent the weekend running Coach's last sentence through my brain until my head pounded. It was like when you get a song stuck in your head but can't remember the words, so your brain runs through it again and again trying to finish the lyrics. Maybe it was nothing—Coach is never satisfied with his team. But maybe the new week would bring the call I'd been waiting for all season.

Monday, I dropped my stuff off in the locker room when I saw Coach talking to the sports reporter for the *Recorder*, a local weekly paper that covered high school sports in the area. It wasn't unusual for Coach to be interviewed, but the player next to him was Ty Jackson. He was a starter, but our best player was Oscar "Big O" Anderson.

Why are they interviewing Ty?

At practice that afternoon, I was startled to see a large, moping figure going through the motions of warm-ups. It was Darryl Nicholson, who had been on varsity all year, now here at JV practice.

I turned to Eddie Benson. "What's Darryl doing with us?"

"Coach sent him down," Eddie shook his head, then patted my shoulder. "Brought up Chris Jackson."

My breath left me, and then as I breathed back in, rage filled my body. Passed over again. *For a freshman turnover machine.* I clenched my jaw, swallowing the profanity I wanted to hurl on Coach's name.

"Sucks for Darryl," I managed to grunt out. "But he'll help us." And I ran off to the ball rack to start my shootaround.

As I warmed up, the anger left me and was replaced by defeat—*what's the point of any of this*? I moved mechanically through practice, now back at shooting guard with Darryl taking over at small forward. There was nothing new. I knew my offensive and defensive assignments. Defeat gave way to boredom. Junior varsity was no longer a challenge. By the time practice ended, I was ready for the whole season to be done.

The next morning, I spotted a copy of the *Recorder* laying around the locker room featuring the headline, "Wildcats Coach Mays Readies His Team for Another Playoff Run." Curiosity got the better of me, and I grabbed it and took it to class.

In second period, as Ms. Longmire droned on about the upcoming group project, I pulled the paper into my lap and began to read. The article first focused on what the team needed to do to get to the playoffs, then shifted to the recent roster change. There was a quote from Ty about playing with his brother, and then a quote from Coach Mays that made me want to tear the paper in two.

"We brought up Ty three years ago to play with his brother Detric,"

Mays said. "So we had two Jackson brothers on the team when we won regionals in '91, so maybe two Jacksons will bring us some luck this year, too."

I rolled my eyes, trying my hardest to stay quiet while Ms. Longmire kept talking. *He chose Chris because he thinks two Jacksons are lucky? I'm stuck on JV because of some dadgum superstition? Dang it, Coach! Are you an idiot?*

I silently fumed, my head down, my eyes reading the article over and over as I fought the urge to crumple it up and throw it.

Then a voice came from my left, soft and quiet.

"Jay?" It was Nicole. "Do you mind partnering up with me on this project?"

I looked up, everyone was moving around. I had stopped listening to Ms. Longmire twenty minutes ago, but she had released us to group up, and everyone had a partner but Nicole and me.

"Yeah, sure," I stammered. "That's good." I was kind of shocked. Normally, if I had hesitated, Nicole would have been the first person to get a partner, leaving me with Charlie or someone random. But we seemed to be the last ones left—the guy not paying attention and the pregnant girl no one knew how to talk to.

Nicole pushed her desk next to mine and we got to work. Our conversation stuck to the assigned task (the themes of *A Farewell to Arms*), but underneath the Hemingway talk, I wondered what was going on with her—what she was thinking, feeling, and how she was navigating all of it. I wondered if I would embarrass her to ask about the baby—or maybe it embarrassed her when I *didn't* ask about it.

As these ideas ran as a constant undercurrent below the discussion, a new feeling rose up inside. I was . . . *ashamed.* Nicole was dealing with heavy, real-life stuff, and I couldn't stop whining about my basketball team.

Charlie pulled up beside me in the hallway after class. "Hey, Mac. Sucks that Coach didn't call you up. A couple of us are pretty pissed about it."

I shook my head. "Man, I just can't get worked up about it anymore. I just gotta do what I do. Maybe I'll run up some numbers against Rayburn." I shrugged. "But if Coach still doesn't care . . . Whatever."

"Well, don't give up, man." We paused at the end of the hallway before we had to go separate directions. "Mays is stubborn, but he wants to win more than anything."

After tip-off that night, I ran over to the shooting guard spot at the right wing—I had spent much more time on the left during my time at forward. It was just disorienting enough that I missed my first two shots from that side.

About three minutes in, LaVon grabbed a rebound and threw me a long pass for a fast break. I laid the ball in for two as a Rayburn player bumped me from behind for the foul. But then I missed the free throw—my first miss from the foul line in weeks.

A Rayburn timeout sent us to the sideline. I flopped down on the bench and shook my head. *I shouldn't even be here.* My thoughts were across town at the varsity game as my eyes moved across the bleachers. My eyes stopped at my mom. She smiled as our eyes met and let out a "*Woo!*"

Who cares? That's what Mom would say. I'm not getting called up this year. It doesn't matter how I play. And we're going to beat Rayburn. Just play.

After the timeout, we lined up to defend the inbounds. Dee intercepted the pass, drove down and whipped it out to me on the right wing. I set my feet as the defender flew past me. I released—*three points.*

Bouncing back down the court, I could feel my eyes focus and everything that wasn't right in front of me melt away. A pass came to my man on the wing. As he tried to drive past me, I poked the ball away and grabbed it—an open court in front of me. I raced down the court, then jump-stopped at the top of the key, pursuing defenders stumbling past me. I released another three—*swish.*

I hit three more threes by the end of the first quarter. We were up by fifteen points, and I already had seventeen. Coach put in the second-string guys to start the second quarter but sent me back in with five minutes to play in the half.

I hit a fifteen-footer and then a fadeaway off the block in the next two possessions. A couple of minutes later, I hit a couple of free throws. Then, with ten seconds left, I caught a long rebound, stepped behind the arc in the corner, and drained another three. Twenty-nine points—and it was only halftime. We were up 46-19.

Coach Ward shuffled through his printouts at halftime, then looked up to us. "We're gonna rest our starters most of the second half. You five are just going to rotate in to rest the other guys."

So I sat down and sucked down Gatorade for most of the third quarter, watching LaVon, then Darryl, Dee, and Eddie sub in. Finally, with a minute left in the quarter, he called my name. My career high was 32 points, so I was just looking for a couple of buckets. I grabbed a rebound and hit the follow-up shot before the quarter ended.

Ward looked at the printouts again, then paused. He looked straight at me. "How many points do you have?"

I looked down. *Is this a trick? Am I not supposed to know?* "Umm . . . 31."

Coach stared at his printouts and gave a little chuckle. "Whatever," he said, then laid the printouts on the bench. "Mac, I don't think anyone has ever scored forty before in our program at any level. *Let's just frickin' do it.*"

I laughed as the team gathered around cheering their approval. I couldn't believe it—Coach Bored made a decision, and it was for *me.*

So I went out with our point guard Dee and three backups with the plan to feed me until I scored nine more points. First time down the floor, I went with my signature move—a couple of dribbles to create space and a fifteen-footer. *Bam.* New career high, seven more points to go.

The next time down, I missed a three but followed my shot and got the rebound. I was fouled and hit the two free throws. Five more to go.

I missed another three on the next possession and then I found myself double-teamed for the rest of the game. Dee distributed the ball to other guys for a few minutes, then another rebound, put-back, and a foul. I made the free throw to bring me to 38 points. One more basket. Still four minutes to go.

I battled the double-team for another two minutes, but then, with Eddie in the game, he set a pick for me out on the wing. I cut hard off the screen, caught Dee's pass in stride just as I hit the lane. I spun to the block and released a fadeaway. I felt a slap on my wrist as I released the ball. It rattled in the rim, then went through—40 points!

I saw Darryl go to the scorer's table to sub for me as I went to the free throw line. One more shot. My mom stood on her feet and screamed for me. Dad stood beside her with a wide smile. I could see John mouth to me, "*Is that forty?*"

I smiled and nodded toward them as the ref handed over the ball. I sank the free throw and jogged to the bench. Coach grabbed my shoulder as I went by. I traded fist bumps on my way to my seat, then put a towel over my head. *Forty-one points.* I had to smile—at least I had *something* to remember for this season.

As a team, we broke eighty points for the first time since I had been playing, 87-53. In the locker room, Ward rattled off a few highlights from the scorebook and let us go. But as I walked out of the jubilant locker room, I was blindsided with a sense of sadness.

I'm playing my best basketball ever, but one more game and the season's over. I hung back in the empty gym with my thoughts until varsity got back.

The news when they got back was not so much that they had blown out Rayburn—that was expected—but that Lake had lost their game, forcing a win-or-go-home for both teams for the playoffs in the game Friday night.

As everyone was milling around, I spotted Coach Mays going into the office. A few minutes later, he came out holding the JV scorebook in his hands. "Hey Mac!" he called out.

I froze. I knew Ward had deviated from Coach's printouts. *Mays is the kind of guy to get pissed when someone scores forty, just because it was not done his way.*

"McGee, when are you gonna pay me back?"

I had no idea what he was talking about. "Uh . . . for what, Coach?"

I caught a twinkle in his black eyes as a smirk formed on his lips. He pointed the scorebook at me. "*For tearin' up my nets!*"

Was that a joke? A joke AND a compliment? To ME? I smiled and looked away.

Coach raised his voice. "Hey, y'all! McGee scored 41 points tonight." His face turned serious again. "Y'all have barely been scoring that much—*as a team*—most every game this year. *Pitiful.*" He went back into the office.

Jimmy and a couple of seniors rolled their eyes and looked away from me. A couple of others tried to pat me on the back, but it all floated by me. *Was Coach just in a good mood? Or what even was that?* I got in my dad's Oldsmobile and drove home to a fitful night's sleep.

I tried to go through my normal routine the next morning, but my knees shook as I entered the locker room that morning. I dropped my bag into the locker and turned to leave and head to class. A voice came from behind me.

"McGee!" Coach Mays appeared in the door of his office.

"Yes, Coach?" My heart raced.

He stood on the steps in front of his office so he could meet me eye-to-eye. His hands were on his hips, eyes narrow. "We gotta beat Lake Friday or we miss the playoffs. Think you could help us?"

I nodded quickly. "Yeah . . . yes, sir."

"All right." He turned back toward his office, then called back over his shoulder. "You'll practice with us this afternoon."

"Wait!" I called out, my eyes wide. "Does that mean you're calling me up?"

"Yeah, Mac." He pointed at me. "Show me something."

Chapter 21

EARN YOUR KEEP

Stepping into varsity practice that week felt unexpectedly familiar. I had played with all these guys the whole offseason. I knew I could keep up with any of them. Still, Coach Mays's constant glare kept me looking over my shoulder.

"McGee—you're gonna switch out at the three with Davis and Gonzalez."

Huh . . . Small forward. That's unexpected.

Coach had me at shooting guard during the offseason, even when I worked out with the varsity guys. But Jimmy Schroeder started at the two—and Coach loved him—so I was glad to be working out where I might get some actual playing time.

In addition to normal drills, Coach spent the week implementing a new press break to use against Lake. If all went to plan, one place the ball was designed to end up was in the small forward's hands near the left elbow. When Kelvin Davis or Charlie Gonzalez got it there, Coach had them trying to feed it to Ty Jackson cutting toward the hoop. So when I subbed in, I took the pass and then fired to Ty.

Coach blew his whistle and ran up to get in my ear. "McGee! We didn't bring you here to give the ball up. You're here to score the basketball! If you're gonna be scared, we can't use you! *Grow some hair and take the shot*!" And he ran back to the baseline. "*Run it again*!"

We reset, half the team in Lake's press, the starting four plus me running the break. Ty threw it in to our point guard Tee, then three quick passes and the ball was in my hands at the elbow. I caught it and shot from one of my favorite spots on the court. *Swish.*

I shot a look toward Coach. He gave a stiff nod, but his glare remained etched on his face. His message was clear: *I'm here to score.*

Friday—game day—arrived.

After lunch, there was a pep rally for us, my first public appearance as a varsity player. I tugged on my number 35 jersey over my school clothes and stared at my reflection in the locker room. *Finally.*

The PA announcer called each player out by name to run to the middle of the floor, where we would be surrounded by a packed arena—students competing for who could scream the loudest, the band blaring the fight song, and cheerleaders waving their pom-poms. One by one, I moved closer to the doorway as each name was called.

Number thirty-five . . . Jay . . . McGEEEEEEEE!

I jogged out, my ears ringing and all the sights blurring around me—the mascot running laps, screaming students, fist-bumps from teammates as I moved down the line, the cheerleaders kicking and jumping. And there, just behind them sitting on the front row in her cheer uniform, was Nicole.

Back in Spanish class, she leaned over. "I didn't know you were on varsity now. That's really cool."

I looked down, hand brushing over the jersey I still wore over my shirt. "Yeah, this will be my first game. I don't know how much time I'll get."

"Well, it will be cool to finally see you play," she said.

Really? She doesn't remember watching me play? I wanted to remind her that she saw me score 32 last year at the JV/varsity doubleheader . . . And in middle school—*two full years as our leading scorer*—she was there too.

She sighed. "I just wish I was *actually* cheering tonight . . ."

I stopped. Just as I was called up, she was being sidelined. I knew it was hard on her, but I couldn't tell exactly what she felt. Embarrassed? Mad?

I didn't know what to say, but I pushed something out. "Yeah . . . that sucks."

The arena was packed that night with students, parents, people from the community, and even some reporters. Handmade banners lined the arena: "*Beat Lake*" . . . "*Playoff Bound*" . . . "*This is Wildcat Country*" . . . Fans drummed on the bleachers as the starting lineups were announced.

"Hip Hop Hooray" blared over the speakers, with the crowd chanting "*Hey . . . Ho . . .*" in rhythm as the starting lineups were announced: forwards *Ty Jackson . . . Charlie Gonzalez . . .* Center *Oscar "Big O" Anderson . . .* Guards *T'Marius "Tee" Williams . . . Jimmy Schroeder . . .* I stood in the line, giving high fives as the starters ran out.

Charlie had replaced Kelvin Davis in the starting lineup late in the season. It marked a shift to a smaller, quicker group. Neither player was a great scorer and both were good defenders, but Charlie was faster and could get open more often. I took my seat beside Chris Jackson on the bench and settled in for tip-off.

Everyone was hyped up to start—passes slapped, players diving, shots sailing long. Both teams struggled to a 10-10 score late in the first quarter. After a three-pointer that put them up 13-10, Lake went into their full court press. Coach Mays called a timeout.

"McGee!" he yelled down the bench. "Check in!"

He huddled the team. "We worked on this all week. Avoid the traps, move the ball, and get it to Mac on that left side—that's an easy two for us."

His eyes met mine, eyebrows lowered. His mustache twitched as he growled, "Here's your chance, son. *Earn your keep*."

The press break worked just as Coach drew it up. We moved the ball past the traps as I made my way to the left side. Big O heaved the ball to me while Ty cut toward the hoop. As I set my feet, I heard Coach call out, "*BAM*!" I let it fly. The ball rattled home. My first varsity points.

Part of me expected Coach to yank me right back out—*terrible defensively* was practically his nickname for me—but I hustled to my spot and stuck close to my man. He received the pass and turned toward the hoop, but with my hands in his face, he gave the ball up back to the point guard. The ball came inside where Big O blocked a shot. I grabbed the tip as it floated loose and fired the outlet pass to Tee.

I sprinted to my spot in our half-court offense, on the left wing. Tee drove to the lane, then dumped it to Ty, who snapped it to Big O. When the double-team came, he whipped it out to Jimmy on the right wing as I rotated toward the top of the key. As the defenders crashed on him, Jimmy threw a skip-pass to me outside the arc—an open shot. I didn't hesitate . . . *nothing but net*. Five quick points.

Our next possession, Tee drove to the basket and was fouled. We lined up along the lane for the foul shots. As the ref handed the ball over for the first shot, one of the Lake guys turned to me, staring at my face.

"Did you used to play with those goggles?" He was remembering my "rec specs" that I had to wear on the court before I got contacts. I nodded.

The first shot bounced off the rim. The Lake player called out to his teammate, "Hey, Cal! This is 'Goggles'! Remember him? You gotta stick close to him or he'll light you up all night!"

It was hard to hide my smile. *"Goggles"? I had a nickname . . . they remembered me.*

As we positioned ourselves to block out for the second shot, he turned to me again. "I don't remember you the last time we played y'all. You been injured?"

I shook my head. "No. Just on JV."

He cocked his head. "*JV?!*"

He couldn't believe it—and neither could I. I had spent all season on JV, but as I played my first varsity minutes, I wasn't scared. It was like I had been here all season, right where I belonged.

Tee's shot went in, the buzzer sounded, and Kelvin came jogging in to sub for me. I sat down on the edge of my seat and wiped the sweat from my face. My eyes were fixed on the court as my heart slowed down.

Get me back in there.

I got another chance in the second quarter when we fell behind and Lake went back to the full-court press. I missed my first shot but hit my second one. The next time down the court, Lake had adjusted their scheme and I was covered. Later, I was fouled after a rebound and made my free throws—my second one put us ahead again.

We built a four-point lead going into the final two minutes of the half, when my man spun past me for a layup to make it a two-point game. The next dead ball, Charlie jogged back in and I went to the bench.

We maintained a thin lead for most of the second half. Coach sent me in when we stalled out on offense but pulled me back out when my man scored or he was afraid we were blowing our lead. Then, halfway through the fourth quarter, I watched from the sidelines as Lake went on a seven-to-nothing run to take the lead by two points.

Coach slammed down his clipboard. *"Dadgummit, Gonzalez! You fight through the pick! You're in there to stop plays like that!"* He threw up his hands into a "T" for a timeout and got in the face of each player as they came over to the sideline. *"Pitiful! Brutal!"*

He pointed to me. "*McGee, check in for Charlie!*"

I gathered around Coach as Tee, Jimmy, Big O, and Ty caught their breath, sweat dripping to the floor. Coach had ridden his starters hard this game, with only Kelvin, Chris, and me getting any minutes from the bench—and Chris and Kelvin hardly played at all.

Coach stared into our eyes. "I see y'all suckin' wind, but this is when you gotta dig deep and find that mental toughness. No more easy buckets on D. Move the ball on offense and get it to our scorers—Big O, Mac, or Jimmy. Four minutes to prove we deserve to keep playing . . . 'Cats on 3 . . ."

Everyone put their hands in and we broke the huddle and ran out. Four minutes for the playoffs. The ball came in, and we hustled down into our half-court offense.

Tee drove . . . dump off to Big O . . . kick out to Jimmy . . . back to Ty at the top of the key . . . back down to O . . . double team . . . I fought past my man . . . O hit me in stride. I stopped, faked toward the baseline, then spun into a fadeaway, launching the ball over the defender's outstretched fingers. He bumped me, and I fell backward onto the floor, sliding on my backside as I watched the ball fly.

The ball spun over the front rim and in, and the crowd erupted into a roar that seemed to shake the building, nearly drowning out the sound of the whistle—I was headed to the free throw line to give us back the lead.

Big O grabbed my hand and jerked me to my feet and into a chest bump. "Let's go, boy!" he yelled. It was a bit awkward—my chest only reached his belly—and more than a little slimy, but no one cared.

Cries of "Mac *DADDY*!!!" rang down from all directions, most loudly from the bench, where Charlie jumped up and down, pointing at me. Coach just stood next to him, arms crossed, staring at the free throw line.

I went to the line, dribbled twice, then spun the ball in my hands as I exhaled, staring at the rim. Then I bent my knees and took my shot. *Swish.* We had the lead again.

"*Get back on D*!" Coach screamed from the sidelines. I put my head down and ran back to the other end.

The next two minutes blurred by as we traded baskets. Then, with a minute left, Jimmy hit a three to put us up four points. Coach subbed Charlie back in for defense, and I was back to the bench.

I perched myself on the edge of my seat, elbows on my knees, leg shaking. *Just hold on, guys. Let's do this.*

Lake hit a three with thirty seconds on the clock. One point game. We tried to run out the clock, but a pass from Jimmy to Tee was tipped away with fifteen seconds left, the Lake player streaking toward the hoop. Tee ran him down and fouled him hard. Nine seconds left, up by one. Lake at the line for two shots.

Coach called our final timeout. He pulled us together. "McGee, you're in for Gonzalez." He glared into my eyes and pointed. "*You block out the shooter on the miss.*"

He scanned the rest of the team. "We're out of timeouts. *Do not call a timeout.* We're gonna have to move fast if it's tied or we're behind. Get the outlet to Tee. Tee you are gonna push the ball as far as you can. They're gonna double-team O. If they give you a lane, take it all the way—but when they stop you . . . *look for Mac.*" He circled a spot on the clipboard for emphasis.

My eyes widened. *Mays wanted the ball in my hands.* I scanned the other faces. Tee nodded to Coach. Big O and Ty clapped their hands, looking me in the eye. Jimmy looked away, jaw clenched—he wanted that shot.

My heart raced as we lined up for the free throw. Two shots—if he makes both, Lake has the lead; just one—game is tied. I was in the position closest to the shooter. I could see how his eyes were darting around, how his hands shook. *Maybe this moment is too big for him . . . will it be too big for me?*

The first shot ricocheted off the front of the rim, then the back iron, then off to the right. *At least now we're guaranteed overtime.*

The shooter shifted his feet as he got the ball again. He stared intently at the hoop and bent his knees. I readied myself to jump into the lane to block out. He released. I jumped out in front of him, backing into him as the shot flew. It hit the back iron and flew right back toward me. I snared it out of the air.

Before he could foul me, I threw the outlet pass to Tee. He dribbled down the court for a few seconds, then threw the ball straight up into the air as the buzzer sounded. *Game over. Playoff bound.* The whole team piled on him in jubilation—a bouncing, sweaty mess of release and celebration—as the arena shook.

And I was right there in the middle of it.

Chapter 22

PLAYOFF TIME

Students stormed the court, a group of guys chanting "Lake sucks" as the Lake players slumped toward the visiting locker room. My eyes turned to the bleachers, where my mom was still standing and clapping. Reporters pulled Coach Mays and Big O aside and started interviewing them. But the one who grabbed me was my dad. He had a wide smile.

"You made it, Jay." He put his hand on my back. "And you did great."

"Thanks, Dad." I glanced at the reporters, hoping they might call me over.

Dad grinned. "There's a lot for you to do here before you head home. Why don't you just take the car?"

I grabbed the Oldsmobile keys. "I was going to meet John and Ashley at Chili's later. Is that OK?"

"Sure. Have fun." He stared at me for a minute, smiling, then grabbed my shoulder. "You really did great tonight, Jay."

By the time the gym cleared and we had our postgame meeting, it was well after ten o'clock before I got to Chili's, where John and Ashley had a Dr Pepper and basket of chips waiting for me.

After three months of Ashley being there on outings that used to just be John and me, we were used to each other—though I'm sure in her mind, I was the one tagging along. But it wasn't always—they had plenty of one-on-one time, and I still had my Blizzards with John from time to time.

I took a long swig of Dr Pepper as I slid in the booth across from them. I was still buzzing from the game. "You guys been waiting long?"

John waved his hand. "Nah . . . not too bad. This is only our second basket of chips." He munched on a chip. "That was awesome out there. That fadeaway was unreal! You feeling good?"

I took a breath to consider all that was going on inside me. "Yeah . . . I mean, it wasn't perfect, but I've thought I was a varsity player all year, and I think I showed that. That's what I wanted. And to win, of course."

"I couldn't believe how calm you looked out there," John said. "I thought you'd be super nervous, and you were smiling, bouncing around . . . like it was just a normal game."

I wiped a drip of salsa from my shirt as I thought about what he said. "I guess I wasn't as nervous as I expected. I didn't know how much I'd play, but when Coach put me in and told me to go score—I mean . . . that's what I do. I guess I just knew I belonged out there."

We recapped various moments from the game together for a few more minutes. Ashley mostly just sat and listened, occasionally adding something about what she heard from her place as a trainer at the end of our bench.

As the food arrived, I turned toward her. "Sorry for always being a third wheel with you two."

She shook her head. "No! It's fun being with y'all and hearing you talk on a night like this."

"Besides," John grinned, "Ashley knows someone who might want to be the *fourth* wheel."

"If you say Carol Young, I'm going to punch you," I laughed.

"Carol? No!" Ashley pointed her fork at me. "You haven't heard?"

I shrugged.

"Remember my friend Elise and her cousin Doug from the winter formal?" Ashley leaned in. "Doug and Carol have been inseparable since around Christmas. It's, like, super serious. He says he's gonna marry her."

I shook my head and laughed. *That explains a lot.*

"So *anyway* . . ." John said, prodding Ashley to get to the point.

"So . . . *speaking of Elise* . . ." she smirked. "She thought it was sweet when you danced with her at formal and she's been talking about you since then, and . . ."

My shoulders slumped. *This again? Why can't I just be nice without someone latching on?* I interrupted her. "Ashley, I . . . don't think I'm interested."

Her eyes flashed and she sat back in her seat. "You're not even going to give her a chance? Why not?"

I hadn't thought about her since the dance, and I didn't really think of her *at* the dance, either. Tonight at Chili's was the first time I even caught her name. The only thing I remembered about dancing with her at the end of the night was that her deodorant had worn off (I'm sure I didn't smell great either) and that I was watching Nicole and Cory fight. But I wasn't going to tell Ashley that.

As I struggled to come up with a reason, Ashley offered one. "It can't still be *Nicole Ellis*, can it?"

I shot a look at John. He put his hands up. "Hey, it's not exactly a secret that you liked her, is it?" He turned to Ashley, touching her shoulder. "I don't think this is about Nicole . . ."

I shook my head. "No. I mean, it's just a bad time with the playoffs and all." I paused, looking down. "I know the whole Nicole thing is not an option with everything going on with her. I do feel bad for her, though."

Ashley rolled her eyes. "I don't know why. It's her own fault. Cory said she doesn't even know who the dad is." She was irritated that I wasn't interested in Elise, and it was making her harsher than usual.

John turned to her. "That's what Cory says. But Nicole told Kat that it's definitely Cory. He just doesn't want the responsibility, so he's spreading around that she was with a bunch of different guys and doesn't know."

Ashley turned to me. "I still don't know how you can still have a crush on her. I mean, you're like the biggest Christian I know. And you're hung up on a girl who went and got herself pregnant. It makes no sense."

I sighed. "It's not a crush, really . . . I don't think I'm hung up on her like that. It's just . . ."

John tried to fill in the blanks. "It's just that he doesn't want to be too hard on her when she's going through a hard time, right?"

Ashley's face softened. "I know it's sad and all, but . . . I mean, it was wrong, wasn't it?"

I looked down, picking at my food. "Yeah . . . but I think she feels that herself. I don't need to add to it. You said I'm like 'the biggest Christian you know' or whatever. Nicole knows that, too . . ." I stuffed a nacho in my mouth, trying to think of what to say next as I chewed, but instead I just took another bite.

Ashley broke the silence. "So it's not a crush. Whatever. Then why not give Elise a chance? She's my friend and she likes you."

I shrugged. "I'm just not interested, especially during the playoffs. It has nothing to do with Nicole. I'm sorry."

She picked at her food and shook her head. "I don't understand it."

We sat and ate quietly for a couple of minutes, before I got up to use the restroom. When I returned, John had changed the subject.

"Hey Jay, we went and saw that new Charlie Sheen movie last weekend. Have you seen it? They filmed a bunch of scenes around here . . ."

As John detailed the different local places he spotted in the movie, I glanced at Ashley and she smiled. John was our common ground. It wasn't long before we started laughing again—then looking forward to where I wanted my focus to be: playoff basketball.

I expected intense practices that week to prepare for the pressure-cooker of the playoffs, but Coach Mays seemed less hysterical and more cerebral. We prepped specific strategies and schemes. As always, Coach demanded perfection, but instead of the shouting, it was just an icy glare and "*run it again.*"

One thing I noticed was that only seven or eight of us ever ran our plays—the rest of the roster ran the opposition's schemes. And I was usually one of the first five guys out there, with Charlie and sometimes Kelvin or Chris subbing in.

Coach did all this without a word toward me. He never told me directly that I was going to start or reference that he just called me up after leaving me on JV all year. But sure enough, when he called the starting five for our opening playoff game in Galveston, I was in there at small forward.

The playoff atmosphere was a little subdued compared to the packed school gym for last week's rivalry game. But the junior college arena still crackled as the crowd buzzed with anticipation.

Things started out rough. I missed my first three shots, and Jimmy was off, too. Midway through the first quarter, Jimmy, Tee, and I missed three shots in the same possession, with Big Oscar Anderson rebounding every one, until he finally scored on a follow-up shot. Big O was the only one on his game in the first half, but he kept us close.

Just before halftime, Big O blocked three shots in a row in the lane, tipping the last one to Tee, who hit me with a long pass on a fast break. I was fouled and hit my free throws to finally get some points on the board. Seeing the ball finally go through the hoop a couple of times released some of the tension from all my misses.

Just keep doing your thing, Jay. The shots will start falling.

At halftime, Coach's message was "Feed the big man."

He looked at Tee, Jimmy and me. "Anderson's been carrying your butts all day. Ain't gonna be long till they collapse on him completely. That'll open up some opportunities for y'all. One of y'all needs to produce." I nodded my head. Despite my rough first half, I was feeling ready to go.

Coach rotated me out for Charlie and Kelvin for most of the third quarter, trying to bolster our defense as we "fed" Big O, who was delivering. By the fourth, though, we were still down three when Coach called my name again.

"McGee! Get in there!" He grabbed my arm as I passed and met my eyes. "We need some points from you, son."

The next possession, Tee drove to the basket, tossing up an awkward layup that clanged off the rim. Big O leaped up and grabbed it, then whipped it to me outside the arc. I immediately let it fly. The three-pointer rattled home, and we tied the game.

As I ran the court, I caught a glimpse of a fist-pump from Coach Mays as the bench erupted in cries of "*Mac Daddy*!" I pumped my fist, too.

That shot ignited a ten-nothing run over the next two minutes—a three from Jimmy, a fifteen-footer from me, and a dunk from Big O to punctuate it all, sending our side of the arena into a roar that vibrated the whole building.

The celebration continued as we cruised to victory over the last few minutes of the game. When Big O blocked a shot with a minute left, they announced he had achieved a triple-double—at least ten points, rebounds, and blocked shots in the same game—the first player in our school's history to do that in the playoffs.

Charlie went in for me for defense for the last part of the game. I went to the bench and slapped hands with jubilant teammates, then sat on the edge of my seat. As I wiped away sweat, I scanned the bleachers.

There was John, screaming with the student section, my mom and dad with wide smiles, and then I looked for Nicole behind the cheerleaders. Shannon and Hannah caught me looking, smiling and waving their pom-poms toward me, but I couldn't find Nicole. *Did she not come? Was she feeling sick?*

The final buzzer brought students storming the court in celebration. Shannon ran and embraced Jimmy, who lifted her in the air. Other girls bounced into the arms of my other teammates. Even Ashley rushed from her spot on the bench and ran to John as he followed the crowd onto the court. But I stood there alone, just a few random handshakes and pats on the back until Coach started driving us toward the bus.

We stopped at Whataburger on the way home—a perk of playoff road trips. As we were finishing up, I went for a drink refill, passing by the table where Coach and the school athletic trainer were sitting.

"Hey, Mac," the trainer said, "that three-pointer to tie us up in the fourth was huge. Great job."

"Thanks," I glanced at Coach, then looked away. "We needed that after I was throwing up bricks the entire first half."

Coach dropped his fried pie and pointed at me. "I'm glad you said that. That was a *pitiful* display in the first half." A bit of pie flew from his mouth as he emphasized *pitiful*. "We pulled this one out, but we need to get back to hitting our shots next week."

I nodded, looking down at my cup. "I . . . I will." The win took the edge off his tone—in the playoffs, winning is the only thing that matters—but I knew I was off most of the night. I spent the bus ride home in silence, running through every miss in my mind.

Chapter 23

THIS IS NOT JV BASKETBALL

I was still deflated as I walked through our back door that night. It was nearly eleven o'clock, but my mom was still there waiting to cheer my arrival.

"Woo-hoo! You were *so* good!" Her bright smile quickly faded when she saw my face. "What's got you down?"

"I'm not down, Mom, just tired." I flopped down into a chair in the kitchen.

Mom sat down across from me. "If you're not down, tell your face."

I hung my head. I was embarrassed, both that I wasn't as happy as I thought I should be and also that I couldn't hide it from Mom. "I don't know, Mom. I only scored seven points."

"Did you win? Yes." She slapped the table. "And those last five points practically won the game for you."

I rolled my eyes. "Won the game, Mom? Big O had a triple-double. I could hardly hit any . . ."

She cut me off. "But *you're the one* who hit the three-pointer to tie it late, and then *you're the one* who made it a two-possession game." She stood up, shaking her head. "I don't know what that coach said to you, but he should be ecstatic. This is only his second team to win a playoff game since Roger started high school."

I cracked a smile. It's good to have a fan like my mom.

She grabbed the cordless phone. "Speaking of Roger, he wanted you to call when you got home." She handed it to me.

I went upstairs, flopped on my bed, and made the call. I spent the first half-hour recapping the game in detail, then talk turned to everything Roger had to get done for midterms, the latest drama with Tiffany, and how he was ready for spring break. As midnight came and went, I lay on the bed with the phone leaning on my ear, eyes closed.

"Dude," I droned. "Mays doesn't make any sense."

Roger chuckled. "You just figuring this out?" He knew as well as anyone how hard Coach Mays was to understand or please.

"I'm serious," I yawned. "All year, it's like,"—I turned on my best Coach Mays voice—"'*Mac, you suck. Terrible defensively. Rot on JV, Mac. You're Pitiful . . . That dog won't hunt, Mac . . .* ' And then when the season's on the line, he's all like, '*Save my season, Mac . . .* '"

"He finally decided that your dog *could* hunt, I guess . . ." We both laughed like you do when you are half-asleep and something not funny turns hilarious because you can't stop laughing.

I sat up to catch my breath. "But man, he acts like it's perfectly natural to leave me on JV all year and then make me a starter in the playoffs."

Roger scoffed. "I can just see Mays walking up to you, looking up into your eyes and admitting he was wrong all year."

"Shut up," I said, adjusting the phone on my ear. "It's just that the only time he has ever acknowledged I was new was that '*earn your keep*' line in the Lake game."

"What did you expect, really?"

"I don't know . . . It would just be nice for him to tell me something good, like I've come a long way or whatever." I sighed. "But that's just not him."

"Yeah," Roger yawned. "Just by putting you in the starting five, he's admitting he was wrong. You should take your playing time as his apology."

I nodded my head. "Yeah . . ." But I wanted more than that. I was on varsity, Coach was finally using me, and we even won a playoff game. But I was still left craving . . . *something*.

We got off the phone, and I just felt empty. I could hardly stay awake, but the confusion over what I was feeling kept me conscious. Finally, my thoughts turned to prayer: *God, I got what I wanted. Why can't I enjoy it? Help me to understand.*

The school was buzzing the next week about our first playoff win in three years. People were passing around a copy of the *Houston Chronicle* with Big O's picture on the high school page of the sports section. In English, Charlie was trying to find our names in the tiny print of the box score.

Nicole and I still had work to do on our *A Farewell to Arms* project. We had the presentation ready other than the visual aids—so I sat in awkward silence while she colored with her markers on the posterboard.

She glanced toward me. "So y'all won . . . how did you do?"

"OK, I guess . . . Seven points. Hit a three to tie it late." I watched every careful stroke of her marker as she continued to work. "So . . . you weren't there."

She dropped her marker. Her voice got quiet. "Yeah. I decided not to dress and travel with the squad anymore." She tucked a strand of hair behind her ear.

I stared at the marker on her desk, trying to decide whether to ask why, but Nicole spoke up first. "I'm getting too fat for my uniform."

She said it like a joke, so I let off a half-chuckle. But then she looked me in the eye, and my smile vanished. My voice stuck in my throat.

She flashed a half-smile and started coloring—more vigorously now. "It's OK . . . sorry . . . not your problem. I hate that I'm missing the games."

I looked away, listening to her marker scratching away, trying to find words. "I mean . . . isn't that what's supposed to happen?"

She turned back. "What do you mean?"

"Don't you have to gain weight . . . you know . . ." I closed my eyes. ". . . *for the baby*?" It was the first time I had directly acknowledged Nicole's situation to her.

She smiled weakly. "Yeah, I guess so." She looked at my face, like she was holding her breath, trying to read what I thought.

I met her eyes and nodded slightly. "So it's all good . . . don't worry about it." There were so many whispers about her—so many things to worry about—I wanted her to know I didn't care if her cheerleading suit fit.

Nicole exhaled and picked up her marker again. She finished off the title-lettering on the poster. "Does that look OK to you?"

I nodded and smiled. I wanted to say something else to tell her that it was OK . . . even that I thought she was brave. But she changed the subject, so I followed her lead. "So we're ready to practice the presentation . . ."

Nicole and I got through the project—a fairly easy A. We'd done projects together before, but this one was different. All we really talked about was Hemingway, but I hoped somehow . . . I was there for her.

It was a busy week in all my classes—I had tests in both Physics and History, too—but I hardly thought about any of that. My mind was on our next playoff game Friday against Katy. We were playing at the arena at Rice University for the chance to advance to regionals. And I practiced with the starting five all week long.

We arrived on the bus and walked through the tunnel and onto the floor. It was like nothing I had ever experienced before. As we warmed up, it was hard to adjust my depth perception to the arena. With seating all around the court, it was like playing on a stage.

After we finished warming up, we started jogging toward the locker room, where a group of kids stood near the tunnel, holding out programs and pens. One kid pushed a basketball toward me with a Sharpie. *This kid wants my autograph?*

I laughed as I scribbled my name. *My "autograph" makes this ball worth less, not more.* But the little boy in me was relishing the moment—playing the part of the basketball star.

In the locker room, we gathered around Coach. "Y'all have been hearing all week that Katy's got a good team. They've got some strengths that'll challenge us." Coach moved his eyes around the room, his stare landing on each of us.

"We have some strengths, too. You could say our strength is our defense . . ." He pointed his finger. "You could say it's Big O down low . . ."

Then he nodded my direction. "Or maybe clutch shots from Mac on the wing . . ."

I froze. Coach kept talking, but I couldn't tune in. My head spun with disbelief at what I heard. *I've gone from JV to a team strength in two games.* I had to crack a smile.

His voice rose to that familiar growl. "*We're gonna win this game by being the team that works the hardest! 'Cats on three!*"

As soon as we tipped off, there was trouble. We prepared all week for Katy's man-to-man defense that they played all season. But instead, they dropped into a zone. It clogged the lane, leaving Big O double-teamed without the ball and—if we could even get it to him—triple-teamed when he had it. The scheme we practiced was not going to work.

We fell behind early, but then Jimmy and I hit a couple of outside shots. That loosened things just enough to give Big O room to work, so we hung close, trailing by five points late in the first quarter.

Early in the second quarter, I realized I could use Katy's aggressiveness against them. Pump fakes allowed me to get enough space to get a shot off—and they often fouled me. On my third trip to the foul line, Katy subbed in two new guys—numbers 23 and 33.

Coach started yelling hoarsely from the sideline. "*Jimmy, you got 33! Mac you got 33!*" He was hard to hear over the crowd.

Did he just say the same number twice?

I sank my first free throw, then looked back at Coach. He yelled again.

"*Mac, take 23!*"

Didn't he say 33 the first time?

"*Mac! 33!*"

Or was it 23?

Panic set in. The numbers 23 and 33 bounced back and forth in my mind. My hands started to feel shaky, so I steadied my breath and took my shot.

I barely watched the ball go through before scrambling to find number 33—the number I thought I heard first. But when I got to him, Jimmy was right there too, sticking with the same man.

I looked in horror as the ball swung to number 23, wide open on the other wing. I desperately ran in his direction as he released his shot. It clanged off the back iron. Ty grabbed the long rebound.

I was so out of position that I was wide open for a fast break. Ty heaved a long pass, I ran it down and laid the ball in on the other end, receiving another hard foul as I scored.

Standing at the foul line, I could see Coach Mays storming the sidelines out of the corner of my eye. Charlie crouched by the scorer's table. The buzzer sounded.

"For the shooter!" Coach barked.

I hit the free throw and ran to the bench. Coach practically threw me into my chair and got right in my face, his nose inches from mine.

"*THIS IS NOT JV BASKETBALL!*" He paced away for one step then wheeled back into my face again.

"*THIS IS VARSITY—PLAYOFF—WIN-OR-GO-HOME BASKETBALL! Time for you to grow up and stop making stupid, middle-school mistakes, son*!" Then he stomped away, muttering "*brutal*" under his breath. I put a towel over my head, wondering if I'd even get back in the game.

My lucky three-point play pulled us within two, but we missed every chance to pull even before halftime, as I watched from the bench. I was back on the floor to start the second half, with the team down four.

I shuffled on and off the court during the third quarter as Coach subbed guys in and out, trying to find the right mix to spark a comeback. But Katy's lead swelled from four to twelve.

In the fourth quarter, he surrounded Big O with four shooters—Tee, Jimmy, Chris, and me—and told us to try to shoot threes to get us back into the game. I made one, missed two.

With three minutes left and the deficit at fourteen, Coach pulled out all the underclassmen and let the seniors finish out the game. I watched from the bench as the clock ran out on our playoff hopes.

The bus ride home was long and quiet. Some of the seniors fought back tears. I replayed the game in my head and counted up my points—fifteen. Despite the butt-chewing I got, I did my part. But there's no bright side to losing in the playoffs. I just stared out the window, fogged up from the warm spring night in Houston, feeling numb.

The season was over.

Chapter 24

SPRINGTIME

The end of the season always brought a feeling of emptiness. It was hard to even get up for school when there wasn't basketball at the end of the day. I tossed in bed, debating whether I really needed to get up, finally pulling myself onto my feet and into the shower.

But with varsity and the playoffs extending the season a few weeks this year, it wasn't long before we hit spring break. That Friday, I shoved my gear into my locker and headed home for a week of . . . *nothing*.

The youth group went on a ski trip we couldn't afford, so I mostly just shot in the driveway, watched TV, played a little Nintendo—but it was nice. Not the full "detox" that summer brought from all the social anxieties of school, but it was a week to clear my head, a time to chill and forget about everything else for a while.

John and I did have one spring break ritual: Astroworld. We both usually got season passes for Christmas to Houston's Six Flags park, and we'd make our first visit that week. So that Monday, we loaded into John's old Buick and got on the freeway—this year, I was in the back seat with Ashley riding shotgun.

So in line for every roller coaster, I got to hear from the workers trying to fill empty seats, "Is anyone riding alone?" and sheepishly raise my hand and push through the crowd—the dork with no one to ride with.

A full day of these scenes brought back feelings that plagued me at the end of every season. Those empty afternoons with no practice gave room for memories to flood in where it seemed every other player had a girl bouncing into his arms after every game—while I just stood there and waved to my mom.

It was always fun with John and Ashley—they never treated me like a third wheel—but beneath the laughs we shared all day was a pit of loneliness in my chest. And it was embarrassing. John had a girlfriend, and I was still alone. When the day finally ended, I was glad to be home.

I slept till noon the next day, waking up to the sounds of video game theme music. Roger was home for the week, and we spent the rest of spring break lounging in his room playing *NBA Jam* or *John Madden Football* on the Nintendo with our brains turned off.

Roger and I mostly settled into the comfort of familiar stories and inside jokes. But Friday night, he wanted to vent. Tiffany had been jerked around by another guy and came running to Roger for comfort. She even told him that she wished she could find a guy like him.

I paused the game. "So what did you say? Did you tell her that you're sitting right there in front of her?"

Roger shook his head. "No . . . she was drunk anyway. If something was going to start between us, that wasn't the time."

I felt sympathy for the roller coaster Tiffany had put Roger on for the past three years, but it was hard for me to root for them to get together. She just didn't seem like a good fit.

Roger unpaused the game, played one possession, then paused it again. "She told me that I didn't deserve to be alone all the time and snuggled up against me. You know it's not the first time she's done that, but I was afraid she was coming onto me when she was drunk, so I left before I got myself in trouble."

"That's good." I set down my controller and lay back on his couch. "I know that must have been hard to do."

"Yeah . . ." Roger looked down, then rolled his eyes. "That's apparently how you start a relationship in college. People hook up randomly after a lot of build-up—make out or even sleep together—then they start dating. That's not a good start, though."

It was sort of nice to be talking about Roger's problems for a change. I don't know if I could have left if the girl I liked for three years was snuggled up to me—I wouldn't be strong enough. I was proud of him.

"So did you end up talking to her?"

"Yeah, but when I tried to—*get this* . . ." Roger shot to his feet. "The next time we talked, she started talking to me about her friend *Jessica* . . ."

I laughed. "It's always a good sign when the girl you like is trying to set you up with someone else."

"You know what?" he said, holding out his arms. "Whatever. I think all this—not just last month but the last three years—has taught me something."

"What's that?"

He paced around the room. "I've told you stuff with Nicole Ellis and all that—stuff I was just as much saying to myself, you know? I don't even think Tiffany is the right person for me anyway. And more than that . . ." He stopped, emphasizing every syllable with his hand, "She's *just* . . . *not* . . . *interested*, period. And that's really OK."

He sat back down. "It's OK to just be nice. It's OK to just be someone's friend and never expect anything back. If Tiffany accepts my help, she's not 'using' me, she's just accepting my friendship. And I've gotta be OK with that."

We sat quietly in thought. I nodded, wishing it was easy to "just be a friend" without getting attached—like me and Nicole—or them getting attached to me—like Carol or Elise.

Then I smiled. "So are you going to go out with Jessica?"

Roger threw a pillow at me, laughing. "Leave it to you to completely miss the point." After a few more seconds of hurling objects and dodging, we picked up our controllers and started playing again.

The next morning, I said goodbye to Roger until the summer. After a Sunday of hearing people talking about the ski trip I missed, it was time to go back to school for the final stretch of my junior year.

School is different after spring break. Whether it's the sound and feel of the A/C working hard or the sight of so many girls and guys coming back tanned from a week in the sun, the air crackles with the promise of summer.

I enjoyed the feeling as I bounced down the hall toward second period. I turned the corner into English class and saw Nicole there, smiling and laughing with Hannah and Charlie. She wore new clothes—looser fitting but still in her bright, colorful, t-shirt-and-jeans style. They were talking about Shannon's birthday party over the weekend.

Charlie grabbed my shoulder and shook me as I sat down. "You should have seen it, Mac. Jimmy was pouting like a three-year-old."

Shannon and Jimmy had been together for years, but always with ups and downs. Nicole, Hannah, and Charlie took turns trying to explain to me the drama from the party, but with names and context I didn't know. So I just smiled blankly and nodded—that was normal when people talked about parties.

But I felt like *something* was different—and then it hit me. This scene—which used to happen every Monday—was something I hadn't seen in months. Nicole's smile was bright, she stood confidently, and she laughed like she used to. And even though I didn't have any idea of what they were talking about, I smiled, too. It was good to see Nicole being Nicole.

Then in Spanish, one of the girls' boyfriends tried to sneak into class and stay there. Mrs. Navarro was oblivious at first, and as she called roll, Nicole turned to him with a mischievous grin. "Tell her you're *Martín* . . ."

Mrs. Navarro went down the roll, finally calling out the name of the kid who had not shown up all year: "*Martín? Martín?*"

"Here!" the boyfriend said with a smirk. Mrs. Navarro's head snapped his direction so fast her glasses fell off her nose. Mrs. Navarro angrily shooed him out of the room as the class erupted in laughter. I smiled wide—Nicole was back.

I was still laughing telling the story to Charlie when we walked into the locker room for basketball period. We saw Big O and Ty and the other seniors turning in their gear to Coach, jerseys and shorts piled on Coach's desk—a visual reminder that this year was over and next year was starting now.

There were only six returning seniors—and that was if Coach didn't cut Eddie Benson. In the playoffs, Tee, Jimmy, and I had started, and Charlie got plenty of minutes, too. Darryl Nicholson, who finished the season on JV, was also coming back. Coach pulled the six of us aside, including Eddie.

"*Take a knee.*" Coach stood straight with his arms folded, fixing his glare on each of us. Even on a knee, some of us were almost eye-to-eye with him. "Y'all are seniors now. I expect you to set an example. That means you're gonna work your *butts* off—even you, Benson—or I'll replace you with someone who will."

In the offseason, Coach divided everyone into three groups for strength and conditioning—and he usually designated a senior as a captain. Since I was one of the three returning starters, I assumed I'd be one of them, but then Coach sorted me into the same group as Jimmy.

Coach blew his whistle. "Tee's group is on the boxes and lunges today. Gonzalez . . . take your group to the weight room. Schroeder, y'all're on the track . . . two miles today. Go!"

My jaw clenched and I shook my head as I jogged out toward the track. *How could I be behind Charlie again? Who started in the playoffs? I played better than Tee and Jimmy! I should be the FIRST to be a captain.*

Jimmy must have seen the scowl on my face, because he got right up next to me as we reached the track, doing his best Coach Mays act. "Are you gonna whine about not being captain, Mac? You think three games on varsity means you're a freaking leader now? You were barely even on the team."

I looked around, trying to read the other guys' reactions—*did they think like Jimmy? Was I delusional to think of myself as a "returning starter" instead of just a guy who got called up for a few games?*

I got no answer. Everyone just put their heads down and started running, so I did, too, taking a big lead over Jimmy out of pure anger. My legs and chest burned as I tried to stay out in front, but he passed me on the seventh lap—hardly even glancing my direction as he passed me—and finished a half-lap ahead of me.

It's a new year. I've proven nothing.

While I was looking forward to my senior season in basketball, John was just a few weeks into his junior year of baseball—and he was still proving himself, too. In baseball season, it was my turn to sit in the stands. And when I saw John bat ninth, get pinch-hit for, or even sit the bench in favor of this fat senior who did everything worse than John, I would pace the bleachers in anger.

Why do we both get screwed over all the time?

On the first of April—a Saturday afternoon—we met at Dairy Queen to vent our frustrations, but once we sat down in the booth, we just sat there, poking at our Blizzards.

"What's your batting average now?" I was the first to break the silence.

John shrugged. ".233 . . . but my on-base is .375. I should be doing better, though. This is the worst I've ever hit."

I dropped my spoon. "But you have a different stance every game. Coach Thomas is jerking you in and out of the lineup, constantly screwing with your swing . . . it's not your fault!"

John sighed. "Yeah . . . It's still up to me to swing the bat. It's on me." He took a sip of water and looked down. "I don't want to talk about it."

John stirred his ice cream then took a bite. "Is Jimmy still being a tool?"

"Yeah, he's always been indifferent to me before varsity, but suddenly now he's trying to put me in my place or something. It sucks, but . . ." I paused, shaking my head. "But he's just trying to be a leader like Coach wants. He's like a taller, younger Mays out there right now. He's a brown-nose, but I . . ."

John clapped his cup on the table. "Coach ought to see you as a leader . . ."

"And he just . . . doesn't." I slumped in my chair. "And he's probably right. Guys might respect that I can shoot, but I don't think they respect *me* enough to be any sort of leader."

John sighed—he understood. "Yeah . . ."

We just ate for a few minutes, then I smiled. "Did I ever tell you about what Nicole did in Spanish last week?" I told him about Mrs. Navarro and "*Martín*." John just smiled—almost sadly.

"I, uh, guess you had to be there." I looked down. "It just seems like Nicole is more herself recently . . . and people aren't treating her as weird."

John shrugged. "I guess she's just trying to make the most of her last couple of months with us."

My head shot up. "What do you mean?"

"You know she's due in September, don't you?" John looked me in the eye. "She's missing the fall semester with the baby. So she'll have to go to the alternative campus to make it up to graduate on time."

I froze like he just slapped me—none of that ever crossed my mind. When I could finally move, I just scraped my last bits from my cup, feeling stupid.

I cracked a half-smile. "We're a couple of bummers, huh?" I sat quietly for a minute, trying to shake my emotions, then shrugged. "At least it won't be long until summer."

John looked up. "Speaking of summer, have you started looking for a job yet?"

I threw my napkin at him. That was the *last* thing I wanted to think about.

I drove home that night with my head spinning. I was back to square one, trying to prove myself all over again. Watching John struggle stirred up my own frustration. And just when the real Nicole was coming back—and I was finally okay just being her friend—she was going to be gone.

But springtime was like that. Basketball ends and then spring break, and I taste summer coming. Then April hits, and it's two long months of projects and state testing to endure before the final bell . . . only to work a soul-sucking job all summer. The false hope of spring.

I woke up feeling heavy. I stopped my alarm and put my feet on the floor and opened my eyes to the light hitting my new pastel blue silk shirt, hanging on my door, and a quiet joy crept in. It was Easter morning.

I came down the stairs to see that Mom had laid out a little basket of treats on the table. You're never too old for a few jellybeans on Easter.

We settled into the comfortable routine of Easter—the feel of the new church shirt I'll wear every other Sunday for the next few months, the smell of the roast starting to cook in the crock pot, and the anticipation as we pulled into the parking lot of the church, packed for Resurrection Sunday. I loved all of it.

The crowd wasn't the only thing that felt bigger on Easter. The smiles were wider, the singing louder. Sure, there were plenty of visitors and twice-a-year attenders, but it seemed that all of us repeating to each other "He is risen . . . He is risen indeed," reminded us that we really did believe.

We sang the Easter standards—starting with "Up from the Grave He Arose" and "He Lives." And all the anxiety—the letdowns, the pressure—shrank a little when we sang, "Because He lives, I can face tomorrow." It was like a quiet voice reminding me.

The pastor came up and invited us to really believe it. I can't remember his words exactly, but I know I could feel a shift in my heart.

For one Sunday at least, I didn't care that the other kids at this church were so different from me. And I wasn't thinking about basketball or about why I still didn't have a girlfriend. At least for today, I understood that "putting God first" meant trusting him—even if I didn't get what I wanted—and that was *real* hope.

Then I went home to a rare day of just feeling comfortable as myself.

We had the pot roast, then homemade ice cream with chopped strawberries. I sat on the porch and watched the neighborhood kids hunt eggs while talking to Roger on the phone.

Then I lounged on the couch with Mom and Dad, watching basketball.

That night, my mind tried to push ahead to Monday—school, pressure, everything waiting for me. But something stopped it, and I smiled.

Because he lives, I can face tomorrow.

The thought put my mind at rest, and I went to sleep.

Chapter 25

WHAT HAPPENED?

When my alarm went off Monday morning, I resisted the snooze button and went straight to the shower. I was determined to spend some time reading the Bible before school for the first time in months. My Bible had a six-month reading plan that I had been using on-and-off since I got it two Christmases ago. I turned to my next reading and cracked a smile: Psalm 139 again—the same passage from the youth conference.

I sat at the kitchen table with a bowl of cereal and the Bible open, reading through the next chapter on the checklist, when it hit me that today we were starting in home room for spring paperwork—enrolling in next year's classes, voting on "class favorites" for the yearbook, and (I hoped for me) ordering letter jackets.

I put my nose back down toward my Bible, wanting to allow God to speak to me over the nerves rising in my chest. But I couldn't ignore it. This morning was like a verdict—*did I earn my place this year or not?*

The only ones who could get a jacket were varsity athletes or those who "lettered" in other organizations. I had technically earned a letter last year by making the National Honors Society, but I didn't order the jacket—ashamed to letter in "good grades" when everyone knew I played basketball.

Coach's rule for lettering was that you had to play in half of varsity's district games. I was only there for one district game and the playoffs. But Ty told me that he earned a letter when he was brought up only for the playoffs when he was a freshman. So I was hopeful.

Dad came into the kitchen to grab his coffee and his keys, signaling he was ready to go. I said a quick prayer, both asking for the letter jacket and asking to be OK if I didn't get it.

My stomach churned on the ride to school and when I sat down in home room. We received the paperwork in a stack of color-coded packets. The last page was a yellow sheet of paper for the letter jackets. Heart rate increasing, I grabbed it from the bottom and scanned it.

In the pre-filled blank for "letters earned" was typed NATIONAL HONOR SOCIETY . . . *and nothing else.* I swallowed hard. Lettering in basketball as a senior was basically useless—you couldn't order your jacket until the spring, and you were lucky to get it before graduating.

Any time I pictured myself as a senior, I was always wearing my basketball letter jacket. And now that wasn't going to happen. I set the yellow paper aside and started filling out everything else as my thoughts swirled.

I never should have gotten my hopes up. I was on JV all year, practically. It's OK. Don't get worked up . . .

The buzz in the classroom got louder and louder as people finished their packets. When I turned in my packet, I was right behind Darryl Nicholson. Before I dropped the paper, I saw his letter jacket form on top.

I shook my head. *Coach wanted me—not Darryl—for the playoffs, but he's the one who gets it. Well, Darryl did play enough varsity games. I can't complain. But . . . this sucks.*

I didn't want to spiral back into bitter thoughts. I grabbed my yellow paper and asked the teacher for a pass to go see Coach Mays. I walked down the empty halls with my heart racing. This might be the first time I've ever initiated a talk with Coach Mays.

Coach was in his Geography classroom. I shuddered to think what those poor freshmen went through having Coach drill them on Asian capitals. But this morning, Coach was just reading a newspaper in the room of raucous freshmen who had finished their paperwork.

I stepped into the room. "Um . . . Coach?" I could barely get the words past my throat. I could feel myself starting to sweat as his newspaper dropped.

His stare hit me. "McGee . . . what're you doin' here?"

"I, uh . . . had a question." I stepped closer, tentatively holding out the yellow form. ". . . *about letter jackets*?"

Coach was stone-faced, his eyes going the paper and back at me. "Son, we got rules for this. You gotta play half of district."

"I know." I looked down. "Ty told me he got a letter jacket for playing in the playoffs when he was a freshman, so . . ."

Coach sighed, his expression softening. I looked at him hopefully, but he shook his head. "We won regionals that year. Maybe if we'd made it a little further this year and you played a couple more games . . ."

"Oh." I lowered my paper and started backing away. "Ok." I turned to walk out, heat rising in my face. I felt so stupid. *Just let me disappear.*

Coach got up and followed me to the door. "Sorry, Mac. Keep working. We're gonna need you next year."

I nodded my head and turned away. *Next year? You needed me* ***this*** *year!* I felt like everything I'd done—all that I did to get to varsity and contribute there—had just been erased. I felt empty and numb. *None of it mattered.*

The bell rang for us to move on to first period.

There was only about fifteen minutes left in first period, so we didn't do anything in history class. I just sat there, fighting the familiar rage that always surged when Coach cut me off from what I wanted. I didn't want to go to that place. Getting mad and feeling sorry for myself never helped me.

I walked to second period thinking about what to do about English class. I wanted to ask Charlie if he thought Coach was being unfair—he'd usually side with anyone against Mays—but I also didn't want to whine when he just ordered his own jacket. I decided it was better just to try to have fun with Nicole.

But when I got to class, Nicole's desk was empty. Just as the bell rang, she rushed through the door and flopped into her desk. She looked pale to me.

Ms. Longmire started class, but my eyes went back to Nicole when I heard her shift suddenly in her seat. Sweat was beginning to bubble up on her forehead.

Hannah leaned over. "Nicole . . . you don't look so good."

She let out a whimper. "I don't know what's wrong. I feel terrible."

Ms. Longmire stopped and knelt between Nicole and me. After a few whispers, she said, "Let's get you to the nurse, dear. Hannah, could you take her down?"

Nicole winced, unable to stand up fully as Hannah helped her out of the room. My eyes stayed glued to the doorway long after Nicole and Hannah disappeared down the hallway. I was curious, but I wasn't sure whether to be alarmed or not.

Ms. Longmire stepped in front of the door and closed it, forcing a smile. "She will be all right, everyone. Eyes back to the overhead."

Despite the teacher's best efforts, there was no way I was going to concentrate on whatever grammar was going to be on the state test. *It's been a long time since she's had morning sickness, I think. Maybe just cramping? Is that normal?* I had no idea.

It didn't surprise me that Nicole never returned to class, but when Hannah didn't come back, either, I started to worry.

I went through the next two periods and lunch with one question pounding in my head: *What happened?*

I looked for Nicole. I looked for Hannah. I eavesdropped on conversations, trying to hear Nicole's name. I asked around. No one knew anything.

I rushed to Spanish class, hoping to find her there, feeling better. But time ran out and the bell rang. No Nicole. All around me, people were buzzing about her absence, but I heard no news until a phrase shot through my heart.

"*Something's wrong with the baby.*"

Maybe it was just a rumor. People make assumptions. But at basketball, more fragments of information kept coming out.

"I heard her mom came to take her to the emergency room."

"Someone told me that she was bleeding."

"Hannah was crying about it in fifth period."

When I got home, I called John. Because of Kat and Ashley, John always seemed to know things that I didn't, but he had baseball, so I left a message with his mom to call me when he got home.

I went to the driveway to shoot to pass the time. Sometimes I could concentrate well enough to sink a few shots in a row. Then my mind would drift to Coach Mays and the letter jacket. I shook my head. It all seemed so trivial now.

It was almost seven o'clock before John finally called back.

I got straight to the point. "What do you know about Nicole?"

John paused. "Not much. Kat's pretty sure she lost the baby . . . but Ashley said that there's something else about it that really scared Hannah. I don't know."

I sat on my bed, unable to speak. I didn't know anything about any of this stuff. What was there to be scared about? What else could happen? I didn't know enough to be scared, so I was just . . . *sad.* Sad for Nicole.

John finally broke the silence. "I think she's OK, though . . . Ashley said she'd be OK."

"That's good." We sat quietly for another minute, then I heard John inhale like he was about to change the subject.

I interrupted him. "I gotta do the dishes. I'll talk to you later." I didn't want to start talking about any theories about what happened, or worse, start complaining about our coaches. It wasn't the time for that.

Going to bed, I remembered my final thoughts the night before—"*I can face tomorrow.*" I chuckled at the irony. *This is the "tomorrow" you send me, God? Have I faced it well? What am I supposed to do with all this?*

Just like the night I first learned Nicole was pregnant, I felt utterly powerless. I didn't know anything, and I couldn't do anything.

I tried to remember something from my Bible-reading that morning. God sees everything. He knows everything. And he cares. He's with me—even in the dark.

So I lay in the darkness, my fan blowing cool air across my body, my eyes wide open, staring at the shadows formed by our popcorn-textured ceiling. I always imagined those irregular shadows as animals and faces and characters. But in the morning light, they were gone.

That's what usually came of the thoughts that kept me awake at night, too. I couldn't control what happened to Nicole. I couldn't control Coach or what he did. I couldn't even control myself—not really. I closed my eyes again.

God, I've got another tomorrow to face. And I have no idea what to do.

After struggling to sleep all night, I overslept Tuesday morning. I rushed through my shower and barely made it before the bell. If there was any news about Nicole, I got there too late to hear it.

But second period should bring some answers. When I arrived, I saw Hannah and Charlie talking quietly. I pulled my desk closer.

"Hey, Hannah. Any news about Nicole? What happened?"

She leaned in, voice hushed. "I was just telling Charlie . . . she was having all these pains, and then when we got to the nurse, she started bleeding real bad. I stayed with her till her mom came and took her to the hospital . . . it was *so* scary."

Ms. Longmire pulled down the screen at the front of the room, trying to get everyone's attention. I glanced that way then turned back. "So . . . the baby?"

Charlie gave a short shake of his head. "It's gone, man."

Ms. Longmire flipped on the overhead projector and stared right at us. "I need everyone to quiet down and look this way."

I had to ask one more thing. "But Nicole's OK?"

Hannah's eyes darted to Ms. Longmire and back. "I think so . . . but she's still in the hospital."

The rest of class was Longmire droning through practice questions for the state test Thursday. Normally, the whir of the overhead and the dim lights would have made it hard not to doze off, but my mind was spinning.

I must've heard it a dozen more times: "*Did you know Nicole Ellis is in the hospital?*" Lots of people were talking in the hallways or in classes—some concerned, some stirring drama, and others just being terrible.

"That's so scary . . . I hope she's OK . . ."

"That's awful. I'm *never* getting pregnant."

"I wonder if Cory is going to keep lying about being the daddy."

"That's what happens when you're a slut."

"It's so embarrassing. I'd never come back to school."

Most people showed concern, but it was the ugliness that lingered with me as I got back home. The house was quiet—no one there, no one to call. Mom was at Bible study, Dad still at work. John had baseball, and Roger worked on Tuesday nights. I was alone with my thoughts.

I want to help . . . but there's nothing I can do. I'm not a doctor or miracle worker. I'm barely her friend—just someone she talks to at school.

I paced the living room, shot some hoops in the driveway, ate a whole box of Fruit Roll-Ups . . . I couldn't stick with anything for very long.

All I wanted was for Nicole to be OK—not just physically but safe from the kind of cruel stuff that I heard at school that day. I knew that if she were anything like me, there's nothing ugly anyone could say that she wasn't already telling herself. *But what am I supposed to do about it?*

I went up to my room and lay down. Prayer was the only thing I had to give, so I prayed. I asked God to help her physically and emotionally . . . and then I ran out of words.

So I just sat there with the same thought lingering like an offering to God: *I want her to be OK.*

Someone told me once that when God speaks to you, it's not a voice you can hear. It's more like the look your mom gives you—the one where she doesn't say a word, but you know exactly what you need to do.

Maybe that was what happened that afternoon. Because suddenly, a feeling washed over me. Not words. Not a plan. Just this: *Be there.*

There was something Nicole needed to know, and the way for her to know was for me to somehow show up for her.

Before my brain could fight back and ask too many questions, I heard my dad pulling into the driveway. I went downstairs to meet him at the door.

"Dad, can I borrow the car for a little while?"

Dad was startled a little by my sudden appearance. "Sure . . . Where you headed?"

"I need to visit someone at the hospital."

I grabbed my keys and walked out.

Chapter 26

THE VISIT

I got into the old brown Oldsmobile and put the keys in the ignition. I waited for that old flood of nerves and dread, just as if I were picking up the phone. Nicole Ellis is in the hospital, and I'm about to just show up? *Really*? But that feeling never came. In fact, there was a calmness that hit me right when I expected to chicken out and go back inside.

When someone's in the hospital, you visit them, right? Nicole was one of the most popular people in school. There would be a bunch of people stopping by; I'd just blend in, wish her well, and take off. No big deal.

As I pulled out of the driveway and drove down the road toward the hospital, I pictured a bunch of cheerleaders and other kids from school hanging around the floor and the waiting room with balloons and flowers. *Maybe I should get something, too*? I quickly pulled into Walgreens.

Now flowers—even Walgreens flowers—were out of the question. And just picturing myself walking in with a balloon hovering over my head just made me laugh at myself out loud. So what was left? Not being a hospital gift shop, the stuffed animals weren't imprinted with

"Get well soon," so I wasn't sure they would have the right effect, either.

It was then that I spotted "Pete the Repeat Parrot"—a mechanical stuffed parrot that would record snippets of what was said around it and repeat it in a high-pitched parrot voice. Maybe something a little funny would be good? After testing with a few phrases and hearing it squawk my words back to me, I chuckled.

I picked that up and started to carry it to the counter, picturing Nicole and I laughing together as the parrot repeated Mrs. Navarro catchphrases: "*Martín? Martín?*" But then I caught myself, and another inner voice told me firmly, "*Now's not the time for something goofy.*"

As I was carrying the ridiculous parrot back to its place, I passed the school and art supplies aisle. I spotted a pack of markers where the color would change when you went back over them with a special color-changing marker. I thought about all the signs Nicole would make for cheerleading and, yes, those notes she would write to her friends, with the names colored on the front folded section. I grabbed them and left "Pete" behind, hurrying back to the register. No card, no gift bag. I'll just leave it on the table with the other gifts. I just won't be empty-handed.

I pulled back out of Walgreens and on a few blocks, turning on the hospital road. My head swiveled around in unfamiliar territory, looking for the signs directing me where to park. My heart started beating a little faster as I pulled into a parking spot. The lot was nearly empty this late in the afternoon, and I saw no familiar faces, no other well-wishing classmates meeting me on their way out.

The hospital was quiet as I walked in. Any notion I had of someone I knew directing me where to go or even following a crowd was gone. My only "friend" was the elderly lady sitting behind the information desk with a name tag that said, "Doris."

"Can you help me, er . . . find the room number for . . . N-Nicole Ellis?" Saying her name out loud instantly made me feel vulnerable. Doris smiled back kindly, but no spark of recognition came to her face. The theory that half the school was turning up to visit Nicole today was clearly crumbling before me.

"Ellis, you say?" she said as she typed into her computer, like it was the first time she had heard the name all day. "Nicole, right? That's room 223."

What am I thinking even being here? "When someone's in the hospital, you visit them"? Where did I get that idea anyway? Maybe if you're a pastor or something. I'm just a kid from school. Nobody knows I'm here. I'm gonna leave before I embarrass myself.

I turned back toward the door.

But one person *did* know I was here. "Sir?" Doris called out, pointing to the hallway behind her desk "The elevators are down this hallway on your right."

I cracked a sheepish smile. My mind went blank as I tried to find some excuse for walking back out the door, so I dutifully marched past Doris and toward the elevator, clenching a pack of color-changing markers in my left hand. I reached the elevator, pushed the button, and stepped inside. I was on my way.

No one else is here. I'm the only one who is clueless enough to think I ought to just show up at the hospital at a time like this . . . and holding markers! This is crazy.

When I arrived on the second floor, there was still no sign of anyone from the school present. I looked at the signs on the walls: Rooms 211-229 to the left. Also on the left was a restroom. I walked in, nervously took a leak and washed my shaking hands, looking back at myself in the mirror.

OK, being here is not the normal thing to do. That's obvious now . . . But maybe it's the right thing to do? No one else showed up. Maybe it's on you to be the one who does.

I stared into my own eyes, alternating between that strange resolve I had in my driveway and the familiar clammy self-consciousness that plagued me with doubt. All at once, I grasped the door handle and walked out.

And coming out of the room across the hall was Shannon Roberts. She saw me right away. She spoke in her typical cheery tone. "Jay! What are you doing here?" With her were two adults who must've been her mom and dad.

Now someone other than Doris and I knew I was here. The only thing to reply to Shannon's question was the truth: "I, uh . . . came to see Nicole."

"Is she here?" she said, glancing down the hall where I was looking as I answered her first question. "I didn't know. I was here visiting my grandma."

"Yeah, room 223. Sorry about your grandma. Is she OK?" I was glad to change the subject.

"Oh, she's OK," she said, looking at her mom to affirm what she was saying. "Minor surgery. She's going home in the morning. How is Nicole?"

OK, fine. Just please don't ask about the markers. "I haven't seen her yet."

She looked around. "So you're here by yourself?"

I could feel blood rushing to my face. "I guess I thought a lot more people would come. I actually feel pretty awkward about even going in," I chuckled nervously.

"No, it's sweet," she said with a reassuring smile. "Don't worry about it. She'll be happy to see you."

"I guess so." I stood there silently, hoping Shannon would offer to go with me to visit her cheerleading teammate. But instead, her dad hit the elevator button and gave her a look of his own.

"Sorry, I've got to go with my parents. Tell her I said 'hi'!" And they disappeared into the elevator, leaving me alone in the hallway. There was nothing left to do but to walk to room 223.

I reached the room and found the door cracked half-open. I saw a heavyset woman with curly blonde hair sitting in a chair near the foot of the bed. She looked up as I tapped lightly on the door, causing it to swing open more.

Our eyes met. "Nicole, sweetie, you've got a visitor. It's a boy."

Among some rustling on the hospital bed, I heard a sleepy voice: "Who is it, Mom?"

Nicole's mom smiled at me. "I don't think I know him." Then she motioned to me. "Come on in." Nicole was sitting up in bed now. She saw me and gave me a kind of smile I didn't expect. It was a *shy* smile.

"Oh, this is Jay," she told her mom. "He's from school. You know when I went to that baseball game with Rachel?"

I stuffed my hands in my pockets. "Yeah, that was me and my friend John Agee."

"Oh, we've known John since Nicole was little," she said. "He's a really great guy."

Nicole's mom tried to make a little more small talk, but it was going nowhere. Nicole lay back down on her side. I inched toward the door, trying to figure out the words for my escape.

Instead, Nicole's mom stood up. "Well, I'm going down to the cafeteria to get some coffee," she said. "I'm going to let you two visit. Love you, sweetie. Nice to meet you, Jay." She placed her hand gently on my shoulder as she passed me out of the room. "It was so nice of you to come."

And I was left behind in the room with Nicole.

I walked around to the other side of the bed and stood near the window, facing Nicole. I smiled at her as she looked back at me from the hospital bed. "So, uh, how're you feeling?"

She wore a nervous smile. "I'm OK, I guess." She fidgeted briefly with her hair and added, "I bet I look awful."

I had to laugh at that a little bit, but I reassured her, "Don't worry about that. You look fine." It was the first time I even thought about what she looked like since I got there. Now that I looked at her there, I wasn't noticing anything about her hair or about her face, just that she somehow looked *smaller* laying in that hospital bed.

I shifted my feet a little. "So you're going to be OK? A lot of people at school were worried about you.

"You know," I added with a self-conscious chuckle, "I expected a lot of other people to be here visiting."

"It's actually been pretty lonely . . . Just me and Mom and the doctors and stuff." She looked up at me. "I can't believe you came to the hospital to see me."

"If someone's in the hospital, you visit them, right? At least that's what was in my head when I decided to come." I looked back down at my feet. "I don't know."

"I guess not everyone thinks like you . . ." Her eyes flashed with a slight smile. "But that's no surprise, right?"

We shared a brief laugh. "No, I guess not."

She sighed. "It's no big deal, though . . . I'm probably going home in the morning. They just wanted to observe me for another day."

She looked up at the ceiling, and I could see a slight shimmer of tears forming in her eyes. "It's my own fault anyway. I can't expect a lot of sympathy when I got myself into this mess. It's just so embarrassing."

Except for my mom, I don't think I'd ever had a girl cry in front of me, at least not like this. I didn't come here to make her cry. My mind raced for what to say.

I think somewhere in that frantic searching was a sort of prayer. I had read somewhere that the Holy Spirit speaks through you sometimes when you don't know what to say.

Now I don't know if that's what happened here; I'm sure what I said wasn't particularly memorable or profound. But I do know that it was the first time I ever spoke to Nicole without scrutinizing every word either before I said it or after, or both.

"You don't need to be embarrassed," I looked her in her eyes and then away again. "Lots of kids have done what you've done, but they haven't had to go through what you're going through. I think you've been brave in all this."

"Well, yeah, I tried to be," Her tears were getting larger and starting to escape down the side of her face. "I thought that maybe the baby would be the good that came from the bad, but I didn't even get to have it. It's like when I tried to do the right thing, it still turned out bad. I don't understand it at all."

"I hate all this has happened to you," Now I was trying to fight tears myself. "I don't understand it either."

We were both quiet for a moment. Fighting my voice from cracking with emotion, I looked straight at her. "It's not your fault, you know. Losing the baby wasn't your fault."

"I'm not even sure that's true." She wiped her eyes. "I was *so scared* about having the baby. Maybe I caused my body to, you know, *reject* it or something." She took a deep breath and exhaled, staring at the ceiling. "Anyway, none of this would have happened if I hadn't been so stupid in the first place. And now everyone knows."

She closed her eyes and shook her head in silence for a moment.

I wondered what was going through her head, then she looked back at me. "Of all people, I'm sort of surprised you would be here."

I took a slight step back, startled and embarrassed. I started to stutter out an apology, but she interrupted me.

She reached her hand toward me. "Don't get me wrong . . ."

Her arms folded back across her chest. "It's just that I know that you go to church and are real serious about all that. I know you '*know better*.' I just figured that when you found out about all this, you probably thought I was a bad person."

A twinge of shame and regret flashed across my heart, as I thought about how I was initially disappointed and repulsed when I first heard that she didn't meet the "good girl" standards I hoped for. It sickened me to think that I might have somehow communicated I thought of her as "bad" during that time.

I pursed my lips and shook my head slightly. "It doesn't matter what I think any more than it matters what anyone else thinks."

I shuffled my feet. "But I don't think that. I mean, you've been a friend to me when you didn't have to be."

Nicole turned her head inquisitively. "I don't really know what you're talking about."

"I mean that you've always treated me like . . . a *person*." I closed my eyes, trying to find the words. "Ever since we moved here—five years ago or whatever—I always felt like most people didn't want to bother with me. That I was just the weird kid who got good grades and thought about basketball way too much."

She pushed up a little in her bed. "I don't think anyone ever thought of you like that anyway, Jay."

I pointed to her. "That's the point. You've never treated me that way, and when you're around, neither does anyone else. But it was really hard for me my first few years to believe I was worth anything.

But these last couple of years, that's changed a little. If a girl like you likes to talk to me in class and seems to want me around, maybe I'm not so bad. You've helped me."

She shook her head. "If it doesn't matter what you or other people think of me, it doesn't matter what I—or anyone else—thinks of you, either."

"I guess you're right," I shrugged. "I guess it really only matters what God thinks." The words came out of my mouth before I knew I was saying them. My heart started beating faster; I never talked about these things openly with anyone except my family and sometimes John.

My voice was hesitant, the words coming slowly. "Maybe . . . God wanted to help me stop thinking I was such a loser. Maybe he just sort of used you to do it."

"You're giving me way too much credit, Jay." She slumped back down into her bed. "I haven't been any nicer to you than you've been to me."

Her voice faltered a bit as she spoke. "I don't think God wants much to do with me anymore, after all that's happened."

I thought for a minute, my nerves strangely calmed. "You know, after seeing you in such pain yesterday and then hearing about everything else at school today, I was scared for you. I didn't know how to help except to pray. I just wanted to pray for you to be OK, but two things kept coming to mind, but they were more feelings than thoughts. One was that I felt like I should come to the hospital to visit. The other . . . it's sort of like . . ."

As I paused to try to put that other feeling into words, I looked back at Nicole. I think part of me—the part that's always screaming, *nobody wants to hear this* whenever I start talking about God—expecting her to turn away or roll her eyes. But she just said, "What was the other thing?"

I took a breath. "What I really felt was this—that you need to know God loves you the same no matter what."

No matter what. The words that haunted me from the Letter were now coming out of my mouth directly to Nicole. Nerves and self-consciousness surged back through my body. I quickly mumbled out, "I know I sound like a cartoon character saying stuff like '*no matter what,*' but . . ."

"No, it's ok . . ." She had a faint but warm smile, then she added softly, "Thanks." She turned her head to wipe her eyes and then looked back at me again. "I bet my eyes are all puffy now."

I shrugged my shoulders a little. I didn't even know what she was talking about, and it didn't matter. We were in silence for a few moments, each nervously fidgeting, her with her hair and hospital gown, me with my feet.

She motioned toward my left hand. "What are those?"

"Oh," I looked down at the markers that I had almost forgotten about, suddenly aware of the sweat in between my hand and the box. "I got you these markers, you know, for your cheerleading stuff and the notes you like to write. Sort of a get-well present, I guess. They, um, change colors when you go back over them with the special marker."

She stifled a small yawn. "Oh, cool. Thanks."

"I'll leave them over here." I walked over to the table holding the one bouquet of flowers that was in the room. I set them down and stayed there, closer to the door. "I guess I'm going to go ahead and go and let you rest. I'll see you back at school, OK?"

"Yeah," she said, "I'll probably be back next week, I think."

"OK, well, see you later, I guess." I gave a half wave good-bye and started walking out the door.

"Bye . . ." She sat back up as I left. "Thanks again."

I lingered for a moment as we shared a smile, then I turned and walked back toward the elevator.

Chapter 27

NO MATTER WHAT

I had so much adrenaline running through me that I almost broke out into a run on my way to the elevator. By the time I got to the parking lot, I couldn't hold myself back anymore, and I jogged to the car. The feeling was almost like when I hit the fadeaway against Lake, but instead of wanting to jump up and pump my fist, I just grinned.

I caught that big, goofy smile in my rearview as I backed out of my spot, and I had to laugh. Just about everything I feared about that visit had happened—I was the only one to visit (but someone still saw me), I was pushed into a one-on-one conversation with Nicole, and she even *cried*—and yet . . . it was good.

Back home, I went through the back door just as Mom was putting an electric skillet full of Hamburger Helper on the table for dinner. She poured me a tall glass of cold milk and smiled. "You're back just in time."

We were only a few bites into the meal when Dad looked up at me. "So who was in the hospital?"

Mom's head popped up, alarmed. "Hospital? I don't know anyone . . ."

"Mom," I interrupted, "I was just visiting a friend . . . you remember Nicole?"

I didn't really know what they knew or remembered. I had only had a couple of conversations about Nicole with either one of them—Dad after the Sunday school class and Mom around the date at the Astros game.

Mom's eyes widened. "Nicole? Is she alright?"

"Yes . . ." I gulped down some milk and took a deep breath. "Well . . . she's going to be." As we ate, I told the whole story. I told them about Cory, the pregnancy, and how she seemed to shrink as people whispered around her. About the English project, how she seemed better since spring break, and then yesterday's emergency. Finally, in front of empty plates and cups, I told them about the visit.

They listened intently, occasionally asking clarifying questions but otherwise silent as I spoke. When I ran out of words, Dad quietly got up and started scooping some ice cream for each of us.

Mom grabbed my hand. "Jay . . . you were carrying so much. I only knew what your dad told me. But I've been praying for you . . . and Nicole."

Dad set the ice cream down in front of us. "I remember you telling me about her after that Sunday school class. I told you your spiritual instincts were good."

"And I told you I don't think I have any instincts at all," I said through a spoonful of ice cream. "I never know what I'm doing. What are you talking about?"

Mom pointed her spoon. "You showed up for her, when no one else did."

"I guess." I shrugged and stirred. "But it's weird being the only one."

Dad looked me in the eye. "Like I told you before . . . being the one who cares is a *good* thing."

We ate our next few bites in silence, though Mom inhaled a few times like she was about to say something but stopped herself. Finally, she spoke.

"So Jay . . . you still *care* about Nicole?"

I sighed. I knew this question was coming, and I wasn't sure how to answer it. Of course I still cared about Nicole, but that's not what Mom was asking. She wanted to know if I still had a thing for her, and it was hard to pinpoint how I was feeling.

"I don't know, Mom." I slumped in my chair. "In some senses, yeah. I care about her more than any other girl I know. But . . ."

As I tried to answer, a dozen pictures of Nicole flickered through my mind—that first smile from sixth grade, the surprised "sounds like fun" when I asked her to the game, her curled up, asleep in that Oldsmobile on the way home, the way she tucked her hair behind her ear when she was nervous, and the sight of her in that hospital bed. Each memory was close to my heart, but the thought of her didn't carry the desperation and longing it once did.

Mom urged me to finish my thought. "But?"

"I guess things have . . . changed." The words came slowly, because I was just then coming to realize these things. "I think I stopped thinking about wanting her for a girlfriend a long time ago. Even though I liked her, she never wanted that from me. And that really is OK with me."

I scooped up the last bits of my runny ice cream as my parents let me gather my thoughts.

"I care about her, but I don't *need* her, you know?"

Mom got up to gather bowls. "What do you mean, 'need'?"

I sat back, thinking. "I guess part of why I wanted her so bad was because maybe it would prove something about me, but I don't want to use her for that anymore. I don't need to."

I nodded toward Dad. He smiled back. "That's right, Jay."

Mom sat back down. "But Jay, what if Nicole realizes the guy who showed up for her in the hospital is pretty special? What if she decides she needs *you*?"

"That's not happening, Mom." I laughed and stood up from the table. "But if it ever did . . . I guess I'd figure it out then."

Mom and Dad got up, too. Mom reached over and squeezed my shoulder.

I grabbed the phone. "I think I'm gonna call John and Roger. I'll be in my room." I jogged upstairs, dialing John's number.

Ashley was there with him, so we didn't talk long. But as I told him about the visit, he kept finding new ways to say, "I can't believe you went up there, man."

Roger had the same reaction. "If you'd called me first, I would have talked you out of going."

I sighed. "I just figured if someone's in the hospital . . ."

Roger cut me off. "No! I'm *glad* you didn't ask me. You did the right thing. You loved her more today than you did back when you wrote that letter."

I sat up. I wanted to throw the phone. "You're as bad as Mom. It wasn't about that! I wasn't trying to get a girlfriend at the dadgum hospital!"

Roger laughed. "Chill, Jay. That's not what I meant."

"Then what's your point?" I flopped back down on my bed.

I could hear that Roger was pacing with the phone. "You took a risk going up there—a risk I would've been afraid to take. Why?"

I paused. "I guess because I prayed . . . I felt like I was supposed to."

"Right! You went there for her, not for yourself. So at least for today, you loved Nicole. It's not about having her for yourself."

I stood up, holding the phone to my ear. "Mom made that comment about all this maybe making Nicole change the way she sees me, and I know there's still part of me that wants it to. But I don't want to go back to that place in my mind."

"Then don't." Roger paused. I could hear the creak of his desk chair as he leaned back. "I always did things for Tiffany thinking I'd change her mind. It's miserable—and I realized it was self-serving and self-defeating. It made me want her and almost hate her at the same time. Don't go there."

I didn't say anything. I just wandered to the mirror across the room. I never really knew what I'd see when I looked. Sometimes I saw someone who was smarter, more talented—*better*—than anyone else at school (and not bad-looking, either). Other times, I despised that person—a loser, a nerd, a joke. But neither was the truth. I just stood there, looking.

Roger's voice broke through. "But don't let it keep you from showing up like you did today. I think that's what God wants from us."

I smiled at myself. I'd always been afraid to bring this person I saw in the mirror to people—to burden them with "me." But today, I showed up, and maybe God somehow lifted Nicole up. And knowing that lifted me up, too.

I nodded, feeling a lightness in my body. "I think you're right."

I went to bed that night feeling like I'd hit a turning point, but the next morning, life just sort of went on. When I heard people whispering about Nicole, I would sometimes let them know she was OK, but I didn't want everyone to know I went to the hospital to see her.

When she finally came back to school the next week, nothing much changed. Nicole never spoke to me about my visit, and I never brought it up. She didn't start calling or writing me notes or anything like that.

Our relationship was basically what it always was, but I enjoyed having her back.

Still, not everything was the same. Nicole was never going to rewind her life back to the way it was before Cory. She carried grief that I could see behind her smiles, a weariness that weighed on her even in those usually carefree last few weeks of the school year.

The first Friday night in May, I went out to the ballfield to watch John play for a shot at the playoffs. Just like my team earlier, they had to beat Lake to get in. For the first time all season, the bleachers were packed. I sat in the top row behind home plate, where I could see both the game and the crowd.

I spotted Charlie wearing his letter jacket—newly arrived that day—over a basketball tank top and some jean shorts, laughing and mingling through the crowd. I laughed—anyone else would have looked ridiculous in that heat, but Charlie somehow pulled it off. I probably would have worn mine, too, if I had one.

I shook my head. He'd have other chances to wear his in cooler weather. My only chance to wear mine will be on a night like this next year.

I watched John ride the pine for the first few innings, yelling for his teammates, reading the opposing coach's signs, and pacing the dugout. I knew the pain he felt being sidelined on a night like this.

In the fifth inning, the starting catcher was lifted for a pinch-hitter, and John finally went in for defense. My heart swelled seeing him in his element—not the quiet little man who could barely open his mouth or speak above a mumble—a real field general, barking out bunt coverages, positioning infielders, running out to calm his pitcher.

Then came the seventh inning—the final inning in high school ball. Two runners on, one out, and down by two. John's spot came up.

I expected Coach Thomas to call him back for a pinch-hitter. But instead John knocked the weighted donut off his bat and strode to the plate, looked to his coach for the signs, and stepped into the box.

On the first pitch, he squared to bunt, and my heart sank. *Let him swing, Coach!*

But John pulled the bat back. Ball one. He worked the count to 3-1, and Coach let him swing away.

Ping!

A line drive into the left-centerfield gap. The Lake outfielders scrambled for the ball and heaved it toward the infield as the tying runs scored. When the throw trickled past the cut-off man, John scrambled to third.

The next batter lifted a long fly to left field, an easy sacrifice fly. John stomped on home plate for the winning run as his teammates mobbed him.

The creaky wooden bleachers rocked under the jumping and screaming fans like they might collapse. I hopped off the side of the bleachers and followed the crowd spilling out toward the field, heart racing.

I craned my neck, looking for John in the chaos. When I spotted him, our eyes locked—John, standing near the third base foul line, arm around Ashley, drenched in sweat, huge smile across his face.

He pointed at me, and I pointed back, pounding my chest with my other arm. “You go, brother!” My voiced cracked as I shouted, tears in my eyes.

When I turned to push closer, I had to duck as Charlie spun his letter jacket above his head in celebration. Near the dugout, I nearly ran right into Coach Mays. He was shaking hands with Coach Thomas, a hint of a grin peeking out under his mustache as he congratulated him. Our eyes met as I slipped by onto the field to find John.

It’s funny that I think of Coach Mays at all from that night. But there are points of time in high school that define you—loud, adrenaline-filled moments of triumph like these or quiet moments beside a hospital bed. And when I look back on them, I think of the one word of real wisdom that I remember from Coach Mays:

> "*Everyone says life is short. That's bullcrap, fellas. Life is long. Whatever you end up doing, you do for a long, long time.*"

And now, picturing those scenes that defined my junior year of high school, I realize that Coach was on to something.

It's true that moments like these are fleeting. These *years* are fleeting.

But the person you become in these years lasts a long, long time.

Final exams came a couple of weeks later, and the last day of my junior year of high school began with one last test—a half-hour Spanish final in a two-hour class period. We counted down the rest of the time playing cards and passing around yearbooks to sign.

When Nicole finished her final, she got out her color-changing markers I gave her at the hospital. We shared a smile. I was glad she was using them. But when she got busy working on one of her notes, I moved to the back of the room and spent the rest of the time playing hearts with three other guys.

The bell finally rang. Just two hours of basketball class stood between me and summer. I passed by Nicole on the way out of class.

"Have a nice summer, Jay!" There was something just a little different—maybe a bit mischievous—about her smile.

"You too!" I waved and watched her for a few steps before I turned and went to the gym.

I dumped my backpack when I got home. When I picked up my yearbook, a carefully folded note fell out and slid out onto the table. On the front, in bubbly multicolored letters: "**Jay**."

I took a moment to admire my name in Nicole's artwork, then quickly unfolded the paper and began to read.

Jay,
It's been a crazy year . . . but we're seniors now!
I just wanted to write to say . . .
You've been a great friend to me whenever I needed one.
Thanks for being there.
No matter what.

ACKNOWLEDGMENTS

Special thanks to Trudy and Debi, for listening to every chapter during "story time" in the office and always encouraging me to keep going. Debi, thank you for laughing at the funny parts. Trudy, thank you for pushing me to share this book beyond just friends and family.

Thanks to Stephen Fontenot, Melissa Harley, Jon Norvell, and my brothers Jeff and Christopher for reading the manuscript and helping me in the final steps.

To my family—Liz, Joseph, Hope, Susanna, and John—thank you for inspiring me every day, for reading and listening as I told stories, and for giving me reasons to tell this one.

To Dad and Mom, whose wisdom and encouragement are reflected throughout my story (in the book and especially in my life).

And to my wife's parents, Jesse and Beverly, whose constant support helped make this publication possible.

www.ingramcontent.com/pod-product-compliance
Lightning Source LLC
LaVergne TN
LVHW010611100826
845148LV00014B/2925

9781684881550